An AMERICAN *in* LONDON

OTHER BOOKS BY LOUISE BAY

New to Louise Bay? Start with *Mr. Mayfair* or *The Boss + The Maid = Chemistry*

Colorado Club Billionaires

Love Fast

Love Deep

Love More

New York City Billionaires

The Boss + The Maid = Chemistry

The Player + The Pact = I Do

The Hero + Vegas = No Regrets

The Doctors Series

Dr. Off Limits

Dr. Perfect

Dr. CEO

Dr. Fake Fiancé

Dr. Single Dad

The Mister Series

Mr. Mayfair

Mr. Knightsbridge

Mr. Smithfield

Mr. Park Lane

Mr. Bloomsbury

Mr. Notting Hill

The Royals Series

The Earl of London

The British Knight

Duke of Manhattan

Park Avenue Prince

King of Wall Street

The Player Series

International Player

Private Player

Gentleman Series

The Wrong Gentleman

The Ruthless Gentleman

The Nights Series

Indigo Nights

Promised Nights

Parisian Nights

Stand-Alones

The 14 Days of Christmas

Hollywood Scandal

Love Unexpected

Hopeful

The Empire State Series

For more, visit www.louisebay.com.

An

AMERICAN
in **LONDON**

LOUISE BAY

 Montlake

Published by Montlake, Seattle

www.apub.com

Amazon, the Amazon logo, and Montlake are trademarks of Amazon.com, Inc., or its affiliates.

EU product safety contact:
Amazon Media EU S. à r.l.
38, avenue John F. Kennedy, L-1855 Luxembourg
amazonpublishing-gpsr@amazon.com

ISBN-13: 9781662532092 (paperback)
ISBN-13: 9781662532108 (digital)

Cover design by Logan Matthews
Cover photography by Regina Wamba of ReginaWamba.com
Cover image: © Mistervlad / Shutterstock

Printed in the United States of America

An
AMERICAN
in LONDON

CHAPTER ONE

For the last ten years, I've been living a life in Manhattan most people can only dream about. Cool apartment on the Upper East Side? Check. Soaring career at a bank on Wall Street? Check. Handsome boyfriend who proposed with his grandmother's ring? Check and *mate*.

In the last week, things have changed.

I've been thrown out of my home. The bank announced a merger, which means my job is on the line. And my fiancé ran off to Iowa with a ballerina named Fifi.

But there are still things to be positive about.

The bank has sent me to London to "demonstrate my talent" for the new CEO and to get myself on the new management fast-track program. At least it won't put a strain on my nonexistent relationship.

Then there's the fact I'm in *London*. That's London, *England*. It's my first trip abroad, and I'm not half-assing it with a long weekend in Cabo. I'm across an ocean. On a different continent from Jed and Fifi. That's gotta count as a win.

I'm prepared for the unexpected—it's on my travel checklist just below *remember passport*—but even the most fastidious planner wouldn't have anticipated checking into her London hotel and finding herself surrounded by . . . women. Not that I expected *not* to see women. I'd just subconsciously anticipated seeing members of both sexes, like I normally do. There isn't a man to be seen.

Instead, there are all kinds of women—blond and brunette, short and tall, thin and curvy. All smiling almost giddily at each other, chatting away conspiratorially and laughing like they've each had a cocktail, even though it's only just past noon. Not that I'm judging. New York brunches are nothing without a mimosa.

I slide my passport onto the check-in desk and pull my eyes away from four women by the door, all my age, huddled together over a map.

"Good afternoon. Is it a business or personal trip?" the neat blond woman behind the desk asks.

"Business," I reply, half wondering whether I missed something when I checked the hotel's website after the bank's travel department booked me in here. I file through the likely explanations in my head: It's an all-women hotel, ensuring women feel safe when traveling; a bachelorette party has taken over the entire hotel; a huge, women-only birthday party has spilled out into the lobby. I crane my neck to see whether any of the other receptionists are men.

"Are you working the convention?" The receptionist's eyes are dancing, and her smile is wide and genuine. She looks positively giddy herself.

"Er, what convention?"

She reaches forward and tugs at something on the desk. In front of me, she sets down a ten-inch-high cardboard cutout of Daniel De Luca—a man, at last, and one I'm very familiar with. "The Daniel De Luca convention, of course! It's our third year."

"Daniel De Luca?" I ask, like I don't know she means the British movie star famed for his Hollywood romantic comedies. He's underestimated as an actor, in my opinion. His finest work was in the thriller *Watching Me*. He was robbed of the Oscar nomination. "There's a convention?"

"DDL Con. You didn't know?" She looks at me like she's just awarded me a big check I wasn't expecting. "Yes, there's a five-day and a seven-day package," she says. "If you have time outside of work, you should sign up. It starts tomorrow, so you haven't missed anything."

A loud rattling sound behind me catches my attention, and I snap my head around to see a short woman in a polka-dot sundress just like the one Mary McDorney wore in *Every Day* when she and Daniel De Luca went to a polo match together. The woman is pulling up a retractable banner, but she's having trouble securing it. At first glance, it looks like she's trying to dry hump an overly large picture of Daniel De Luca's face.

Not exactly what I expected from London, but international travel is supposed to broaden the mind.

I turn back to the receptionist. "I'm not sure I'll have time, but thank you."

I've flown over on a Saturday to give myself time to recover from jet lag and settle in before the start of my five-week stint as the bank's new project manager, working directly with the CEO. I'm planning to find a great coffee shop, figure out how long the journey to work is likely to take, and get to grips with the public transportation system; I've got a list of all the things I need to do tomorrow before I show up at the bank on Monday. I want to be prepared—I can't lose my boyfriend and my job at the same time. My life would veer into pathetic territory, and I'm not going to let that happen.

"Oh. Poor you." The receptionist tips her head and pushes her bottom lip out, like missing the convention is the worst thing that could happen to a woman like me.

Girl, please. Let me introduce you to my cheating fiancé. In another life, maybe missing DDL Con would be the biggest tragedy going. After all, I've seen a lot of Daniel De Luca's movies. When I was a teenager, Mom and I would spend hours watching his films, looking up facts about him, and researching his movie locations. But my mom is dead, I'm not a teenager anymore, and I'm in London to save my career. I'm not here to gush over a movie star.

The receptionist slaps a booklet on the sleek white counter between us. "This is a schedule of events," she says. "You have to be part of the convention for most of them, but you can book some of the tours even if you're not. Oh, and . . ." She reaches under the counter and produces what looks like a tourist map. "There's a Daniel De Luca map. It sets out all the filming locations for his movies in London. There are even some outside of London, too, if you fancy a trip into the countryside."

What my fifteen-year-old self would have given to be here. Come to think of it, my forty-year-old mother would have sold every last one of her collector's-edition holiday snow globes to attend this conference. My heart clenches a little at the memory of her face when she opened the last Christmas present I gave her: the first and only Daniel De Luca snow globe I ever managed to find.

The edges of my grief for my mother have worn and softened since the sharp pangs of the first couple of years, but the pain of her not being here never goes away. It sits and waits under my skin, ready to surface at the mention of her favorite movie or whenever the first chill of fall means I slip on a jacket. Autumn was her favorite season.

"Oh, goodness," the receptionist says, typing away on her computer keyboard. "You're booked in for thirty-six nights. You'll be like family by the time you leave." She clicks the mouse. "There. I've upgraded you to one of my favorite rooms." She hands me my key. "Welcome to London. I hope you run into Daniel De Luca himself."

I can't help but laugh. "Thank you. I hope so too." If nothing else, my dad would get a kick out of me meeting the man my mom and I were borderline obsessed with during my teen years.

When the elevator doors slide open, they reveal the walls of the interior, which have been decorated with stills from every Daniel De Luca film ever made. It's almost like stepping into a time capsule. I'm surrounded not just by Daniel De Luca but also by my memories of watching his movies and how it felt to be a teenager snuggled up with my mom on the couch, eating popcorn and talking about the future as if it were a magical dreamworld filled with love and romance and happily-ever-afters.

When the elevator arrives at the seventh floor, the doors ping open, revealing a blank wall, low lighting, and a distinct lack of signage. Much more like the real-life future I *actually* encountered, rather than the one I'd dreamed up with my mom.

After first going in the wrong direction, I find my room, which is all cream and pale blues. The beachy theme and sun coming through the window make me almost feel like I'm on vacation. I dial my best friend, Melanie, before I've even kicked off my shoes.

"You've landed?" she asks.

"I'm at the hotel. I just got here, and you're not going to believe where they've got me staying."

"Buckingham Palace?" she asks.

"How did you guess? Kate Middleton and I are going for mani-pedis later. No, this hotel is hosting a Daniel De Luca convention. Isn't that . . . weird or funny or something?"

"Oh, Tuesday."

I skim right over the sympathetic tone to her voice. "Funny, right? They gave me a map to all his movie locations."

I put the phone on speaker, unfold the map, and move the fruit bowl on the small table by the window so I can spread the entire city of London out in front of me. "Hang on; let me switch to video. You gotta see this."

I switch the camera around so she's seeing what I am.

"Oh, God. There are hundreds," she says.

Different-colored lines starting at locations on the map lead out to the edge of the paper where there's an image of the scene shot there.

"Which movie is that one on the top left, where he's wearing the hat?" she asks.

I know even before I've found the image which scene she's talking about. "*Never on a Sunday*, where he borrows the kid's hat to make the mom laugh."

I trace my finger along the top of the map, trailing through stills from his movie catalog before landing on the one from *Never on a Sunday*. It was always one of my mom's favorites. I often wonder if she considered whether Dad would remarry if she ever died, like Daniel De

Luca ended up doing in that film. Not that she knew she was going to die. And not that Dad ever did remarry.

"If you could monetize your Daniel De Luca knowledge, you wouldn't need the job at the bank. You could come back to New York today," Melanie says.

I laugh. "Yeah, I should be running this convention." My knowledge is probably a little out of date now. It's been a while.

"Maybe if it doesn't work out at the bank, you can throw a convention in New York."

I laugh again because the idea is ludicrous. I don't indulge my *own* fantasies, let alone those of thousands of strangers. "My mom knew far more than I ever did."

"That's bullshit. You knew everything."

I turn from the map and unzip my suitcase. "No, my mom was obsessed with him. I was just along for the ride."

Melanie bursts into laughter. "It was totally the other way around. You were so in love with him. Don't you remember your vision board?"

I'd started my vision board to copy my mom. She was always tearing images from magazines and flyers—a field of daisies, a pretty sundress, a sunset over the Rocky Mountains. Then she'd pin them to the giant corkboard in our kitchen or stick them to the refrigerator using my old alphabet magnets. Mom always said it was good to be surrounded by things you wanted in your world. And I wanted Daniel De Luca in mine.

I suppose Melanie's right. My mom was just my partner in crime when it came to worshipping him. It feels like such a long time ago, when life was far simpler than it is now. "I thought I was going to marry him."

"Yes!" Melanie says. "We dressed you up in your mom's veil and a white apron. Do you remember?"

I'd carefully cut out the picture we took of me dressed as Daniel's bride and stuck it next to a picture of him in *Sunshine on a Rainy Day*. That's how my vision board started. I gradually added members of the congregation and then the house we'd live in—in England, obviously. I was planning to relocate after the wedding.

"Maybe your vision board is finally coming to life. I read yesterday he split from his girlfriend. He might make an appearance at the convention, and he'll realize, after dating all those twenty-two-year-olds, it's you he wants."

I sigh. "Don't hold your breath, Melanie. Life isn't a movie." I learned that the hard way and far too young.

"No, if it was, you'd have the chance to go to London for a month. *London*, where there are tons of British guys. If not Daniel De Luca, then maybe someone else."

Melanie's desperate for me to be "over" Jed. She doesn't need to worry. He and I were together a long time and being dumped is never fun, but I'm fine. I don't need to get under a British guy to prove it.

"This isn't a vacation," I say. "This is an opportunity to get onto the management fast track. You know I'm about ninety-eight-point-seven percent likely to get fired if I fail. They've already announced layoffs of junior analysts. If they don't think I'm good enough for the fast track, why would they keep me?"

Melanie sighs, and I appreciate that she doesn't fill the silence with platitudes like "You're going to be fine" or "They're lucky to have you. Of course you won't get fired." We both know New York is a tough city.

"How is apartment hunting?" I ask. Melanie's lease is up next month, and we're looking for a place to share.

"Depressing. Everything's so expensive. And since Covid, all the landlords are asking for so much more."

I take a breath and try to unknot the irritation in my chest. Jed always enjoyed our fancy apartment, even though I could only just make it work on my salary. I would have been much happier with a smaller place where I could have saved something. He earned more than me, so it wasn't such a stretch for him. But after my subway pass, meals out, and other expenses, there wasn't anything left to save. I was living paycheck to paycheck. I kept telling myself it was okay because my salary would continue to go up at the bank and my fiancé was already outearning me.

Except it wasn't okay.

In some ways the London trip came at the right time. It means I have a few weeks to save my paycheck instead of signing it over as a rent payment. I wish I'd tried a little harder to persuade Jed to take a one-bedroom downtown instead of a two-bedroom on the Upper East Side. But the location was really important to Jed, and so I agreed.

"Maybe we should think about Brooklyn," Melanie says. "It's definitely cheaper."

I turn and sit on the bed. "Really?" I love Manhattan. I love the way the streets are busy no matter the time of day, the way no one bats an eye if you're making your way home with only one shoe (true story), and the way on every corner there's something happening I want to tell my dad about.

"I'm going to start calling agents this week. Let's see what's around."

"Sounds good." I really hope we don't end up in Brooklyn.

There's a beat of silence before Melanie says, "What happened with you and Daniel De Luca? Did you just fall out of love with him?"

I shrug. "I grew out of silly fantasies. Like *most* people." I fake a cough. Melanie has never grown out of her Harry Potter obsession, and I love her for it.

"Why, though?" Melanie asks. "Why do we have to grow up and become sensible?"

There's a simple answer to that: Because life isn't a fairy tale.

"So, London men," Melanie continues before the silence can grow uncomfortable. "You'll have to do lots of due diligence and report back."

I straighten, pulling back my shoulders. "I don't need anyone else."

Jed and I met in college. It was his realistic approach to life that had attracted me. There were no butterflies, no blind passion or days spent lost in conversation. Our relationship wasn't like in the movies; it was better because it was real. Practical. Focused. We wanted the same things out of life: a Manhattan apartment, a place in the Hamptons, a fat 401(k). I wanted a life where I never had to worry about anything. I wanted a stable, dependable man who would fit into a stable, dependable life.

Except the stable, dependable man I picked decided he wanted a much less stable and dependable ballerina sister of a mutual friend. They're moving to Iowa together to run a farm, which leaves me to go get my stable, dependable life on my own.

And that's exactly where London is going to lead: saving my job, getting a place on the management fast track, and securing the future I want for myself.

"Don't you think it's a little . . . unusual to stumble across a Daniel De Luca convention?" Melanie asks. "And not just stumble across it but be staying in the same hotel that's hosting it? Maybe it's fate."

"It's coincidence," I reply.

"Right, but a strange one. And it's in London, for Pete's sake. How often do you travel for work? Never. And the one time you do, you're staying at a hotel that's celebrating Daniel De Luca? It's . . ."

"Totally random?" I suggest.

"It's fate, I'm telling you. It's the universe throwing you a rope. You need to cling on and see where it takes you."

"Cling on?"

"*Lean in* is probably a better way of putting it. I can't help but think you being at this hotel, surrounded by . . . memories . . ." She pauses, and we both take a breath. "Enjoy it. Maybe take a tour. Or just go to a couple of locations on the map. You might find what you're looking for."

"Like a job?" I suggest. "Or the life I was meant to have with Jed?"

London won't give me my old life back, but it might help me keep the job I need for the new solo life I'm left with. At the moment, it's the best I can hope for.

CHAPTER TWO

If I count from the time the plane touched down, I've been in London twenty-seven hours and six minutes. In that time, I've seen at least three hundred and fifty-six thousand images of Daniel De Luca. Being in my hotel is like living in fourteen-year-old me's brain.

And it's terrifying.

There's also something comforting about it. My mom's death threw me into adulthood with such force, I never looked back. But being here is making me do just that. Every time I turn around, I come face-to-printed-face with my teenage crush. And even though I don't believe the universe is sending me a sign by having a Daniel De Luca convention in the hotel I'm staying at, I'm going to take Melanie's advice and lean into it. Not because it's a sign, but because . . . maybe it's a sign?

I have so many happy memories of my mom and his films that I may have snuck my Daniel De Luca map into my bag along with my phone, water, and sunglasses. The hotel is walking distance from the office, and I want to check the route in advance of Monday morning so I know what to expect—and what shoes to wear. I imagine London is a lot like New York when it comes to shoe-swapping to and from the office.

I have the entire afternoon, and I need to shrug off my jet lag so I can show my boss how perfect I am for the management fast track. At least that's my excuse for heading for a short detour through Green Park. I feel a little guilty, because I'm here on a work trip, but I justify the detour by reminding myself it's the weekend. A particular scene in Daniel De Luca's first ever big movie was shot in the park; as a teen, I'd longed to go to the place where Daniel's career took off. He didn't have top billing in *Love Me Like a Boss*, but he played opposite the queen of rom-coms, Julia Alice, and it launched him into superstardom.

If I thought the roads in New York City were busy, London is on a different, very chaotic scale. They don't follow a pattern, so blocks aren't easy to make out, and there aren't places to cross at regular intervals. What are you supposed to do? Fly across the street? Even the sidewalks are confused—sometimes cobbled, sometimes asphalt, and sometimes slab. Pick a lane, Londoners!

I fall in behind an American family—mom, dad, and two teenage children—and try to be subtle about following them as they're clearly trying to cross the mammoth road in front of us called Piccadilly. Not Piccadilly Street or Piccadilly Road—just Piccadilly, like we have Broadway back home. The family look as if they've been here a couple of days already and have a map without Daniel De Luca's face on it, which probably means they have a higher probability of crossing this road without being run down by a red bus. Good enough for me.

We finally reach a crossing and get to the other side. They head left, but according to Google Maps, I need to go right. "Thank you," I call out in their direction before realizing they didn't even know I was following them.

When I reach the park, my guilt fades and my insides start to fizz with excitement. I can't remember the last time I felt this . . . light. Inside, the park is magical. Pathways meander in all directions, all covered in a canopy of bright-green leaves. Sunshine finds its way through the tunnels, reflecting a web of tattooed leaves on the ground. It looks like a setting for a fantasy story, because real life couldn't possibly be this beautiful. Somehow, even though the road is only a few paces away, I can't hear the traffic. All I hear is birdsong and the whoosh of a passing cyclist.

I stand on my tiptoes to try to make out the sign up ahead. I'm trying to find the Canada Memorial. It was in the background of the scene where Daniel's character, Tom, ran into Julia Alice's character. As I glance through the trees, I spot the metal structure lifting from the ground, almost like a half-open trapdoor. I'm on the exact road where Daniel De Luca must have walked.

I try to picture the scene in my head so I can find the exact right spot when something—or someone—catches my eye.

As the stranger nears, my heart lifts in my chest, the ground tilts, and I have to stop to make sure I don't fall over. It can't be . . . Can it? Coming toward me is the one and only Daniel De Luca.

Holy shit.

His almost-black hair is swept up and back from his face, revealing high cheekbones and the square jaw that sends my stomach up, up, up, like I'm inching toward the summit of a roller coaster. He's dressed in a navy suit and looks ready to boss someone around. I mentally raise a hand to volunteer. His stern frown suggests he's far from the easygoing, charming, smiley Daniel De Luca I see on TV in interviews and on the red carpet.

Maybe his cat died.

He'll reach me in just a couple of seconds. I have to gather myself and say something, but what?

"Daniel," I call out when he's a couple of yards away. "I'm a huge fan of your work and loved you in *Love Me Like a Boss*. You were simply—"

He doesn't slow down, but he turns his head toward me and deepens his scowl like I'm a rodent he's trying to will away. That's when I realize: I'm not talking to Daniel De Luca at all.

The man in front of me isn't a movie star. Granted, he's hot and looks like Daniel De Luca's twin brother. But he's just a guy. A guy who has just been accosted by an American woman. "I'm sorry," I say, flashing my best smile, hoping he'll skip past my humiliation and chalk up my faux pas to American friendliness. "I thought you were someone else."

He doesn't stop.

He doesn't say a word.

He doesn't even smile or nod an acknowledgment.

He just stalks on by, as if I'm a lunatic and he's got somewhere to be.

Embarrassment creeps over me. What is the matter with me? I'm actually hallucinating and starting to see Daniel De Luca in random men on the street. At this rate, I'll be hiding in the bushes of Daniel De Luca's front yard in an attempt to orchestrate a casual, totally coincidental meet-cute between us before the week is out. I might fully revert to my preteen self and start covering my notebooks in Daniel De Luca scribbles again.

I try to muster up some grace for myself. Between the breakup, job stress, and my hotel being plastered in memories of Mom, it's no wonder I'm flirting with the edge of reasonable behavior. The time in my life that involved Daniel De Luca was so carefree. There were no student loans. No cheating fiancés. No possibility of losing my job. And my mom was still the person I relied on for everything—from makeup tips to pocket money.

After she died, I never wished the clock would turn back or had conversations with her in my head. I was worried I'd never recover if I did. Instead, I marched onward, leaving everything connected to Mom—sunsets and fairy tales and happily-ever-afters—just where it was. In my history. And it's like London is prodding me to look over my shoulder.

I take a breath and force myself to gain perspective about the reality of fangirling over a perfect stranger in the street. Mom never got embarrassed about anything. If she were here, she would have made the unwitting impersonator stop and pose for pictures. At least there's no one here to recognize me. New York's a big place, but I bump into people I know far too often. If I'd been at home, I wouldn't have felt capable of brushing off my mortification and moving on with my day.

For the first time in a long time, I wish my mom were here. I could be buoyed by her ability to laugh at herself, to dust herself off and make the most out of any situation. I'm pretty sure she'd tell me I don't have to be grown-up, fiancé-less, inching-toward-destitute me. She'd assure me I can laugh out loud to myself in public, accost complete strangers, and love Daniel De Luca.

But she's not here, and the only thing that can make me feel even slightly better is the thought that I'll never have to see that familiar stranger again. I need to find the nearest exit and go find a coffee shop. A caffeine fix is the therapy I need right now.

I sigh, glance around . . . and realize I'm standing in the exact spot Julia and Daniel ran into each other for the first time in *Love Me Like a Boss*.

CHAPTER THREE

I could only find chain coffee shops yesterday, despite looking for something . . . new. This morning, I asked the concierge for a recommendation. It's only five after seven, but Coffee Confide in Me is crowded. That's gotta be a good sign. The long queue snakes down the center of the store, leaving room for small tables on either side.

I close one eye, then open it and close the other, trying to figure out whether I'm just not used to being up at this time or I'm really tired. I sigh, take a step back, and tread on someone's foot. I stumble forward, then turn to apologize. "Oh my gosh, I'm so sorr—"

I freeze in shock like someone pressed "Pause" on me. I can't believe what I'm seeing.

The Daniel De Luca look-alike I accosted yesterday is staring back at me.

"It's you!" Seeing a familiar face is like an adrenaline rush to the heart, despite the fact I humiliated myself in front of him. Today it doesn't feel as mortifyingly fresh as it did yesterday. "It's me." I place my palm on my chest. "From yesterday in the park. I thought you were . . . never mind . . . just someone else." Is this guy following me or something?

His expression is no less stern than it was yesterday, but I'm closer today, so maybe that's the reason he looks slightly less menacing. His long lashes sweep up, taking the edge off his masculine jaw and the tightness across his forehead. Would it be rude to ask whether he applies a serum before bed? Whatever it is making those lashes grow, I want a slice.

He still hasn't spoken. I don't know why, but I'm really pleased to see him. Maybe I'm so desperate for a friendly face I'm pushing my embarrassment away, or maybe my mother's spirit is with me, making me immune to shame.

Either way, after one night on a new continent, there's a bubbling in me that says London isn't just an opportunity to save my job. It's a new city, and maybe I can scoop up some of that newness and wear it for a while. I can try on a new me. At the very least, it feels like it could be a fresh start. Or five weeks of one, at least. No one knows me here. This stranger and I will be separated by a whole ocean next month. Who cares if I say hello and he hates me?

"My name's Tuesday." I give him my best upstate New York smile that says I like to pick apples on the weekends and bake my own bread. It's different from the expression I developed when I moved to the city, which gives *don't fuck with me or I'll stab you in the heart* vibes. "We met yesterday," I say.

His eyes are a cornflower blue—so bright they almost look fake. No wonder I thought he was a movie star—on-screen, he'd break box office records. He glances behind me and nods. I turn and see the line has moved forward a little but I haven't. I shuffle forward. "I just arrived in London yesterday. It's my first time here. Do you work around here? You take the subway into Green Park?" New York Tuesday would not be striking up conversations with strangers, but I'm not in New York. Maybe London Tuesday likes to chat with people she doesn't know.

His eyes slide back to mine and he studies me without saying a word. His gaze travels down my face, body, right to my toes, then back up again. "Sunday."

Heat winds through my body as if his gaze leaves a trickle of melted chocolate on my bare skin. I frown, a little irritated at the way my body is reacting to a decidedly un-charming man. "Today's Monday."

"Your name," he says.

Oh, bless his heart, he's trying to make an effort. My apple-pie smile is back. "Tuesday. Not Sunday," I correct him. "Nice to meet you." I hold out my hand, and instead of shaking it—like any normal human being, even if I am a perfect stranger—he just nods. I snap my head around to find the cashier waving at me.

Okay, so the Daniel De Luca doppelgänger is rude, but at least it's my turn for coffee.

I order my venti cappuccino with an extra shot, half almond milk, half oat milk, three pumps of caramel, extra foam, and cinnamon sprinkles. I really hope they remember the sprinkles. Generally, there's a fifty percent hit rate.

The cashier, who has crayon-red hair and a name tag that reads Ginny, looks at me. "American?"

I beam. "Yes. I guess my accent gives me away."

Her expression is blank. "Your order, more like." She bellows my order to the barista, and he openly groans. "Name?"

"Tuesday."

She laughs and shakes her head. "If you say so." She scribbles on my cup; I put a tip in the box and move out of the way.

I stay close to the line so I can hear what Daniel Doppelgänger will order.

"Medium filter coffee," Ginny says to the barista without Double-D saying a word. He pays with his phone, puts a bill in the tip jar, then moves to the other side of me, checking his phone.

Maybe he can't speak. Or not in sentences anyway. He's said exactly one word to me. I suppose I should feel special, as he didn't even manage a "good morning" for the cashier.

The barista calls out a medium filter coffee, and Double-D moves to the pickup counter to collect it. He's tall and broad and shouldn't move as gracefully as he does. Wait . . . They didn't even call his name. He must be a regular.

"Tuesday," someone calls out. I turn to find Ginny holding out my drink to me. The line has almost gone now, and someone else is manning the cash register.

"Thanks," I say, grabbing a cupholder. "I heard this place makes really great coffee."

"We're the best in Mayfair," she says as she begins to tidy the stirrers and the sugar packets. "Maybe even London."

"I have my favorite coffee place in New York."

"That where you're from?" she asks.

"Yes. I'm just visiting, as you guessed. Here for a few weeks for work." I pause, wondering whether or not to say anything else. She's not overly friendly, and I've heard Brits can be a bit cold. But my new Tuesday persona gets the better of me. "Hopefully I'll leave here with a promotion."

"Either way, you'll get to spend time in the best city in the world."

I nod and go to sip my coffee, but change my mind when I remember it's just been served. "Yeah. I'm in *London*." I've been so focused on proving myself in the new role as project manager that I've skipped past the bit about being in a place I only ever dreamed of visiting. I have thousands of years of history around me, and I haven't so much as cracked open a guidebook. I'm going to have to focus on work—there's no doubt about that—but I have weekends to fill.

"That guy after me," I say. "The filter coffee guy. What's his deal?"

She glances up at me, and suddenly, her eyes light up. "He's seriously hot, right? I mean, the suit, those eyes. Have you seen the size of his hands?"

"Does he ever speak?" I ask. "You seem to know his order by heart."

"He must have done at some point. But a guy like that only needs to give me his order once, and I have it memorized for the rest of my life. He comes in seven days a week, but he never makes small talk. I get the odd thanks. He always tips—which ninety-nine percent of customers don't. And honestly, I don't care what he says or doesn't say as long as I get to look at him once a day. He's a walking dose of dopamine."

I can't disagree with her assessment. He looks like a movie star. "He's a dead ringer for Daniel De Luca," I say.

"I guess he is." She pauses and squints at me. "Is your name really Tuesday?"

I know she's not asking me because she thinks my name is beautiful, but I can't help but beam at her. "Sure is."

I love my name. That's not to say I don't get a few raised eyebrows when I introduce myself in New York. Tuesday is the name my mom wanted to call her daughter since she was four years old, because it was her favorite word. Every time I say it, it's like I feel the warm squeeze of her hand in mine.

"It's unusual."

"It is," I agree. I check my watch. Time to go. "Thanks for the coffee."

As I exit the coffee shop, I glance up and down the street, half expecting to see the Daniel De Luca look-alike.

Talk about a coincidence. London has a gazillion people. It makes no sense I'd bump into the same stranger two days running. My mom would call that fate. So would Melanie. But it's just a coincidence. *Right?* Something tells me I'm going to see him again—maybe because I'm going to make sure I'm standing in line for coffee at exactly the same time tomorrow.

CHAPTER FOUR

If I didn't know I had jet lag, I would think I'd accidentally taken acid. Even though today was tiring from the new routines, unfamiliar faces, and a particularly bad health and safety video I had to sit through, I just can't master this *going to bed five hours earlier than I normally do* thing. Last night I listened to every podcast ever made. Tonight, I have a different tactic: cocktails. I don't want to roll into my second day of work with a hangover, since I'll finally be meeting my new boss and the bank's CEO, Mr. Jenkins, but neither do I want to have had thirty minutes' sleep. My plan is to order exactly one perfect cocktail I've never tasted before, then take myself upstairs to my room and meditate myself to sleep.

The bar looks sleek and glamorous every time I walk by. It seems to be the only place in the hotel not plastered in images of Daniel De Luca. I've been desperate to slide onto one of the barstools and order myself a drink, but so far I've resisted. Ordering a drink while waiting for a friend is one thing, but drinking alone? On a work trip? Somehow it feels off.

My need to sleep overrides my concerns. I need the soporific effects of alcohol so I can get my internal clock on local time.

Olive-green leather booths with dark wood tables line the room, and a smattering of burnt orange upholstered club chairs around low tables fill the middle. It's cozy-glamorous. Is that a thing? The uplighting creates a moody, mysterious vibe. It's enough of New York to feel inviting and enough of London to feel new.

They're playing Ella Fitzgerald, reminding me of Friday nights when I was little. My parents would put me to bed before the zip and crackle of Dad's old record player introduced Ella. They didn't know, but occasionally I'd creep out of bed and sit on the stairs, watching them through a crack in the living room door. They'd dance, Dad twirling and dipping Mom until she inevitably began giggling and Dad owl-laughed—how my mother described his effusive *who-who-who* laughter. I wanted to be just like them when I grew up. They seemed so happy. They *were* so happy. And that made me happy.

It's so strange that a visit to a foreign country can bring back so many memories. So far, so much of London is like a love letter from my past.

I lift my head and stroll into the bar. Every table is taken, but somehow it doesn't feel busy. I head over to the bar and slide onto one of the few gigantic barstools still available. "You'd think they'd make these a little more small-person friendly," I mutter to myself. It's like a mini sofa on tall legs, and so comfortable.

That's when I glance to my right and see the one and only Daniel De Luca look-alike.

He's a perfect stranger. But he's at least familiar. I'll take it.

"Hey, doppelgänger! Aren't you afraid of getting mobbed in this hotel?" Frankly, I'm surprised there isn't a gaggle of women surrounding him, thrusting autograph books in his direction.

He turns his head to the left, sees me, and looks back to his drink. He doesn't say a word.

"So how are you?" I reach for the drink menu and settle into my seat. "I haven't seen you since this morning." It's like we're old friends and have arranged to meet here. We're not and we didn't, but *whatever*.

He glances at me again, and believe me, he's no poker player. He clearly thinks I'm off my meds.

"You're probably wondering why I'm talking to you like we're old friends. Well, we are in a way. In the sense that you're my oldest London friend. Met you the day after I landed, and I've seen you twice since.

To a New Yorker, we're practically family." I glance across at him, and he takes a sip of his wine. "You never know; another couple of conversations and you might even speak."

He raises an eyebrow. "Unlikely, Wednesday." I swear the corner of his mouth twitches.

Did he just make a joke? At my expense? I'm honored. A flicker of excitement races up my spine. For the first time since arriving in London, I'm not conscious of anything but this moment, right now.

"You *know* my name is Tuesday, don't you?"

He sighs and sits back in his seat. "How could I not, seeing as you—a complete stranger—have introduced yourself?"

Yes, he's being cold and rude and his voice is clipped and irritated, but I'm delighted I managed to get him to speak an entire sentence.

"What can I say? Americans are just friendly, I suppose."

He takes a sip from his glass of red wine.

"Whatcha drinking?" I ask.

"Wine," he replies.

I should give up and leave him alone to his sad, miserable life, but there's something in me that's drawn to him. Maybe it's his eyes. Maybe it's because he looks like Daniel De Luca. Maybe fresh-start London Tuesday needs to have a conversation tonight and wants to talk to him, even if he doesn't want to talk back. I'm a conscious moth, completely aware the flame is going to burn the shit out of me, yet unable to keep from hurtling headlong toward it, hoping it might change its mind at the last minute.

"I'm definitely here for a cocktail." I study the list, letting my attention be drawn from . . . Hell, I don't know his name yet. "You haven't told me your name. I can't keep calling you the Daniel De Luca doppelgänger."

He rolls his eyes and clearly doesn't give a shit I can see him perfectly fine, despite the low lighting. "You could just stop following me around."

I laugh-snort and turn back to the menu. "You're following *me*. This is the hotel *I'm* staying at. I'm supposed to be here. What's your excuse?"

I don't expect him to answer, but he does. "I'm meeting a friend."

Give me an inch and I'll take half an inch—usually. But I'm in London. And London Tuesday is . . . well, I'm not sure, but I'm making her up as I go along. I can be anyone I like, and right now, I feel like taking a country mile.

"A girlfriend?"

He narrows his eyes. "None of your business, but no."

"A boyfriend?"

He snaps his head around. "I'm meeting a male friend. About business."

"Interesting," I say. It's not that interesting, but I want it to be. "Have you known this male friend long?"

"Since university."

"We call it college," I say.

"So?"

I don't know if he's nervous, uptight, or just an asshole, but his rudeness is grating. I skim the cocktail list and order a cocktail called Life's a Peach.

"Really?" he asks. "Life's a Peach." He shakes his head like it's the final straw. "So typical."

Jed would normally order my cocktails for me if we were out together. Or if I was with girlfriends, I'd just have whatever most people were ordering. But right now, I'm not even embarrassed he doesn't like my order. I can't help laughing at his dramatic response. "So typical of what? Me? Americans? Women? Put me out of my misery; tell me what about my drink order is so abhorrent to you."

"People like you." He lifts his hands and makes air quotes. "Happy people. Optimists." He says it with such disdain it's like he's physically pushed me.

It's my turn to frown.

My fiancé just broke up with me. When I get back home, I have to find a place to live in Manhattan that isn't a shoebox or roach infested and costs less than five grand a month. I've been sent abroad with the threat of layoffs snapping at my heels. I've lost my fiancé and my home, and I'm looking at possibly losing my job. "Happy" isn't how I'd describe myself. But I have to believe things are going to get better and that the future's bright.

He's right. I *am* an optimist.

"Why is being optimistic a bad thing? Why is being happy something to complain about?"

He pauses . . . and this time I know it's not because he's ignoring me; he's really thinking about it. Eventually he turns and looks me in the eye, and I can feel the intensity of his stare in my hips, my throat, my wrists, my toes.

"It's about authenticity." He holds my gaze, and suddenly I'm feeling a little faint. I take a deep breath, and I realize by doing so, my bosom is heaving like I'm in a costume drama and the man next to me is the rake who's about to steal my virtue—just like Daniel De Luca as the title character in *Alexander, Duke of Hearts*. "Are you *truly* happy, Tuesday?" Again, his words are like a physical blow.

I wonder if he's flipped open the top of my brain and can see every thought of mine as they form.

"Of course I'm happy. I'm in *London*," I say, almost trying to convince myself.

He shrugs and sips on his wine.

I shiver. Maybe it's time to give up trying to be friends with this guy.

"You never told me your name," I say, more quietly this time.

He sighs. "Ben."

I'm nodding when we're interrupted by a man who I presume is Ben's dinner date. A shorter blond guy who gives me Bradley Cooper vibes slaps Ben on his back, then catches sight of me and immediately offers his hand. "I'm Nick." He shoots Ben a questioning glance.

"I'm Tuesday," I say, taking his hand. "I'm a friend of Ben's."

I can almost *hear* Ben rolling his eyes.

"I'm delighted to meet you. A friend of Ben's is a friend of mine." He squints at me, and I can tell he wants to ask me what kind of friend I am, exactly.

"I'm from New York," I say. "Just landed two days ago. Ben was the first person I met, and we've been firm friends ever since."

I glance at Ben, and I swear I see the corner of his mouth lift, as if he's given up trying to *not* be my friend and is going to let me say what I like. Nick frowns like what I'm saying doesn't quite add up. He's right, of course.

"Let's get our table," Ben says.

"I do hope you're joining us?" Nick asks, his eyes full of mischief.

"No, she is not," Ben snaps.

I glance between the two men and something inside me shifts. They want opposite things, and I get to decide. Normally, I'd find the idea of choosing impossible. But today it feels easier. The stakes are lower.

"I'll leave you two gentlemen in peace." I glance down at my cocktail. "I have my drink for company."

Ben's frown deepens, and I get the feeling he's just about to say something. But he doesn't and they head off to the restaurant.

I take another sip of Life's a Peach and wonder what in my life would change if this drink were a magic potion that *creates* a peachy life. I scoff quietly. What would change? What wouldn't, more like.

"Have you eaten?" A voice comes from behind me.

I spin, and it's Ben asking me the question.

"Eaten what?" I ask.

"Come and have dinner with us," he says. It's not so much an invitation. More of an order.

I shake my head. "I couldn't—"

He growls. Well and truly growls, like a wolf or something, and it stops me in my tracks.

"Did you just—"

He picks up my cocktail and stalks across to the restaurant. I have no choice but to follow him.

CHAPTER FIVE

"How long are you in town for, Tuesday?" Nick asks as he puts his napkin on his lap. We're seated around a square table with Nick and Ben opposite each other and me between them. I feel a little awkward, but having company at dinner feels good. And with two handsome British guys? I'm not about to file a complaint.

I suck in a breath. "Thirty-four days." I glance across at Ben, but his expression gives nothing away. "The bank I work for has been taken over by a UK bank, and they're trying to consolidate the two management-track programs. We all have to do a stint as a project manager, working directly with a member of the C-suite. Then they decide whether we deserve a place on the new program. I drew the CEO."

"Could be outstanding, could be a disaster—depending how good you are at your job," Nick summarizes accurately, although I've been trying not to think about the disaster angle.

Ben inexplicably growls again, and goose bumps scatter across my skin.

"Thanks for reminding me," I reply.

"Did you grow up in New York?" Nick asks. He's friendly and attentive, but not in a way that I feel he's coming on to me. It's almost as if he's treating me like Ben's girlfriend.

"Raised upstate, then moved to the city when I went to college."

"New York's fun, isn't it, Ben?" Nick asks. "I had my stag do there."

"Your what now?" I ask.

"A party with the boys before I got married."

"Oh, a bachelor party. You came to New York? Where did you stay?"

He nods at Ben. "Ben very generously took us over on his jet, and we stayed at a hotel in Midtown. The Avenue. Know it? The bar there is epic."

I narrow my eyes. A jet? Who am I dining with? "Hold your horses, cowboy," I say, and I turn to Ben, who's perusing the menu. "You have a jet?" I take in his suit a little more carefully. Having hung out with Jed and his corporate attorney friends, I'm used to a nice custom suit. And Ben's is certainly nice. It's a dark navy and makes his shoulders look wide enough to carry the *Titanic*.

"I'm going to have the lamb," he says, ignoring my question. "And I think I'm going to need another glass of cabernet."

"Not like you to be drinking by the glass." Nick points his thumb at his friend. "He's one of those who likes the best of everything, so even if he only wants a glass, he'll order a bottle of something very old and expensive and only *have* a glass."

I shake my head. "How wasteful. You'd never catch me wasting wine."

Nick laughs and calls the waitress over.

She stares right at me. "What can I get you?"

My heartbeat quickens and I glance between Ben and Nick. I can't remember the last time I went to a restaurant and ordered for myself. Jed would always order for the both of us, depending on what he wanted to try. "Uh . . . gosh, I'm not sure. Whatever you suggest."

Ben shoots me a disapproving glare. "Pick what you'd like."

Nick interrupts the awkward pause. "I'm going to have the cod."

"Cod," I say, scanning the menu. "That sounds good. I'll do the same."

Ben orders the lamb and the waitress disappears.

"Tell me more about this friendship you two have," Nick asks. "Excuse me for being nosy, Tuesday, but new friendships aren't really on-brand for Ben in my experience. Is it a holiday romance?"

Ben chokes on his wine and thumps his chest with his fist to try to catch his breath.

I can't help but laugh at his reaction. "I have a confession," I say. "Apart from not sleeping with your very attractive friend here, I'm also not really friends with him. I keep running into him, and if I were a different type of woman, I'd say the universe is telling us we need to know each other. Something in his frown and tight jaw tells me he needs a friend like me."

Nick smiles at me and then glances at Ben. "You know, I think you might be right."

"She's being ridiculous. I don't *need* anything. Or anybody."

Instinctively, I reach for his arm to comfort him and a buzz of electricity dances across my palm. "Don't say that." I think he feels it, too, because he pulls his arm away like I've slathered him in mud. He proceeds to stand, take off his jacket, then place it on the back of the chair.

If I thought he was handsome before—which, no doubt, I did—the bright white of his shirt lights up his face to a truly devastating effect. The contours of his cheekbones are so high, I've got altitude sickness just looking at them. His face is the kind photographers love to take pictures of and painters like to recreate on canvas—he's a classical beauty. An image I'm much more used to seeing carved in marble or up on the big screen in a movie theater. My gaze follows his throat to his open collar and down. There is no disguising his fit, lean body under the thin white cotton.

"Did you just flex?" Nick asks Ben.

"What?" Ben asks, picking up his glass of wine. "Don't be ridiculous."

"I think you're trying to impress our American friend."

"I told you, she's not my friend," Ben says. "She's my stalker."

"Nope," I say. "I've never followed you anywhere. And FYI, I'm staying at this hotel, and you kidnapped my cocktail. Who's stalking whom, exactly?"

Nick grins. "If he didn't want you to join us for dinner, believe me, you wouldn't be here. Ben is not a man who puts up with things he doesn't like."

Ben starts to protest, but before he can vocalize what we all know he's thinking, I interject. "Ben told me you were meeting to discuss business. What business are you in?" I ask.

I want to change the subject. There's no doubt Ben is attractive, but I'm not interested in romance at the moment. I want to focus on work. It feels more solid than being a girlfriend. I was blindsided by Jed dumping me, and although the initial hurt has faded quicker than I expected, I'm not ready for anything new—not even a holiday romance.

"I'm in property development," Nick says.

I nod and turn to Ben. "You too?"

Ben shrugs. "Among other things."

"What are we discussing?" I ask, glancing between the two friends.

"Ben wants to buy a group of hotels, but the owner doesn't want to sell."

"Nick," Ben growls. "We're not going to talk about business in front of—"

"Oh, don't worry about me!" I say. "My ex-fiancé was a corporate attorney. Practically all he did was discuss business. I won't be offended at all."

"I'm not concerned with you being offended," Ben says, his jaw tight. "I'm concerned about confidentiality. I don't discuss my business affairs with strangers, even if I *am* stalking them." He delivers the line in such a deadpan way, I nearly miss it.

"Ha! So you admit it," I say, narrowing my eyes.

Ben's expressionless, despite plenty of evidence that he has a real sense of humor in there, hiding deep down inside.

"And I work in banking," I reassure him. "I'm a professional—completely trustworthy. I'm not going to tell a soul."

"I'm not discussing it," Ben says.

"I think you're going to want to hear what I'm going to say," Nick says. "Because the duke is hosting a shooting party the weekend after next, and I'm invited."

Ben freezes, his glass halfway between the table and his deliciously full lips.

"I'm taking Elizabeth, obviously," Nick continues. "I mentioned I was meant to be away with an old friend and managed to get the invitation extended to you and *your* significant other too."

Ben places his glass back on the table. He seems to lift himself up in his chair by five inches. "Are you serious?" There's a grit in his voice I haven't heard before.

"Completely. So stop fucking around and let's make a plan."

"We need to stop fucking around and make a plan," Ben echoes.

I'm not quite sure who the duke is, or what the hell a shooting party is, but apparently it's serious. And also, honestly, it sounds a little dull. I might ditch dinner and go rewatch one of my favorite Daniel De Luca films. I've got the urge to snuggle up with some popcorn and press "Play" on *The Lady Loves a Loser*. I loved that one so much because Daniel and Olivia Lamb, who gives Elizabeth Taylor vibes, really seem to hate each other for the first part of the movie, but it's completely obvious they're perfect for each other.

"You know, I'm going to leave you guys to eat your dinner and make your plans in peace. I'm hanging up my stalking shoes and gonna slip on my Netflix slippers."

"Please stay," Nick says. "I actually think you might be helpful to Ben."

I pause and stay silent, expecting him to elaborate. How am I going to be helpful planning a trip to a shooting party?

Nick looks at Ben with a serious expression.

"What?" Ben asks.

"Ask her to stay, mate. You might need her help."

"I very much doubt that. But Monday is welcome to stay if she'd like. No doubt she'll make better company than you."

Another joke. A twirling ball of amusement spins in my stomach. *Saturday Night Live* will sign this guy up if he's not careful.

"Stay, please," Nick says again. "I'll explain my plan."

Our appetizers arrive, and when the waitress leaves us, Nick leans into the table as if he's about to tell us the location of the Holy Grail. "I've been working directly and indirectly for the Duke of Brandon for years now," Nick says. "He's a huge landowner in the UK and the only shareholder of the Castles and Palaces Hotel Group. Ben wants to buy the hotel group—it's one of the most prestigious in Europe. Small, boutique hotels, often in some of the most historic houses in the United Kingdom."

"It's good business," Ben says.

"And he has other reasons," Nick says to me. "Anyway, the duke doesn't want to sell."

"He won't even take a meeting with me," Ben says, as if it's completely ludicrous anyone wouldn't cut off their arm to have a meeting with him. Maybe they would. He could be Harry Styles's dad for all I know.

"The duke is notoriously private, but his wife is a little more extroverted. It's the duchess who's encouraged the duke to host the shooting party."

"But the duke will definitely be there?" Ben asks.

"Absolutely," Nick confirms.

"Do we go up on Friday?" Ben asks.

"It depends who you're referring to as 'we.'" Nick winces, like Ben is going to start putting the pieces together any moment now and lose it.

"And who is 'we,' Nicolas?" His tone is one hundred percent Daniel in *The Lady Loves a Loser*—wry and skeptical. Maybe that explains my sudden urge to rewatch after all these years.

"Well, that depends. I'm finally going to get you in front of the duke; it's going to be your chance to sell yourself."

"My offer sells itself. It's more than generous."

"He doesn't need the money. I don't know how many times I need to explain to you that the duke is all about legacy. Not money."

"Everyone's got their price."

Nick pauses, shakes his head, and rolls his wineglass in one hand and then the other. "No. He doesn't. You could offer him double what you're thinking, and the answer would still be no."

"Then why am I wasting time going to a shooting party?" Ben asks.

I'm ready for the answer. This sounds like the start to a cozy mystery, and I'm here for it. Daniel De Luca's brief foray into television with *Hamish McPhee Investigates* might not have had the ratings to secure a second season, but my mom and I loved it.

"Family means everything to him," Nick says.

"So you keep telling me."

"As you know, the duke and the duchess's son died in a boating accident when he was just two," Nick says.

The mention of death sparks a flash of memory—the summer I turned fourteen, and the last vacation Dad, Mom, and I took together before everything changed. I thought we'd have those lakeside summers every year, because I didn't understand yet that nothing lasts forever. Life can't always be rowing in lazy circles on calm water, toasting marshmallows while watching the sun go down. Not always. Maybe not ever.

"I heard the reason he won't think about selling the hotel business is because he always expected an heir would run it before taking on the entire estate. He's always wanted to pass it down to the next generation."

"Does he have nephews?" Ben asks. "Nieces? A daughter?"

Nick shakes his head. "No one. If you really want to buy the hotels, you're going to need to go in there and prove to him you're a worthy successor."

Ben pulls in a steady breath. "Okay. That's not a problem. I'm committed to owning the business long term. I'm not some private equity house that's going to prop it up with debt and drain it of cash. I'm certain I can convince him I deserve it."

"No, not on your own, you can't," Nick says. "You need to become a man who thinks like he does, who thinks family is everything. Someone who's all about creating a legacy to pass down to your children."

"Children?" It's like someone has put sour milk under his nose. "I'm not thinking about a family."

"Then you won't get the hotels. It's as simple as that," Nick says. "You need to paint yourself as a family man, working to create something your children can one day inherit. The duke wants to find a home for some of his assets, but he won't make compromises to do it."

"So what do you suggest? I kidnap a baby and bring it along for the weekend?"

Nick tilts his head one way and then the other, as if considering Ben's suggestion. "Probably not the best idea."

"Okay, so I'll kidnap a woman instead and take her to Gretna Green."

Nick winces. "Kidnapping probably shouldn't be part of your plan. And Gretna Green isn't Vegas. You'd still have a two-week wait to get married."

"So what's your suggestion?" Ben asks.

"A fiancée would do it. You're looking forward to the big day, can't wait to start a family, you want five kids and to move out to the country—just like him."

Ben chuckles, takes another sip of wine, and then picks up the drink list. "No problem. You think they have fiancées on the menu?"

Nick fixes his mouth in a straight line, raises his eyebrows, and then looks pointedly at me.

It's like someone's pressed "Pause" on the scene. While the men are busy not speaking, my brain catches up to what Nick's thinking.

He can't be serious.

"Absolutely not," Ben says at the same time as I blurt out something slightly less eloquent.

"Why not?" Nick asks. "You're following each other around. You need someone who isn't actually trying to get you to commit. Because we all know how that goes."

I like Nick. Ben is clearly rich and powerful and in a permanent bad mood, but Nick doesn't pull any punches with him. Ben needs someone like Nick in his life.

"I don't need a fake fiancée," Ben says.

Nick winces. "I beg to differ."

"Well, I'm certain *I* don't need a fake fiancé," I say. These next weeks are about keeping a job. Stopping my life from completely falling apart. They're not about pretending to date a stranger, even if that stranger has biceps of steel and cheekbones I want to lick. Even though my default position is to say yes if I can help someone, this time, I have to say no.

We fall silent as the waitress clears our plates and tops up our wine.

"You heard her. Even if I was prepared to entertain your harebrained scheme, Saturday Afternoon here won't hear of it."

"Name's still Tuesday," I mumble under my breath.

"You can solve that problem," Nick says, ignoring me. Does he know something I don't? "You said it yourself: Everyone has their price."

"Nick! I'm not for sale, no matter what you might think." I push my chair out and scrabble in my bag. This is getting weird and I need to get out of here.

"He didn't mean that." Ben places a hand on my upper arm, and I freeze. All I can feel is the heat of his hand and the way it rockets through my body like a firework.

"He's out of line and thinks money can buy everything—and most of the time, that's true," Ben says, his voice low and serious. "I don't think that of you. And neither does he. Please stay."

It's the most he's spoken to me since I met him, and there's something so reassuring, so knowing, so completely protective to his tone, that I put my bag down.

Our entrees arrive and our table is completely silent.

"I'm sorry," Nick says. "I was out of order. I thought it might be the perfect solution . . . and I wasn't trying to imply you were . . ."

"A prostitute?" I suggest.

Nick shrugs. "It's just like Ben says. Most things can be solved with money. We need to think of someone else, though. What about that Paula you were seeing?"

Ben gives a brief shake of his head, and Nick doesn't push it. I focus on the cod. The sauce is really salty, but I'm not that hungry, and I don't want to upset anyone by complaining. I eyed some cashews in the minibar in my room. I've been wanting an excuse to open them.

"What about her friend Rosemary?"

Ben's jaw tightens. "No." He glances at me. I pull my mouth into a smile. He looks down at my plate. "You don't like it?"

"I'm just not that hungry," I say with a shrug.

"If none of your exes, then who?" Nick asks.

Ben beckons over the waitress, and I send up a silent prayer, hoping he's not going to say anything more about my cod. I really hope I haven't offended him.

"We'd like another main course. What would you prefer?" he asks, looking at me.

I smile at the waitress. "I'm fine. Really."

"A selection of starters, then," he says to the waitress. She nods once and disappears.

I start to apologize. "I'm sorry, I—"

"No apologies." He turns back to Nick. "We need to come up with a different solution," Ben says. "I'm not getting fake-engaged to anyone."

"I'm telling you, there is no other solution, and not even transforming into the ultimate family man is a guarantee. The duke isn't driven by logic when it comes to his hotel group. He's entirely driven by emotion. If you're not willing to be the man he wants to sell to, then you need to give up on your desire to own those hotels."

"Never," Ben says.

I try to focus on the embossed pattern on the tablecloth and my plans for the next day and the way my arm still buzzes, even though it's been at least twenty minutes since Ben touched me. Nick and Ben continue to argue about the approach to take with the duke. I'm happy to not be included at all in their discussion. I'm not pretending to be an almost-stranger's fiancée just so he can buy some hotel.

"Accept the invitation on my behalf," Ben says. "And I'll bring a plus-one."

"Finally," Nick says.

Well, it won't be me, I don't say, just as a selection of appetizers appears. "I'm planning a day trip to Stonehenge this weekend. It's where Daniel De Luca filmed the most heartbreaking scene ever—when his wife dies in *Antonia*." I wasn't actually planning on that trip, but I happened to notice it listed on the convention roster, and it sounds plausible. Ben doesn't seem to be listening.

"That was a terrible film," Nick says.

Everyone thought it was a terrible film, but I still feel like I should defend it. "That movie showcased some of his greatest acting." I take a forkful of rice studded with pine nuts and fat, green olives. It's delicious.

"Would twenty thousand dollars be useful?" Ben says out of nowhere, and I do a cartoon gulp, visible to everyone in the restaurant.

"Are you asking . . . me?" I ask.

He doesn't answer but continues to hold my gaze in a way that might be terrifying if he wasn't so completely attractive.

I look away because my lips begin to buzz like they're impatient for a kiss, and I'm a little concerned I'm going to lunge at Ben. "When isn't twenty thousand dollars useful?"

"That's a very good point," he says. "So would you be my fiancée for the weekend for twenty thousand dollars?"

I open my mouth but words don't come out.

Of course I don't want to disappoint Ben. I never want to disappoint anyone, which Melanie would tell me is both my best and worst quality. Twenty thousand dollars is a lot of money. Money that's particularly useful to someone with no savings and an apartment in Manhattan to find and finance. But I can't take money for . . . lying. It seems wrong. And I can't provide a girlfriend experience. Even for free. Ask Jed.

"I'm sorry, I can't."

Ben looks disappointed. It sounds like he really wants these hotels and has to have a fiancée to get them. I need to leave. Right now. Or I'm going to find myself doing something I shouldn't and saying yes to something I should definitely and completely say no to.

"Please excuse me . . ." I hold my hand to my ear. "I can hear Netflix calling my name. See you tomorrow morning at Coffee Confide in Me, Ben. Nice to meet you, Nick."

And before either of them can say anything to stop me, I race toward the life-size cutout of Daniel De Luca that's been placed by the elevator.

CHAPTER SIX

It's seven thirty-seven and I'm at my desk outside Mr. Jenkins's office, ready for when the man himself arrives. If I ever get to the point in my career when I employ a project manager, I will definitely want them to arrive before me.

The offices here are very different from New York. Long, dark, narrow corridors and poky rooms, compared to the spacious, bright, floor-to-ceiling-windowed space of our Wall Street offices. If I didn't know better, I'd say Daniel De Luca filmed *Big Money* on this exact floor of the building. It has the same brown leather chairs opposite the elevators and the same mahogany paneling on every wall. If only Daniel De Luca was about to arrive to boss me around. I've seen Mr. Jenkins on Zoom and can guarantee he's not going to get mistaken for my teenage crush anytime soon. Then again, I'm definitely not going to get mistaken for America's sweetheart, Julia Alice. My thighs are way too wide, and my hair is not nearly as shiny.

I can't help but think I drew the short straw ending up here. The CFO is based in New York, and one of my counterparts is doing his stint as project manager there and has his own office. The director of compliance is based there too. Why I got shuffled halfway around the world remains to be seen. I'm sure some people would think working so closely with the CEO is a better gig, but it feels like the stakes are too high for comfort.

"How's the hotel?" Gail asks from where she sits opposite me. I've only known Gail, executive assistant to Mr. Jenkins, for a day, but I like her already. She's in her mid-forties, and both today and yesterday wore a headband color-coordinated to her outfit. You gotta respect someone who matches their headband to their shoes.

"Good," I reply. "They upgraded my room, so that's nice."

"So nice." She pauses, but I get the impression she's got more to say. Frankly, I'm here for it. Anything to take my mind off my meeting with the boss at eight. "Am I right in thinking there's a convention on there at the moment?"

I laugh. "Daniel De Luca. Yeah. Can't miss it. There are life-sized cardboard cutouts of him everywhere."

Her eyes grow wide like she wishes she had a life-sized cardboard cutout of him next to her right now. "Are you a fan?" she asks. "I do hope so. I read about the conference, and when it came to booking you in somewhere close by, it seemed like a good idea. Less so if you hate him."

Honestly, if I'd known about the convention before I arrived, I would have probably tried to get the booking transferred to another hotel. There are so many memories of my mom wrapped up with him and his movies. To stay on track, moving forward, I've spent years avoiding things I thought would bring me pain. But now? I'm pleased I'm there. Remembering my mom so vividly and often isn't as painful as I expected.

"Yeah, I'm a fan. I've got a lot of happy memories of watching his movies," I reply. "I was totally in love with him when I was a teen."

Gail gives me a goofy grin. I'd put money on that she'd be squealing right about now if we weren't at work. "Me too. Except I *still* think he's wonderful."

I smile at Gail, getting giddy.

"You know, we have a very important client who looks a little like Daniel De Luca." She looks wistfully into the middle distance, like she's traveled back to a time where women swooned. Maybe it's an English thing, and she has a ready supply of smelling salts stashed in her drawer for when she actually faints. "He actually owns the building and has offices on the top floor. Sometimes I catch a glimpse of him crossing the lobby, and every now and again he pops in to see Mr. Jenkins."

Is she talking about Ben, or is there more than one Daniel De Luca doppelgänger in this city? Before I can ask her more about the object of her swooning, the elevator doors ping. In a Pavlovian response, Gail pulls her shoulders back and straightens in her seat.

"Gail," a man yells as he rounds the corner, waving a folded-up newspaper.

"James," Gail responds, leaping to her feet as he reaches her desk.

Mr. Jenkins, I presume.

"Bloody traffic is a nightmare on Piccadilly. I've had to walk and it's just starting to rain." He sweeps a hand across his balding head as Gail rounds her desk and helps him out of his coat.

"We've got Tuesday with us today," Gail says.

I stand and feel suddenly awkward and very American. How do Brits greet each other in the office?

He turns to me, his eyebrows knitted together in confusion. Gail obviously catches his bewilderment and adds, "The new project manager from the New York office, Tuesday Reynolds."

I hold out my hand and he shakes it firmly. "I'm very pleased to be here and excited about being able to be of assistance."

"Very good, and what do I call you?" he asks.

I smile. "I answer to most things, but Tuesday is what most people settle on."

"Like Wednesday?" he asks. "Just a day earlier?"

"Exactly." I press my lips together to stop myself from smiling. I don't want to offend anyone on my second day, but Mr. Jenkins is funny and I'm not sure if it's intentional.

He narrows his eyes like he's not sure whether he's entirely convinced. "Righty-oh. We have a meeting." He thrusts out his arm, revealing his watch, sharply bends it at the elbow and takes in the time. "Gail, please get us some coffee. We'll start early. We have a lot to get through. Follow me, Tuesday."

In my experience, the more senior to you the person you're meeting with is, the longer you're kept waiting. But things with Mr. Jenkins don't seem to work like that. Maybe it's a British thing. Maybe this is why he's the CEO. I scramble for a pen and my notebook and follow him into his office.

"Take a seat, Tuesday. I'm afraid I don't do well at chitchat, so let's get straight down to it, shall we?" There's an old-fashioned mahogany coat stand to the side of the office, and he slots his umbrella into the bottom and turns to me. "I'm responsible to the shareholders of the bank for the running of the business. Yet as you might expect, as CEO, I'm not all that involved with the day-to-day operations."

I furiously write notes as if I'm going to take a test at the end of the day.

"The private-client side of our business is small, but that's where I started, and I still act as accounts manager for one or two ultra-high-net-worth individuals. Clearly, I'm just the figurehead. I can't take any credit for the actual work managing the portfolios of those clients. The Private Client Team does that, but I still have the necessary face-to-face contact with those clients." He takes a seat at his desk and flips open his laptop in front of him.

"I understand," I say.

"One of those clients uses us for some of his UK-based investments—shares and bonds. Most of his wealth is managed for him in-house. He really only still uses us for legacy reasons—I'm close with his father. But his name attached to our business is only a good thing, and I do everything I can to retain his investments. It's a fact that, as a client, he gives our bank a gold stamp of approval many other private clients take very seriously, as well as the boards of various pension funds that invest heavily with us."

Mr. Jenkins obviously wants to be very clear about the importance of this wealthy client, but why? Nerves start to swirl in my stomach as

I suspect the answer involves me, this prestigious client, and my entire professional future.

"As you must know from the New York office, we give all our clients an annual health check, which goes beyond the day-to-day portfolio management. When we do this for ultra-high-net-worth individuals, we like to look at their wealth more holistically to make sure we're best serving their needs." He sounds like he's reading from the bank's website, but I nod like what he's saying is riveting. "But these annual reviews have a secondary purpose. One that benefits the bank."

He looks me in the eye as if he's about to draw back the curtain on a secret known to only five people on earth. I do my best to look riveted.

"It allows the bank to demonstrate value. It's a platform from which we can show the client why we are the perfect, most trusted partner for them."

I try not to let my shoulders drop with disappointment at his lack-luster revelation.

"It's also an opportunity to see if we can be managing more of their wealth," Mr. Jenkins continues.

"Client retention. Client growth," I paraphrase.

"Exactly," he says. "In relation to the Kelley account, client retention is paramount. Client growth is . . . almost impossible, but we try, nonetheless." Before I can ask why it's impossible, he leans toward me and drops his voice. "Last year we had a hiccup with the account. Some of the numbers were wrong, and Mr. Kelley was able to identify the mistakes during the meeting."

The thought sends a shiver down my spine.

"It was embarrassing. For the bank. For me. I don't want it to happen again. I want everything scoured for mistakes a thousand times."

His eyes bulge and he fists his hands, almost as if he's reliving the embarrassment in the moment.

"I understand," I say. Although I'm not exactly sure what my role is in all this.

"Good!" He bangs his fists on the desk, his voice returning to full volume. "I want you to be my eyes and ears on all this. Obviously, the Private Client Team is all over it, but you're going to be the final pair of eyes on everything. I don't want to see a graph, report, or table you haven't personally signed off on."

I grip my pen a little tighter. That seems like a lot of responsibility. "I'll make sure it's all exactly how it should be."

"Good. The meeting is in four weeks. Don't leave anything to the last minute. Kelley has a habit of moving up our meetings. I think he'd like to catch us off-balance again this year if he can. The man is too smart by half." He switches his attention to the laptop in front of him. "That's all, Tuesday. Don't let me down."

I scoop up my pad and stand. There's no chance I'm going to let him down. I'll work day and night if I have to. If it's within my power, Mr. Kelley—whoever he is—will be skipping out of his meeting with Mr. Jenkins, he'll be so impressed with his health check.

"Just one more thing," Mr. Jenkins says. "Kelley likes to drop into the office now and then. Usually only when Chelsea's lost. He's a bloody Arsenal supporter, just like his father. Make sure there's nothing lying about that may catch his eye. I don't want to start a conversation I can't finish."

I nod and head to the door. As I grab the handle, it moves, and before I know it, I end up pushed behind the door as it opens.

"I just wanted to come and pay my respects," a familiar voice announces.

Gently, I push the door closed so I'm no longer squashed behind it, and I almost choke at the sight of Mr. Jenkins's visitor. Is that who I think it is? I can only see the back of his head, but isn't it—

"And to give you this." He holds up a blue-and-white key ring. "It was on sale."

"Ha, ha," Mr. Jenkins says, clearly not amused. "You're no funnier than your father."

I take a couple of steps around the door, unable to tear my gaze away from the office interloper, when the door creaks and both Mr. Jenkins and my oldest friend in London turn to stare at me.

I pull my mouth into an apple-pie grin. "Hi," I say.

Ben frowns but doesn't say anything.

"This is our new project manager," Mr. Jenkins says. "She's going to be helping me prepare for your health check, among other things."

Someone's hooked a cannonball onto my insides as realization dawns. Ben, the Daniel De Luca doppelgänger, the guy I flat-out refused to help last night, is my boss's most important client.

CHAPTER SEVEN

As I'm climbing Cowcross Street—and "climbing" is accurate, since the road is as steep as Everest—I make a mental note not to visit San Francisco anytime soon. I also remind myself never to look up the origins of London street names ever again. Cowcross sounded like a cute, eccentric name. A Google search set me straight. Apparently, the name pays homage to the cows that have been herded up this road to their slaughter. I'm in Smithfield, the meatpacking-slash-slaughtering district of London. It's probably not an area I would have visited, but I have a front door to find.

In *Sunshine on a Rainy Day,* Daniel De Luca played a down-on-his-luck artist on the brink of giving it all up when he meets an heiress in front of his favorite painting at a gallery. I'm trying to find the front door of his studio flat in the film. It might seem odd to want to visit a front door, but the scene where he and Jennifer Elm, my second-favorite actress of all time, argue and he runs out after her, barefoot, into the rain-filled street is one of my favorites.

Daniel barefoot in a rainstorm is a scene to be savored. And I'm hoping it will bring me luck. Finding out the guy who may or may not lose an important deal because I declined to be his fake fiancée was my boss's most important client wasn't the highlight of my week. I don't think Ben will say anything directly to Mr. Jenkins, but he might be predisposed to nitpick the health check documents because he knows I prepared them.

After Ben dropped off the key ring, we had an awkward introduction where we kinda sorta acknowledged we'd met before. Mr. Jenkins was distracted and didn't push for details. Since then, I haven't stopped thinking about Ben and whether I should have accepted his offer. Twenty thousand dollars is a lot of money. And Ben? He seemed like a nice guy who needed my help.

My phone buzzes and I take a climbing break to see who's calling. Panting, I think of the added insult to injury for those poor cows, who were forced into a grueling workout before being put to their death.

It's Melanie. We still don't have the time difference figured out, so we've been missing each other's calls. I have so much to tell her.

"Finally," she says as I answer.

"I miss you." It isn't how I'd planned to start our call, but hearing her voice triggers something in me.

"I miss you too. New York City isn't the same without you."

It's only been a week, and it wasn't like we saw each other every day when I lived with Jed, but I know how she feels. There's something about knowing your best friend is a cab ride away that's reassuring.

"How are you?" I ask, wanting to hear all the news. Coming to London was so sudden. I haven't seen our group of girlfriends since Jed and I broke up, and I've only heard from Melanie. They probably don't want me to think they've been gossiping, but of course they know we're not together. And they must know I'm in London—I posted an image of Green Park to Instagram a couple of days ago.

"Same old, same old," she replies. "I want to hear about you. Are you leaning in to rediscovering Daniel De Luca? Have you come across the man himself during your quest? I'm convinced you're going to. I feel it in my soul."

Daniel De Luca quests. Maybe that's a business idea I could run with if I get fired.

"I haven't seen the real thing, but a Daniel De Luca look-alike offered me twenty grand to pretend to be his fiancée, and I turned him down and then found out he's my boss's most important client so . . .

London is interesting if nothing else." London is more than interesting. Setting work aside, I love how very different it feels from New York, and how similar it is, too—like the cities share the same bass line but have different melodies or something.

"Okay, I'm going to need you to break that down for me."

I start walking up the hill again, taking my time, trying to keep an eye out for Daniel's blue door as I tell Melanie about Ben. I explain how I met him in Green Park at the very spot Daniel De Luca met Julia Alice in *Love Me Like a Boss*, then how I bumped into him again and again. I recap dinner and how we went from strangers to discussing engagements. "So I received my second proposal of marriage in London. Who'd have guessed?"

"And he has a jet? Have you googled him? What did you say his last name was?"

"No idea," I reply. "I never asked." I pause for a second. "Of course I know his last name. It's Kelley with an *E* before the *Y*." I put Melanie on speaker and type his name into my phone.

She must be doing the same thing because she squeals. "He's gorgeous. And you said no because . . . ?"

Melanie sounds incredulous, like I turned down a marriage proposal from Daniel De Luca himself. Panic starts to echo in my ears. Did I do the right thing? I thought my best friend would be high-fiving me through my phone for saying no. She was always encouraging me to voice more of an opinion with Jed.

"To be clear, you're looking for a reason beyond the fact he's a total stranger? And I didn't know he was a client of the bank at the time." The panic grows louder.

I'm met with silence on the other end of the line. I can't believe Melanie disapproves of my decision. We're usually on the same page about most things.

"You think I should have said yes?" I ask. "He could be a people trafficker. Or a drug baron. Or—"

"A handsome, single guy who needed a woman to pretend to be his girlfriend and was prepared to give you a hefty chunk of savings, which you've been complaining about not having."

Melanie sounds *disappointed*. We probably could get a bigger place if I had a little more cash. My stomach curdles as the panic mixes with regret. Was my refusal too rash? "But you know the saying—there's no such thing as a free lunch. If he was offering me that much money, there had to be a reason."

"Sounds like you didn't stick around long enough to find out. Maybe he just really wants those hotels. This Ben guy sounds super wealthy. He probably just picked a number he thought you couldn't say no to. Although, if it were me, I would have negotiated him up fifty percent. Can you call him and tell him you've changed your mind?"

"I don't have his number," I say. I could probably find it in the bank's system. Hell, I could probably run into him at Coffee Confide in Me, although I haven't this week. "Didn't I come to London to keep my job? Not to follow some rich guy around pretending I'm engaged to him. I don't want to lose focus on the end goal here." The pretending bit wouldn't be that hard. My broken engagement is still fresh, but the tingles I felt when I touched Ben revealed that my vagina isn't as loyal as my heart.

"Maybe," Melanie says. "Or you could be killing two birds with one stone by saying yes. In fact, I count three birds. First, you don't make an enemy of the bank's important client. I mean, that's a win. Impressing your boss is why you're there."

It's a compelling argument I can't ignore.

"Second, you don't have to worry about not having money for an apartment, plus some savings to fall back on. Then finally, and I think this is most important, pretending to be a gorgeous billionaire's fiancée sounds *fun*. And a fun injection is exactly what you need about now."

Everything she's saying is true, and I feel terrible for not talking it through with her before saying no.

"You don't think pretending to be a stranger's fiancée for money is too weird and sex-workery?"

Surely she'll see my point. She'll understand why I said no.

"So if he didn't pay you, it'd be better?"

I spot the blue door on the other side of the street. Except it's not blue. It's been repainted peacock green. I recognize the tarnished brass doorknob and the lantern hanging outside.

"I'm serious," Melanie says. "Say that when you bumped into him in Green Park, he hadn't been so grumpy. Maybe the two of you had a brief flirtation. Perhaps he recommended a restaurant and took a picture of you so you didn't have to rely on selfies. Then you bumped into him at the coffee shop . . . Let's say he bought your coffee, and the two of you sat down for a chat. Maybe he asked you to dinner, and you found out about his dilemma."

Melanie should have been a lawyer.

"You're right, it's a good way of looking at it," I confess. "But isn't it different when he's offering to *buy* my time?"

"Why?"

I don't have an answer. "I don't know. Do you remember the scene in *Sunshine on a Rainy Day* when a barefoot Daniel rushes after Jennifer after the fight and gets locked out?" I stand in front of the door and just stare at it.

"Of course I do." Melanie has also watched every single DDL film ever made. One of the perks of being my best friend. "That was your mom's favorite."

It didn't matter how often we watched the movie together. When we got to the scene, she'd always say, "Make sure you marry someone who'd run after you barefoot in a rainstorm." Then she'd talk about the time she and Dad got locked out of the car at a music festival. "It didn't rain, and we didn't argue," she'd say. "But if circumstances had been different, your father would have come after me no matter the weather or his footwear."

"You okay?" Melanie asks.

"Yeah. I have so many happy memories," I say. The bit I leave unsaid is, *I wish she was here with me.* But Melanie knows.

"She would be so happy you're in London."

I nod. "I know."

"I think she'd want you to pretend to be this guy's fiancée." Melanie certainly does, and I can't ignore her opinion. She's my best friend.

I turn away from the door. For all the nostalgia it inspires, a door is only interesting for so long.

"You really think it would be a good idea?"

I'm not sure what my mother would say. She'd probably tell me to follow my heart. She was a romantic like that. It's moments like these when the grief surfaces. They don't happen very often now. I still miss her, but I don't rail against God in the way I used to. I've accepted things how they are. I got to have her for as long as I did. I have wonderful memories and I knew her heart. I know what she would have done in most circumstances I come across. Being asked to be someone's fake fiancée, though . . . Amazingly, it never came up in all our *what would you do if* scenarios.

"Your mom was a dreamer. A lover of fairy-tale romances. She'd tell you to pretend to be this guy's fiancée because even though it might start off as pretend, it might turn into a love story."

"That's ridiculous. You've seen how hot this guy is. And he's rich AF. He can date any girl he wants." I haven't told Melanie about the surge of electricity I felt when Ben touched me. Just because I felt it doesn't mean he did.

"Okay, so take the romance out of this. It's practical. You get the money *and* you don't make an enemy of a client. You could even negotiate. See if he'll pay you more."

The scales are tipping. Melanie's making really good points. "You think I should try and call him?" I ask.

"Maybe," she says. "Or maybe fate will intervene and you'll bump into each other again. Didn't you say you work in the same building?"

Gail said Ben's offices are in the same building as the bank's and that she sometimes sees him in the lobby. Ginny says he goes into Coffee Confide in Me every day. It shouldn't be too difficult to "coincidentally" run into him. Although with my luck, I'll never see him again.

CHAPTER EIGHT

It's Sunday, so I'm late getting to Coffee Confide in Me. My conversation with Melanie is still replaying in my head. It didn't occur to me she'd think agreeing to be Ben's pretend fiancée was a good idea. I'm worried I've done the wrong thing, that I should have said yes. Melanie's right—the money would be really useful. But if he thought I was a stalker before, if I track him down and tell him I've changed my mind, he'll probably have me arrested. I'm going to need an espresso chaser this morning.

Ginny with the bright-red hair is on again, and she beams when she sees me. I know this isn't her normal greeting—she's British, after all. I expect a grunt that's supposed to pass for hello or a tense smile.

"It's you," she says, her eyes widening. "Filter Coffee Guy has paid for your coffee."

It's like my brain is upside down in my head today. I can't make sense of what she's saying. So I order. "Can I get a venti cappuccino two extra shots, half almond milk, half oat milk, a shot of caramel, extra foam, and cinnamon sprinkles?"

"Absolutely. I was trying to remember what you had before. I forgot about the almond milk and the extra foam." She calls out the order, still grinning at me, like we're in on a joke or something. "Can you believe he paid?"

"*Ben* paid?" I ask, making sure I haven't misheard her. I'm distracted watching the barista put all almond milk into my coffee, but I don't say anything.

"Yes. Are you going to go speak to him?" She lifts her chin toward the tables at the front of the store.

Everything tips into place. "Ben's here?"

I snap my head around to find the man himself staring back at me. My heart trips and skips. I'm half nerves, half anticipation. But I have to chew the inside of my cheek to stop myself from grinning. I shouldn't feel this excited to see this grumpy British dude who's pretty much a stranger, even if it gives me a second chance to say yes to his offer of twenty grand.

I look back at Ginny and she's still grinning. "Go and speak to him. At least to say thank you for your coffee." She nods vigorously. "He's clearly waiting for you. It's so cute. If you two end up getting married, you absolutely must have me as a bridesmaid. I insist. I don't care that it might be weird because we barely know each other."

"Happy to agree to that," I say, moving to the pickup station. I glance back at Ben's table and he's gone. My stomach plunges as my opportunity to change my mind about his offer goes with him. The coffee was a nice apology.

I turn back to wait for my coffee and electricity buzzes through my jacket sleeve as someone touches me. "Hey," a gravelly voice says, and I don't need to see him to know Ben didn't leave.

"Hey." I turn to face him. "Thanks for the coffee."

He nods. "Do you have five minutes?"

I have the entire day, but I don't tell him that. I ditched the Stonehenge idea given the journey time. I've decided to take a bus tour around London today; my Daniel De Luca quest is on hold while I do some straight tourist stuff. I can't come to London and miss the big attractions because of my movie-star crush.

"I do," I say and feel my cheeks burn at the reference to marriage. "You're a client, after all."

He guides me back to the table he was at previously and pulls out a chair. Is that a British thing? Jed never pulled out my chair, and it had never occurred to me that he might until now. I take a seat and pull off the plastic top of my coffee cup before taking a sip. Oh, I can taste those extra shots of espresso. Hopefully, I'll find the words I need.

He sits opposite me and pulls in a breath. In the beat of silence, I enjoy watching him—the contours of his cheekbones, the strong jaw, that glossy black hair that looks like he's got his personal hairdresser three feet behind him, making sure it's entirely perfect at all times. "I wanted to apologize about the other night," he says. "Nick is a little . . . He sees a problem, then a solution, then he just wants to get on with it."

I nod. "I got that about him."

"It's useful."

"He works for you?" I ask.

"He used to. Then he set up on his own, so I pay him three times as much to do the same thing as he did when he was working for me."

"He's smart," I say.

The corner of his mouth lifts, and warmth floods my chest at the thought I've been able to elicit a smile from him. "You're right. But he can be like a bull in a china shop at times. I'm sorry you were—"

"The china?" I suggest.

"I hope you're not entirely broken by the experience." He clears his throat, as if completely uncomfortable discussing my potential brokenness.

I smile. "Not broken at all. I was on a high shelf, watching while I enjoyed a lovely dinner." *With a pretty view,* I don't say. He really does have the most beautiful eyes.

He nods. "Glad to hear it."

I lift one shoulder in a semi-shrug. It really doesn't matter. "Seriously. It's forgotten."

"I want to assure you there was never any intention that sex would be part of the deal. Not on Nick's or my part. It wasn't a case of me wanting to sleep with you. If I wanted to pay for sex, there are plenty of options in this city." He blushes and shakes his head. "Not that I take advantage of any of them—I'm speculating."

He sounds awkward, like everywhere he turns, he's stepping on land mines.

"I never thought it was some elaborate scheme to get me to sleep with you."

"Good," he says, clearly relieved he can stop rambling about prostitution. He blows out a breath. "But the thing about Nick is, he does have incredibly good ideas, even if he's a little impatient to execute them." His tone has shifted from embarrassed and awkward to serious and studious. Nerves start to trace circles on my lower back. I suppress a shiver. "I would like you to consider an offer I have for you."

I thought he'd never ask.

He opens a manila file I hadn't noticed on the table in front of him and pushes it toward me.

"That's an independent background check on me." He guides my eye down the page as he points to various items. "My full name, my current address, confirmation I have no criminal or civil convictions. Details of where I went to school, university." He turns the page and reveals a list of company names. "This shows all the companies of which I'm a shareholder, either directly or through a shareholding of another company." The list continues on the following page. On the next page, he stops. "I'm a director of all these companies," he says. He turns the page once again. "This is a printout of my Wikipedia page."

I glance up at him, but he's focused on the file. "You have a Wikipedia page?"

He meets my gaze but doesn't say anything before he looks back down at the file and turns the page again. "These are character references."

I scan down the page and recognize a few of the names. I'm not sure why he's shown me his file, like I'm some investigative journalist or something. I pull my mouth into a forced smile. "Congratulations?" I'm not sure what he wants me to say.

His half smile is back and tugs at something in my stomach as the penny drops.

He wants me to feel safe with him.

"I want you to reconsider Nick's suggestion."

"Why would you pay me to be your fiancée when you could get any girl in England for free?"

His jaw twitches, and I get the sense he's trying to decide how to answer. "There's more than one answer to that question. Obviously, you know I need someone to go with me. You fit for more reasons than Nick even realized. He thought the priority was finding someone who didn't actually want to be my fiancée. I could have picked any one of my exes if that was the only requirement."

Did moody, serious Ben just make a joke that wasn't about my name?

"It's helpful to me that you . . ." He exhales loudly. "It's helpful to me you don't live in London. The fact you're American means when people ask you where you went to school or whether you know the so-and-so family and whether you grew up skiing in Val d'Isere or Verbier, you can say no to all the above and won't be judged for it. Yes, people will judge you for being American, but that's something we can get past."

"Wow, so you don't like this duke guy, then? Sounds like a horrible snob."

"To be fair, I don't know him, but I do know how aristocrats think. They like people to be one of them. Not that they won't welcome outsiders into their homes and joke with them like you're their best friend. They just don't want their sons and daughters to marry them."

"Oh. And . . . I'm an outsider."

"Yes, but not because you didn't go to the right school or don't know the right people. It's because you're American. It's almost a thrill for them, like seeing a lion in a cage or something. And then there's the issue after the split. They're not going to run into you and find out our story was an elaborate hoax. You'll be back in America"—he pauses—"doing whatever it was you were doing before you came here. And the likelihood of bumping into someone you met during the charade will be almost zero."

I nod. "How very convenient."

"I told you, Nick's smarter than he looks."

I take another sip of my coffee. When I'd chatted to Melanie last night, she'd had some good ideas—negotiating for more money, for a start. But would that look weird? I don't want Ben to think I'm greedy.

"I want to be very clear, I would not expect to sleep with you," Ben continues. "Not even stay in the same bed. It's likely we'll be given one bedroom between us, but I'll take the floor. My goal is to buy a luxury hotel chain, not add a notch to my bedpost."

"So what *would* you expect, exactly?"

"From a physical perspective, just hand-holding. Maintaining an illusion of intimacy typical for a couple in company."

Without thinking, I stretch out my fingers as if preparing to have Ben reach across the table for my hand. He glances down, and I ball my hands into fists.

"And from a nonphysical perspective?" I ask.

"We'd need to do some prep. Realistically, we'll need to work hard to make our relationship seem authentic."

"What kind of prep?"

"We need to get to know each other. You'll need to visit my house. We'll need to learn each other's backstories and foibles. I offered you a lot of money to be my fiancée because there's a lot at stake, but it requires work and preparation."

"What about Mr. Jenkins? The bank? I'm trying to get on the management fast track. If I start hanging out with a client . . . Well, it could be a conflict of interest or something."

Ben sighs. "I can talk to James. I'll get you on the management fast track."

My stomach swirls with a mixture of emotions. I shake my head. "No. I want to get it because I deserve to be there. Although . . ." My voice trails off. What was it Melanie said about negotiating for more? She meant more cash, but maybe I could ask for something more valuable than that. "You could agree to keep your investments in the bank."

Ben frowns. "What are you talking about?"

"You've got your annual health check with the bank coming up. Mr. Jenkins really doesn't want you to withdraw any funds."

"I'm not going to withdraw any funds," he says simply.

"Can you put that in writing?" I ask.

"I don't need to. I'm not going to withdraw funds. I never have. I don't invest with the bank because of account performance. I do it because of a personal connection. James and my father are close. As long as James is there, my money will stay."

That's good news, I suppose, but it wasn't exactly a negotiation. "There will need to be an NDA," I say. "I would hate for Mr. Jenkins to hear about any of this."

He lets out a small groan I feel between my thighs. "I definitely don't want James to hear about this. An NDA is a good idea. You should take some time to think about this. I know I'm asking a lot."

I nod. It feels like a lot. Melanie made it sound like a bunch of fun, and she's probably right—I don't want to regret anything about my time in London. Still, I'm nervous. Ben is a powerful guy who could make life difficult for me. I could do something wrong, say the wrong thing and ruin everything for him. And myself.

"What are you thinking?" he asks. "I'm not pressuring you to make a decision, just wondering if there are any concerns I can address."

"If I mess up, then what?" I ask. "If I say the wrong thing to your snobby duke and we get tossed out on our asses. What happens?"

"Risk allocation," he says simply, like I'm supposed to know what that means. He must see the error message my brain spits out in my expression. He adds, "It's a risk taking you, but it's my risk. If something goes wrong, then I lose out. It won't affect your payment or the other terms of our agreement. That said, we can mitigate the risk by doing the prep."

"You're not going to sue me for being a bad fiancée?"

He shakes his head. "Americans—you love a lawsuit. No, I'm not going to sue you. We can set out a limitation of your liability in the contract, if that helps."

He has a solution for everything. "You really need my help, huh?"

He looks at me with a stare so heavy and intense I have to look away. "I do need your help, but you shouldn't say yes to this unless you feel entirely comfortable."

I suck in a breath. Entirely comfortable being someone's paid fiancée for the weekend? Is that even possible?

He pulls out his phone and starts to type. "I'm going to call you in forty-eight hours. If it's no, you don't need to answer. If it's yes . . . pick up. But make sure this works for you just as much as it works for me."

I can feel this conversation coming to a natural conclusion, which means the window of opportunity to ask for more money is closing. I could wait until he calls in two days, but it feels dishonest to keep my demands to myself.

"And what did you say you'd pay?" I ask. "Twenty thousand dollars?" My pulse is racing as I try to summon up the courage to ask for more when it's already so much.

He nods, glancing between me and his phone.

"It's a lot of money for a weekend," I say. My palms are starting to sweat, and I pick up my coffee to distract myself. He's still looking at his phone. This is it. If I don't ask now, Melanie will never forgive me. "But you want the prep time too."

He looks up and waits for me to elaborate.

I wince and say, "What do you think about . . . twenty-*five* thousand?"

His expression softens, almost like I've said something to please him. "Let's make it an even thirty. There's a lot to do."

We lock eyes but neither of us speaks. Eventually, Ben looks away.

"Nick has accepted the invitation for me and my fiancée," Ben says. "The plan is to arrive on Friday evening and leave on Sunday night."

Two entire days? I'm not sure I can fake anything for that long.

Ben must see the concern written on my face. "The other thing about you being American is if something goes wrong, we can put it down to your nationality."

I sit back in my chair. "Because all Americans are idiots?"

"No, because there's an inevitable cultural divide. It's easier to pass off little inconsistencies as misunderstandings when we're from different countries. That means there's not so much pressure to get everything perfect. And if we say we've only been together for three months, that gives us some wiggle room too."

Wiggle room? I start saying "wiggle" over and over in my head. It just seems such a strange word to come out of sensible Ben's mouth. "No one's going to believe we're already engaged after three months."

"Of course they will. When you know, you know. I decided to put my bachelor years behind me when we met because I knew instantly you're the woman I want to build a life with. You're the one I want to be the mother of my children. I'm a man who's used to seeing value and locking that value down as soon as possible. They'll understand that."

"Wow," I say, feeling less than charmed by his cool, calculated assessment of marriage. "I feel like a pile of stock certificates."

"It's an analogy, Tuesday. I'm sure you have them in America."

Jeez, he's brusque. But *so* pretty.

Melanie was right when she said I'd do this for free if I'd met him under more . . . romantic conditions. And if I hadn't just had my heart ripped out by my college sweetheart. I need to stop overthinking and just say yes already.

"So when do we start?" I ask.

"I'll call you in forty-eight hours."

"But I've made my decision."

"I want you to be sure you're getting what you need from this."

I've said yes. What more does he want?

"I'm good. When do we start?" I ask, a little more forcefully.

He holds my gaze for a second, two, three, then says, "Now." He folds the manila file and stands. "I'll have my lawyers draft a contract by lunchtime. Then you can be certain you'll get your money. I have a car waiting outside. Let's go."

CHAPTER NINE

This month is going a little differently from the last. First, I'm on a different continent and in a different time zone. And second, instead of being Jed's fiancée, I'm shopping for engagement rings with a British guy I mistook for a movie star just a week ago.

"Wait, this is Bond Street?" I ask as I finally spot a street sign. One of the weirdest things about London is it's hit or miss whether or not you find a street sign, and I don't get it. Why don't the British like to know where they are? "This is where Tiffany is!" Daniel De Luca only made one Christmas movie, and it has some pivotal scenes on Bond Street, including a proposal in front of Tiffany.

"I believe it is," Ben says. "But that's not where we're headed."

I told Ben to get any old ring, but he insisted we come and pick one out. He said the duke would never believe he's romantic enough to have picked it out himself, so we might as well pick one out together. Plus, the experience gives us a genuine story of a shared experience. Win-win.

"Will we have time to get a picture *outside* Tiffany's?" I ask. Multitasking at its best: enjoying some DDL time while pocketing thirty grand.

Ben doesn't respond. His driver pulls to a stop at the side of the road.

He gets out and holds the door open for me. I slide across the seat and can see the Tiffany-blue flags a few buildings up. "I gotta get a picture," I say. "I'll just be a second."

Before Ben has a chance to stop me, I chase up the street and tip my head back as I take in the imposing black brick building. It's so different from the New York City Tiffany, but somehow this one looks like the flagship. It's such a perfect fit—traditional and beautiful and part of history.

I spin around and find the exact spot Daniel De Luca proposed to Rachel Joshi. The setup was a little cheesy, but Daniel always has a way of pulling it back from full fondue. It must be the British sense of humor or something. Maybe it's just his accent. I shuffle to my right a little and bring up the camera on my phone. Even if it was years ago, I've seen *The 14 Days of Christmas* at least a hundred times, so I know the exact angle I'm trying to get.

"You want me to take it for you?"

I spin around, and Ben is standing there, one hand in his pocket. He looks like the film-poster version of Daniel for this movie. He just needs a Santa hat.

"Let's take one together," I say. I'd never pass as Rachel Joshi—who starred in *and* produced *The 14 Days of Christmas*—but it would be fun to take a shot and send it to Melanie.

"I don't do pictures," he says.

"Not without your stylist and makeup artist?" I tease.

He rolls his eyes and whips my cell from my hand, then takes a couple of steps back before pointing my phone at me. I tilt my head to one side and give him my most natural smile.

"Did you get it?" I ask with gritted teeth. Is he messing with me? How long does it take?

He doesn't say anything but nods as he stares at the screen with an intensity that tells me there're a thousand things going on in his brain. But what? What's he looking at? Me and my rigor mortis smile?

"Ben?"

He snaps his head up as if he's been caught doing something he shouldn't. "What?"

Never mind.

"Now for one together," I say and take the phone from him. I link my arm through his, enjoying the heat of him so close. For a split second, it feels like we're a real couple. I hold up the phone, and you'd think someone just told him his cat died. "Smile," I say, giving an exaggerated grin to the camera.

"Like *that*?" he asks. Our image on the screen reveals him looking at my smile like it's curdled cream.

"I'm trying to be encouraging."

"Selfies and I aren't a thing," he replies.

"Maybe they should be." I take a couple of shots. "These next few days, you think you're getting a fiancée for hire, but what you're actually going to experience is a *wild* ride. First on the list is selfies. Next we'll be driving with the windows down, and by next Sunday night, you might have even loosened your tie."

The corner of his mouth twitches, and I manage to capture it. It feels like a victory. Until he takes a step back and I feel a chill at my side in place of his warmth.

"Let us take one of you two." A short, light-brown-haired American woman who sounds like she's from Virginia sidles up to Ben. The look on his face is priceless—like she's just told him he'll be milking cows for the rest of the afternoon. Before he has the chance to turn her down, she gives him a gentle shove toward me and takes my phone.

"Are you sure you don't mind?" I ask. We might as well get couple practice in now. And there's one final picture I'd really like to have.

"You're American!" she says. "We're here from Virginia. I'm Pat and this is Bobby, my husband." She nods at the guy next to her with the sandy-blond bowl cut. "Where are you from?"

"Originally from upstate New York." Say you're a New Yorker to another American and they make their mind up about you right away—they'll either love you or loathe you. Upstate New York is perfectly acceptable to most people. "But now my fiancé, Ben, and I live in London."

I slide my arm around Ben's waist. It's probably just an excuse to touch him again, but I'm supposed to be playing a part, right? It's not like he's going to think I'm into him. And he smells so good, not getting close to him when I have the chance would be like passing up a winning lottery ticket. He's taller than Jed. And bigger. There are muscles under the suit you'd never know about just by looking at him. Okay, so maybe I had an inkling from dinner the other night.

I look up as he puts his arm awkwardly around my shoulder. Is he not smooth with women in general, or just women he's fake-engaged to?

"Relax," I whisper, then let out a small laugh. I thought it was going to be me who was going to have a problem faking things between us.

"You're engaged?" Pat asks, beaming. "That's so nice. We've been married thirty-five years. It's gone so fast, hasn't it, Bobby? And now that the kids have flown the nest, we're finally taking all those trips we said we would when we first got engaged. Have you got any plans to travel when you're married?" she asks. "Smile," she adds, and points the phone at us.

"I hope so," I say. "I'd love to go to Italy." All the advice I've ever heard about lying is that it's best to stick as closely to the truth as possible. Who doesn't want to travel to Italy?

The woman narrows her eyes. "You know you look awfully like that actor. The British one. Daniel De Luca."

I can't contain my laugh. "He really does, doesn't he? The first time I met him, I thought Ben here *was* Daniel. In fact, you know that movie he was in, *The 14 Days of Christm*—"

"Of course I do," Pat says. "It's one of my favorites, and definitely my favorite holiday movie. I watch it every year."

"This is where the proposal scene takes place. I'd love to get a shot with us pretending to be Rachel Joshi and Daniel De Luca."

Pat squeals. "Well, of course you do. That would be just the cutest thing."

I turn to Ben. "You need to stand like this." I grab his forearms and move him into position like he's a giant mannequin. He's standing in front of Tiffany, facing up the street. Then I stand opposite him. "You need to put your hands on my hips, and I'm going to put my hands on your chest."

This situation is so weird. The man I'm ordering about is almost a perfect stranger, yet I'm maneuvering him into what I'm just now realizing is an extremely intimate pose. And he smells so freaking good. I'm going to find out what makes him smell like clean laundry and wood chippings, just so I can make sure my next boyfriend smells exactly the same.

Ben slides his hands over my hips. Despite the fact I asked him to, his touch chases the air from my lungs, and I gasp. We lock eyes as he hears my response to his touch, and maybe it's me, but his gaze feels intense.

"Oh, that's just perfect," Pat says, breaking the momentary spell. Ben looks away. I'm both disappointed and relieved. "You two look like you're actually from the movie. Now put your hands on Daniel's chest."

I'm hyperaware of my hands as I hover them over his shirt before placing them down. His chest is hard but has heat, like I'm touching a rock warmed by the sun.

"You need to look at each other," Pat squeals. "This is better than the movie. You two don't need to pretend you're in love—you have the real thing."

A smile threatens at the corners of my lips before Ben looks at me, and I forget everything I was thinking.

"You two are just perfect together," Pat says. "Don't you think, Bobby?"

Ben clears his throat and reaches for my phone from Pat. "It was very nice to meet you. But we must be going." He takes my hand and practically drags me down the street.

"Bye," I call over my shoulder. "And thank you!" I do a little half skip to catch up with Ben. "Well, that was a little rude. They were just being friendly."

"In this country, it's rude to strike up conversations with strangers."

I scoff. "No, it's not."

"Maybe not, but we need to find a ring. And I don't have all day."

He lets go of my hand, and I feel the loss of heat as if his has always been holding mine. He nods, encouraging me through the door being held open by a doorman.

Immediately, a male sales assistant appears in front of us. "Mr. Kelley. We're delighted to have you in store. How may I be of assistance?"

Why would Cartier know Ben by name? I get it, he's rich—but he's not *actually* Daniel De Luca.

"I'd like an engagement ring," Ben says flatly. "Something we can take away today." He couldn't sound more brisk or businesslike if he were telling his broker to go short on Japanese tech stocks.

"Congratulations, Mr. Kelley." He turns to me. "And . . ."

"Tuesday Reynolds." I plaster on a smile and attempt to push away an intrusive thought about how close I was to being Mrs. Miller if I'd married Jed.

But . . . *was* I close? Maybe he had no intention of marrying me. We never set a date. Jed suggested—and I agreed—that we wouldn't move forward with wedding plans until we'd grown our nest egg to a quarter million dollars—which seemed high to me. He said it would be best to start our marriage off with financial comfort, since money problems are the leading cause of divorce in America. Yet here I am, shopping for a fake engagement ring with a near stranger, precisely because there *was* no nest egg. And if there was no nest egg, was there ever really a plan to get married? What rankles most is that I'll never know.

"We would be delighted to find something that will suit you. My name is Edward. Let's go to the suite."

Edward leads us through the shop, where the number of sales assistants far outweighs the number of customers. We go through a door the assistant unlocks with a key card.

"Please take a seat," Edward says. There is a red velvet sofa with a low table in the middle of the room and to the side, a small desk with two chairs tucked underneath it. "Can I offer you any refreshments? Tea? Coffee? Champagne?"

Ben looks sideways at me and then back to Edward. "Her coffee order is ridiculous. You'll be sorry you asked. I'll have a black coffee, please." He guides me to the sofa and we take a seat.

"I'll take a green tea," I say, determined not to be irritated by Ben's assessment of my coffee order. "Thank you."

Edward presses a button under the small desk, and almost immediately, someone knocks at the door. A tall Asian woman who looks around twenty appears. Edward goes to speak to her, presumably to give her our drink order.

I nudge him with my elbow and lower my voice. "Calling me ridiculous in front of people might not be the best way to convince them we're in love—*FYI*."

"*FYI*, I didn't call you ridiculous," he replies as if such a suggestion is in and of itself entirely ridiculous. "I would never do that. I was referring to your coffee order."

"Semantics," I say.

"Which are important. *You're* not ridiculous. *Your coffee order* is ridiculous. You are not your coffee order. Just like your name is ridiculous. But you're not ridiculous."

"Ben!" I say. "You gotta stop calling me ridiculous. You might try and argue I'm not my name or my coffee order, but you're adding to the list of my ridiculous qualities fast and thick. Before long, everything about me is going to be ridiculous, and that's a red flag when you're supposed to be falling in love with someone."

He pulls in a breath, not in an exasperated way, more like he's weighing what I've said. "I see where you're coming from. For the record, everyone is ridiculous in one way or another."

"I agree. But the man who's in love with me has to think those ridiculous things are adorable."

"I can't sleep unless I wear an eye mask. Ridiculous or adorable?" he asks.

I scan his expression, trying to determine whether or not he's making this up. He's not. "Adorable," I reply. "Do you have to have a lavender-scented pillow as well?"

He narrows his eyes at me like he's going to get me back for making jokes at his expense. "No, but that sounds *adorable*. Can you get me one?"

I laugh, but before I can think of a reply, Edward's back. "Do you have any styles in mind?" he asks.

"No." I don't want a replica of the engagement ring I returned to Jed. That would be . . . weird. "Just not an emerald cut." I don't really know how to describe my previous ring other than that. "I'd like something a little . . . different."

"Of course, miss. Excuse me, and I'll bring through a selection." Edward does a little bow and wafts out.

"So you come here a lot?" I ask Ben, now that we're alone.

"No," he replies.

"Then how do they know your name?"

"I've made a couple of purchases from them. I suppose they know who I am."

I don't feel jealous, exactly, but my mood takes a turn toward jealous-adjacent. It doesn't make sense. I'm not with Ben. I'm not his girlfriend, and I'm certainly not his fiancée. I barely know the guy. But there's a bubble of something I'm not used to feeling in my stomach.

"What kind of purchases?" I ask, trying to sound nonchalant.

He leans back on the sofa and stretches his arm across the back, behind me. "A couple of watches. That kind of thing."

"No other engagement rings?" What is it with this guy? He's gorgeous and rich. Okay, so he's a little grumpy, but there are men on death row in relationships. Why doesn't Ben have a girlfriend?

He lets out a half laugh. "No. The only women's jewelry I've ever bought has been for my mother."

"Well, that's disappointing," I say. "As your fiancée, I was looking forward to lots of expensive gifts for birthdays and Christmases."

"I'm not averse to it."

"What? Buying me expensive jewelry?" I flatten my palm on my chest and flutter my eyelashes like I'm thrilled at the idea. Which, of course, I would be. Name a girl who says no to expensive jewelry.

"I've never been serious enough about a woman to buy her jewelry. It's just never occurred to me."

"You're engaged now. Don't hold back, my friend."

"I'm not sure our arrangement counts."

I pretend-pout, and I finally get that smile from him I was looking for when we were posing outside.

"So you're a mommy's boy?" I ask. "Buying your momma expensive jewelry and all?"

"I love my parents. They worked hard all their lives and gave me everything they could."

"So you didn't grow up with money?"

"No. We weren't poor, but my mother worked part time as a teacher, and my father was . . . in client relations. We got a new car every three years and went on holiday every summer."

"And you became this uberwealthy guy . . . how?"

"Like most people who have done it themselves: self-belief, hard work, and luck."

"In hotels?"

He shakes his head. "No, tech stocks. I was a nerdy teenager. Started trading money on the stock market that I earned through my Saturday job at Halfords. Then I reinvested it and reinvested it. When I got to a hundred thousand, I told my dad and . . ." He shakes his head, and a dimple on his right cheek appears. It makes him look younger than he normally does. "He completely freaked out. He'd opened the trading account for me because I'd been bugging him about it. He knew I had less than a hundred pounds, so didn't worry too much—thought it would teach me a lesson about not spending what I couldn't afford to lose. I'd started with ninety-two pounds."

"How old were you?"

"Seventeen. It didn't seem like a big deal at the time. Looking back, I was so precocious."

"A hundred thousand pounds is a lot of money for a seventeen-year-old." I could barely remember seventeen. Those first few years without my mom are all a blur.

"I'd made a million by my eighteenth birthday."

"Wow," I say. "That's impressive."

He shrugs. "What about you? What's the Daniel De Luca thing all about? Are you one of those crazies who hang around his film sets and try to break into his hotel room when he's traveling?"

I smile. I suppose it must look like I'm obsessed with DDL. My fourteen-year-old self most definitely was.

Thankfully I don't have to begin to explain because Edward returns with a large tray, placing our conversation on temporary hold. How strange that we're about to pick out engagement rings, yet this guy doesn't know much about me other than my coffee order. That's going to have to change over the next few days.

Edward places the tray on the low table and starts to take us through the various settings and stones.

"Which one do you like?" Ben asks me.

There's no ring in front of me I don't like. They all gleam like they're vying for my attention. I shrug. I can't help but think back to my engagement. Jed presented me with his great-grandmother's ring when he proposed. It was pretty enough, but it hadn't been my choice.

"Why don't you tell me the ones you like, and that will narrow it down," I say. It feels wrong to be excited about all this beautiful jewelry in front of me. It's not like I'm going to be keeping it. And it's most important that Ben is happy. "All these feel a little overwhelming."

Ben works methodically down the rings and picks out three. Three of the prettiest engagement rings I've ever seen. I might have seen bigger on the fingers of some of the wives of the people Jed worked with, but I haven't seen nicer. I know my favorite without having to think about it.

Edward places all three on their own separate stands.

"This one's pretty," I say, pointing at the middle one.

"This is particularly beautiful—a yellow cushion-cut diamond in a double-halo setting," Edward says. "Let's try it." He hands me the ring, and I slide it onto my left ring finger.

It looks bigger on my hand.

"I'm not sure," I say, suddenly really uncomfortable. What the hell am I doing? I'm picking out engagement rings with a stranger. I'm here in London for work, not to pretend to be someone else.

"It's beautiful," Ben says. "Impressive without being gaudy, and classic without being boring." His eyebrows are pinched together, and his expression is hard to read, almost like he expected to see something other than the ring on my finger. "I think this is the one."

"Really?" I ask. "I'm not sure it's me."

He nods. "It suits you. It's a little unusual."

I laugh, and my anxiety ebbs away. "I'm unusual?"

"You're definitely that," he says. "You're American, after all."

"There are three hundred million of us," I say.

"But not another one like you."

Our eyes lock, and I can't think of anything to say. It's like he's stolen the words right out of my mouth.

CHAPTER TEN

I'm super aware I'm wearing a veritable rock on my left ring finger as we step out onto the street. I glance around us to see if there's anyone about to attack me for the yellow diamond I'm pretending is mine. It's noticeably heavier than the engagement ring I had from Jed, and it feels strange having something on that finger again.

"Next, I was thinking Ralph Lauren. It's classic enough to be acceptable, but American enough to be authentic."

"What are you talking about?" I slide my ring around so it's facing in; all people can see is the band of gold.

"You're going to need a suitable wardrobe, unless you came to London with a case of clothes appropriate for shooting and cocktails." We cross the street toward the large Ralph Lauren store adorned with stars and stripes, navy awnings, polished brass, and dark wood.

"It depends on what we're shooting. I'm pretty sure I can point and shoot a Glock 19 in jeans and a sweater." I've watched enough of *The Crown* to know he's not suggesting we shoot handguns, but does handling a rifle really require more shopping? When I signed up to pretend to be Ben's fiancée, I hadn't factored in ring shopping and a wardrobe refresh.

Ben doesn't say a word, just guides me into the store with a hand at my lower back.

An assistant greets us immediately. "Good morning, can I help you with anything?"

"We need women's wear. Two evening outfits, two traveling outfits," Ben says like he's shopping for a quart of milk and some trash bags. "Something for shooting, and two outfits for a smart-casual weekend in the country. We need shoes and coats—everything."

I try to give Ben a look that says, *Have you lost your mind? She's going to think you hired me to dress me up*, but he isn't focusing on me at all. So here I am, a human Barbie, ready to be outfitted.

"Certainly. I can help you with all that." The assistant glances at me, then back at Ben as she leads us farther into the store, like she's trying to figure out whether she should ask my opinion about anything. After all, I'm the one presumably having to actually wear what she and Ben are going to pick out.

I pull my face into a smile. I'm getting thirty thousand dollars for this. I shouldn't care what she thinks. As for Ben, well, I need to accept that a rich, good-looking man spending a small fortune on clothes for me is going to want his opinion taken into consideration. It's not exactly a hardship, being the center of this man's attention.

"Jeans and cashmere always make a great traveling outfit," the assistant says, stopping at a rack of camel-color sweaters.

Ben turns to me. "You like these?"

I raise my eyebrows to say, *Does it matter?* "Sure," I answer instead. Who says no to cashmere? Even if it's only temporary ownership.

"A classic mac is a good traveling coat for this time of year—protection from the odd spots of rain. And we'll pick up a jacket for hunting." She calls over another assistant, and they exchange a few words in hushed voices.

Suddenly another assistant appears. Apparently the assistants have assistants here. They clearly know Ben is about to spend some money. For a moment, I want to ask whether the money for the clothes is going to be taken out of my thirty thousand, but it doesn't seem like the right time to bring it up.

We wander from display to display, the assistant in charge asking our opinions about this and that. Ben doesn't say no to anything, and neither do I. There's absolutely nothing to complain about in this store. Maybe that's part of the reason he chose it.

"Let's go to the fitting room. We can start trying things on, and I can send out for other pieces as we need them."

The first assistant ushers us into a large room with a separate changing area. After Ben places a drink order—green tea for me and black coffee for him—I head behind the changing curtain while the first assistant goes off to find shoes.

"This feels weird," I say. "Are you going to rate me on a scale of one to ten?"

"I'd rather not, but if you insist." Ben's tone is always the same, so I can't tell whether he's joking.

"Of course I don't want you to grade me. But it feels weird to be dressing up for your approval like this." Or maybe it feels weird that it doesn't feel weirder? I pull off my jeans and try to figure out what I should try on first.

"If it makes you feel any better, we're not slap-bang in the center of my comfort zone right now either. I've never bought a woman clothes before. And it wasn't on my grand plan for the things I wanted to achieve in the next five years. But needs must. This weekend has to be perfect."

"You have a five-year grand plan?" I ask, pulling one of the cocktail dresses from the rack. I've never worn pink before, and I'm sure it won't suit me.

"No . . . Well, yes, in that my business has a five-year plan, and I am my business."

"Does it include doing things with women?" I scrunch up my face in embarrassment. That didn't come out exactly right.

He doesn't respond right away, probably wondering whether he should answer at all. "What kind of things?"

"I don't know. Do you put girlfriends in your plan? Fake fiancées? Have you penciled in a personal life?" I manage to reach the low zip at the back of the dress and adjust the straps before turning to the mirror.

The pink is pretty, and I don't hate it as much as I thought I would. I wouldn't wear it in *black is the only acceptable color* New York, but I'm not in New York now. My old life there has disintegrated. Maybe the new me likes pink. I twirl, loving the way the pleated skirt lifts. I'm a cross between Marilyn Monroe and Julie Andrews—an unexpected but delightful combination I didn't know I needed.

"I told you, it's a *business* plan."

"I've only ever had a personal plan—at least, I did back in the day. As a teenager." I think back to my vision board. "But it wasn't even a plan, really. More like . . . I had a vision of how I wanted my life to be."

"How did that work out?"

"Not well." I step out of the changing room. "The skirt lifts when I twirl," I inform him, like I'm selling him a car and I want him to know about the built-in safety features.

"Do you twirl a lot?" he asks, looking thoroughly confused.

I pull in a breath and lift my arms to the sky to check it's not too short. "Not as a general rule."

"Good," he says. "I think it's acceptable, so we'll take it. What's next?"

"Acceptable?" I ask. "Gee, you really know how to make a girl feel good."

He blinks, holding my gaze. I'm not sure what he's thinking until he announces, "It's a nine out of ten. Next."

I flit back into the changing room before the heat in my cheeks turns my face the same color as my dress. I want to ask him more about the score. What makes it a nine? Is me in the dress a nine, or does the dress meet some kind of suitability criteria he has in his five-year plan? I hunt through the different garments for the next outfit.

"What would a person even put in their personal life plan?" he asks out of nowhere, like he's been mulling over the idea of my vision board and suddenly wants details.

"I had a lot of pictures of Daniel De Luca on mine."

"The film star? How old are you?"

"I *was* fourteen. What images would fourteen-year-old you have in your personal life plan? A copy of *Forbes* and a tie?" I laugh as I imagine Ben at fourteen, super serious, wearing a suit to play basketball and asking girls about their favorite element on the periodic table.

"Strawberry shortcake," he answers.

"Is that a cartoon character?" I ask. "Or a porn star?"

"A pudding." His tone is wistful, as if he's remembering something important.

I internally decode "pudding" to "dessert" for my American brain. It seems too unbusinesslike to be on Ben's vision board, even when Ben was fourteen.

"You have a sweet tooth, huh?" I pull out a black dress from under the other hangers and compare it with a green one hanging next to it. I absolutely hate wearing green. For some reason it always makes me feel like a frumpy aunt who may or may not have psychic abilities. I'm not sure whether to get it out of the way and try it first or try the black and hope he likes it so we don't need to look at the green one. "Do you come to New York much?" I ask. I tug the green one off the hanger. This is on Ben's dollar. He should see all the dresses. "You should try Serendipity 3 next time you're in town. Best desserts in the city. I used to take Jed on his birthday."

He pauses. "Jed?"

I step out of the changing room and put my hands on my hips. "What do you think?"

He glances down my body and then back up to my face. He holds my gaze for a beat, then two. "Clearly you don't like it, so it's a no."

Heat balls in my chest. I hope I didn't offend him. "It's fine if you like it," I say.

"Try the black one and tell me about Jed."

I disappear behind the curtain, a combination of embarrassment and thrill mixing in my veins. Part of me feels bad that I didn't like the green dress. It's not me paying, after all, and I'm in Ralph Lauren. Nothing's so bad I couldn't make it through an evening wearing it.

But another part of me is kinda excited that Ben took my feelings into account. He was nice when he didn't need to be, and he paid attention to my unspoken feelings, which he also didn't need to do. What does it say about my relationship with Jed that Ben's attention and thoughtfulness feel like a novelty?

I tuck the thought and the green dress away, content to hide them both from sight. "What do you want to know?" I call.

"Is he a recent ex?" he asks.

"Define recent?" I ask. But before he responds, I reply, "He called it off a couple of weeks back. Decided he wanted to move to Iowa with a ballerina." I still don't understand how I didn't see any signs. I shake my head and busy myself stepping into the black dress. It looked weird on the hanger, probably because it's one-shouldered.

Once I've actually managed to get it on, I feel sexy for the first time since Jed dumped me. It hits just above the knee, and the fabric has a subtle sheen. I absolutely love it.

I slip out of the changing room, and Ben looks up from his phone. His gaze wanders down my body like a downhill skier enjoying the sun.

He looks up, and his softened expression makes my heartbeat stumble. "Jed was an idiot."

His words bring my heart to an abrupt stop. I have to pull in a breath to start it again.

He blinks. "I don't remember us picking that one up. It's a no." He looks back to his phone.

What?

I'm completely confused, and my neck aches from the whiplash. He seemed to really like this dress. He told me my fiancé was an idiot for dumping me when he saw me in this dress. Maybe I misunderstood. My brain starts to push away the question I have for him: *Why is the dress a no?* It will sit alongside all the other questions I've never asked.

The ones for Jed: *Why haven't we set a date yet? Is our life together what you want?*

The ones for my dad: *Do you miss Mom? Do you think she's proud of me?*

The ones for me: *Are you happy?*

I don't want to push my question to Ben away. New London Tuesday wants answers. "It's a *no?*" I ask. He doesn't reply. My heart sinks a little. I guess I read him wrong. Not difficult when he's such a closed book. "Not a nine, then?"

He looks up and his brows are pulled together like he's confused. "What's not a nine?"

I sweep my hands down my body. "The dress. You . . . don't like it?"

"The dress is a ten on you. But for the weekend it's a two." He says it like he's telling me water is wet, like it's a law of the universe I look good in the dress, but the law can't apply this weekend.

I push my lips together to avoid a smile. Waves in my stomach crash together, taking me by surprise. I think that might have been a compliment, and I get the impression Ben doesn't dish those out very often. I'll take it. "Right. It's not suitable for the weekend."

He still looks confused, but it's more that he's confused at why *I'm* confused. "Right."

Ben is so direct, so clear about everything. It's refreshing. And only now is it obvious that Jed wasn't like that. At all.

I bet Ben doesn't harbor any secrets about wanting to move to Iowa.

"What about you?" I ask. Ben's engrossed in his phone. "Do you have any ex-fiancées I should know about?"

"No," he says simply, not even looking up.

But I want more than a syllable about his relationship history. Who is this guy as a boyfriend, fiancé, husband?

"Wives?" I ask.

"No."

"Serious girlfriends?"

He pauses, and for some reason my heart sets off like a hen's at the sound of a circling fox.

"No."

"Are you gay?" I ask.

He doesn't miss a beat. "No."

"Good chatting with you, Ben," I reply before slinking back into the changing room.

"Would you like me to make something up? I don't have any serious relationships in my history. That makes it easier, doesn't it? Nothing for you to remember."

"I guess. But is there anything you want to tell me about your personal life?"

He sighs on the other side of the curtain. "There's nothing to tell. I'm focused on my job. I'm not saying I'm a monk, but you're asking about important romantic relationships. And I'm telling you there's nothing notable in my history."

"How does that happen?" I take off the black dress and try the more-than-suitable gray silk maxi skirt with a matching shirt. The white pearl buttons are so tiny it takes at least two and a half hours to do each one. "You really haven't dated anyone seriously?"

"I didn't realize it was obligatory."

"It's not, but you're a good-looking, rich, powerful guy. You must have women lined up round the block wanting to have dinner with you."

I'd never dated in New York. My girlfriends are always complaining about how rough it is. I suppose I'll find out for myself when I get back home. Fake-dating Ben might sharpen my skills—a dating test case as well as a fake fiancé. Spending time with him might help me figure out what kind of guy I'm looking for. Ben's directness burns sometimes, but at least I know where I stand with him. It's a good quality in a partner, and one I might want to put toward the top of my Qualities to Look For list when the time comes. I'm just not used to it.

"I'd have to look it up, but I'm pretty sure dating has to be consensual," he says. "I'm not interested in dinner."

He just wants sex.

Like I said—Ben is direct.

The head assistant comes back, rolling a rack full of clothes, all of which appear to be in my size, and her assistant follows, holding a tower of shoeboxes tucked under her chin. "That looks gorgeous, and I have just the shoe," she says. She pulls out a simple black strappy sandal and fastens it for me.

"You've never asked me my size, and yet everything fits perfectly."

She grins up at me from the floor. "That's my job."

"You're really good at it."

"Thank you. That is completely stunning." She sweeps her arm in front of me, encouraging me out of the fitting room to show Ben.

He looks up from his phone and his expression is all business, the softness I saw when I tried on the black dress nowhere to be found. "We'll take it."

CHAPTER ELEVEN

During one afternoon on Bond Street, Ben has spent more on my wardrobe than I have in my entire life. I bought myself nice things back in New York, but I mixed them with cheaper stuff.

"Are we done now?" I ask as we exit Ralph Lauren, my feet aching and my hair looking like I've been wrestling alligators for the last couple of hours.

"Most women wouldn't complain about shopping for a new wardrobe."

"First, that's sexist. Second, I'm not *most* women."

"True on both counts. Now back to my office."

"On a Sunday?" He doesn't respond. "Can I ask you a question?"

"Don't do that," Ben replies. "Don't ask permission to ask a question. It's a waste of time. Does anyone ever say no when someone asks them if they can ask a question?"

"Jeez, you're a stickler."

"I'm efficient."

I bend my arms and move them jerkily around like I'm pretending to be a robot. "Yes, sir," I say in my best robot voice. I drop my arms and switch back into my normal tone. "What happens to the clothes when this weekend is over?" I ask.

When Ben finished choosing all the pieces for my weekend wardrobe, he simply handed over his business card, asked that everything be de-labeled and laundered, then delivered to my hotel. He hadn't handed over a credit card or anything. I didn't even know stores would do something like that. I've certainly never seen anything like it.

Ben glances down at his phone and then nods as his Range Rover pulls up across the street. "Is this a trick question?"

There is definitely more of a language divide than I expected there to be between me and the rest of London. Maybe it's cultural? "No, I just wonder whether they're on loan or I need to pay for them or . . ."

"I'll pay for them. After, they'll be yours to do with what you wish. If you don't like them, I suggest you donate them."

"I love them," I blurt. "I was just wondering. It all feels a little . . . *Pretty Woman*."

"Except you're not a prostitute and this is reality."

"True on both counts," I say, echoing him. We reach the car, he holds the door open, and I climb inside. *Is* this reality, though?

I have to move a pile of papers off my seat so I can sit. Ben closes the door, rounds the trunk, and then slides in next to me. The driver pulls off; presumably, he knows where we're going.

"Oh, good," Ben says as he sees the papers in my hands. "There should be two sets there. One for you and one for me." He takes the stack from me and flicks through them. They seem to be divided into separately stapled bundles. "These are yours." He hands me three bundles and keeps three for himself. "The first one is information about me. The second one is information I'd like about you, and the third one is things we need to decide on."

"Wow." I clear my throat. "Efficiency is key," I say, using my robot voice again.

I pull out the section titled "Tuesday Reynolds," which looks remarkably similar to a college application. *Name, date of birth, place of birth, parent(s) name, parent(s) age, parent(s) occupation.* I turn the page. He's a man who clearly likes details. The questions continue. *Pets (breed, name, age, idiosyncrasies if applicable).* I turn the page again. *Favorite foods. Favorite books.* The questions go on and on and on.

I put down the questionnaire for me and pick up one of the other packets. It seems just the same as the one I'm supposed to fill out, except this form has already been populated with details about Ben. "This seems very thorough."

"Like I said, everything has to be perfect."

"Is this a form you ask people to fill out a lot?" He can't have prepared this form just for me. Thought and preparation went into this.

Perhaps he gives this to his potential girlfriends to see whether he wants to have dinner with them, and that's why he doesn't date—no one's made the grade so far. I keep skimming through the pages, wondering whether I'll uncover something interesting. Is there a section detailing his favorite sexual positions or penis length? I glance across at his crotch, catch myself, and focus back on the questionnaires.

"You said yourself you like to be efficient. It could make dating easier if you prescreened potential sexual partners with this form."

I'm kidding. Sort of. It's nerves. I'm partly impressed with his organization and commitment to our ruse. It makes sense; we've got a lot to cover in a short amount of time. But it's also freaking me out. Has he done this kind of thing before? Does he have a hidden agenda? My instincts say no. From what I know about Ben, he's a straight shooter. But it's weird he can just produce this questionnaire out of nowhere.

"I'll keep it in mind. Although I'm not interested in this level of detail regarding the women I sleep with. It would have to be a streamlined version."

I slide my gaze to his face to see if he's kidding. He gives me a look that says *Of course I'm not being serious; get back to work*, and I can't help but smile. There is a sense of humor lurking deep down in this man. You just have to mine it like gold.

"Stop freaking out," he says, reading my mind. "I have a resourceful and clever assistant who put this together for me while we were . . . shopping."

That makes sense. "What does she think about you taking a fake fiancée?" I ask.

"I haven't asked her."

"She didn't say anything when you asked her to compile all this?"

"No," he says simply. "Now let's go through the information we need to decide between us. First things first: How did we meet? Shall we say we were introduced by mutual friends?"

"But then which friends, and would the duke know them? I think we stick to the truth. We bumped into each other in Green Park, then I ran into you the following day at the coffee shop."

The silence starts again. Ben sure does like pauses.

What? I want to scream at him.

"I'm not a natural talker," he says eventually. "I'm not sure it's believable I'd just strike up a conversation with a perfect stranger."

"You didn't. You glared at me as if I'd just set you on fire the first time we met. The second time, I just chatted at you in the coffee shop. The third time, the seat next to you was the only one in a busy bar. You asked me to dinner."

His frown is back, though I'm starting to realize this isn't necessarily because he's disapproving. He's assimilating and trying to see the advantages and disadvantages of what I'm suggesting.

"Why would I ask you to dinner?" he asks.

"You're attracted to me. You're going to have to fake some of it."

"I *am* attracted to you. That's not the problem. It just wouldn't necessarily mean I'd ask you to dinner."

My stomach tips and sways. He finds me attractive. *Well, the feeling is mutual,* I want to say, even though he's grumpy and bad-tempered and borderline rude seventy-eight percent of the time. "What would make *you* say yes to dinner?"

More silence.

More thinking.

"Okay, so I say yes to dinner." He pauses. "Just because I'm attracted to you." He says it like he's rehearsing the idea in his brain.

"Okaaay," I say. "And I'm over here for work, trying to save my job and nurse my broken heart, when I run into the love of my life."

"Is this the plot of another Daniel De Luca film? You never did tell me what the obsession is."

"No, it's not the plot of a movie. We're staying as close as possible to the truth, remember?"

He flips over the page and without looking up at me says, "Like I said, he was a complete idiot."

Warmth blooms in my cheeks. Honestly, even if Ben weren't tall, dark, and handsome, with his own plane and a black Amex, I'd still want to kiss him right now.

"Okay, so that's how we met," I say. "What's next? Let's do the pets section. Easy for me. I don't have any. You?"

"I have a goldfish named Strawberry Shortcake," he says.

I turn to him, intrigued by his strawberry shortcake obsession. "Really?"

"No. Neither of us has pets. Good. Next?"

I laugh and take in the wrinkles at the corners of his eyes from his smile. They suit him.

"Brothers and sisters?" he asks. "I have neither."

"Same. No siblings."

"What about your parents? What do they do for a living?"

The question brings me back to my past with a jerk. "My mom died when I was seventeen." I stare out the window, watching the gray London streets whizz by that my mother would have so liked to have seen for herself. "She always wanted to come to London."

"Her death must have been very difficult," Ben says simply. There's no apology, no dressing up death into "passing." Always the straight shooter.

I nod. "It was. It still is."

I hear Ben sigh, but it isn't impatience. Almost like he's commiserating with me that life can be a real fucker at times.

"My dad . . . It was almost worse for him, I think. I got to move away to the city, but he still lives in the house I grew up in. He's surrounded by memories of her."

Ben pulls in a breath and shifts in his seat, but not in a way that makes me think he feels awkward. More he's making himself comfortable. "Maybe he likes it like that."

"Yeah," I say, thinking about the curled list still pinned to the refrigerator door. "I guess he does."

"I think my dad would be exactly the same if my mum died. He worships her."

I give out a small smile. "That's nice." I like the idea of Ben growing up with parents who worshipped each other. Every kid deserves to see devotion growing up. "Did you grow up in London?"

"On the outskirts. Hertfordshire. Dad used to commute into town to work."

The questionnaire falls away and we're just talking. Two people getting to know each other, simply for the pleasure of it. If I didn't know better, I'd think the moment was real.

CHAPTER TWELVE

I haven't studied so hard since college. Every evening this week, I've pored over the papers Ben filled in. I've spent hours in my hotel room, reading and rereading until my eyes watered. But I have thirty thousand dollars to earn, so here I am, in front of an almost-stranger's house. Obviously, I was expecting Ben's place to be impressive, but as the door opens to reveal the marble floors, sweeping staircase, and an elaborate chandelier, I realize I've underdressed. I'm in jeans and my old Sarah Lawrence sweatshirt. This is supposed to be a casual dinner.

"Ben is just on a call," the slight, older lady who opened the door says through a beaming smile. "I'm Lera, his housekeeper. He won't be long. Do come in. Can I get you a cocktail?"

"Sure," I say, tipping my head back to take in the circular window in the ceiling at the top of the winding staircase. This place is grand but somehow also cute AF.

"Anything in particular you'd like? Ben said you enjoy a Kir Royale?"

My heart trips in my chest. Ben has clearly also been studying his comprehensive guide to Tuesday Reynolds. Him mentioning my favorite drink to his housekeeper was thoughtful and charming and kind—the sort of thing a real boyfriend would do. I meet her gaze to find her twinkling at me. "That would be wonderful. Thank you."

"Let me show you through to the drawing room."

The walls of the drawing room are almost black, and one wall has backlit bookshelves that give the room a book-shrine feel. The furniture is dark wood and burgundy velvets with lush, expensive cushions and billowing drapes. It has a definite feel of romanticism about it, like I might find Lord Byron behind the sofa, passed out from too much opium.

I'm about to start examining the bookshelves when the door sweeps open and Ben appears. It's the first time I've seen him in anything but a perfectly tailored suit, and my stomach swoops at the sight. At-Home Ben is sockless, in cuffed sweatpants and a white T-shirt, his hair ruffled like he's just come off a difficult call, his brow tight, and his eyes trained on me.

I might be recovering from heartbreak, but in Ben's presence, it's hard to remember. He's like coming into the AC on max after a walk from the subway in August.

"The sweatpants suit you," I say. "And here I was thinking you might be Dracula."

"I only wear my cloak on special occasions," he says without missing a beat.

"But seriously," I reply, nodding at the room. "It's moody. Dramatic. I feel like I should be in a corset and carrying smelling salts."

"I'd never discourage you from listening to your gut. Feel free to wear a corset next time you're here." Does he know how funny he is? I can't decide if he's cooler than a fan or just plain uptight.

Would there be a next time? Soon we'd be heading to the country, and then on Sunday evening, when we arrive back in London, my job will be done. I'll be thirty grand richer, and I'll likely never see Ben again before the bank's annual health check.

"Shall I show you around?" he asks. "You should be familiar with the place at least."

I nod. "Absolutely. I get to see the coffin too, right?"

He doesn't respond but leads me straight to the kitchen. It looks like something in a magazine, only nicer. It's big and expensive, but not showy or brash. The dark-color theme continues with what looks like tarnished bronze accents, dark-stained cabinets, and swathes of backlit black-and-white marble.

"Where's your refrigerator?" I ask.

"Over here." He indicates what looks like more cabinets. He pulls it open to reveal a huge larder fridge, with a smattering of fresh fruit, vegetables, and dairy. "You hungry? Or are you trying to discover where I hide the dead bodies once I've drained their blood?"

A chill melts down my spine. "Can you stop being so nonchalant about being a vampire? At least pretend to be offended."

"I've heard worse."

"You have? What's worse?"

"Maybe I'm wrong, but I'm assuming you don't actually think I feed on people's blood. So why would I be offended?"

He's unlike any man I've ever met. Cool. Cocky. Unreadable but kinda funny, and charming in his own way.

"You really have an answer for everything. It's exhausting."

"Then maybe stop trying to trip me up. Let's get down to business. Where was I born?" He turns and heads out of the kitchen. I follow.

"Hertfordshire. Me?"

"This is my office." He opens a door off the magnificent hallway and steps aside to let me in first. "Madison County, upstate New York. Where did we meet?"

I stand in the middle of the booklined room and spin around, taking it all in. The room is more library than office, with built-in shelving lining the walls floor to ceiling. I move toward one wall of shelves. It's not just business books, though there are plenty of those. There's also fiction that looks well thumbed, including a particularly worn copy of *The Hotel New Hampshire*—the seminal modern classic of misfits and oddities—and next to it, a huge coffee-table book simply titled *Washington State*. I want to be left here for a week to do nothing but investigate every corner and page of this room.

Ben moves behind me, and I spin again to take in the parts of the room I've not seen yet. There's a heavy mahogany desk on one side and two large navy couches facing each other by the window. I could live in this room. Other than bathroom and kitchen access, I wouldn't need anything else. I hadn't exactly envisaged what Ben's house would look like, but the warmth here is unexpected. I suppose I was expecting his home to reflect his aloofness, but instead of cold and clinical, this place is a warm blanket and a bucket of popcorn.

"I love it," I say and glance at Ben.

I swear there's a flicker of a smile before he lowers his head and pushes his hands into his pockets. "Where did we meet?"

"Green Park, of course. I was a tourist wanting my picture taken. Was it love at first sight for you?"

His brow furrows and he looks up, catching my gaze. "Not love, exactly, but I was intrigued."

I try to disguise my smile. "How did you know you'd fallen in love with me and decided to ask me to be your wife?" The question wasn't part of the packet, but it is something people ask. I remember Jed being stumped by the question when his grandfather asked. Maybe that should have been a warning sign for us both.

"The first night we had dinner, I knew it was special. I'm used to people being . . . relatively subservient. Not because I demand it," he rushes to add. "People self-edit. But you didn't. It caught me off guard. You saw yourself as my equal, and that shifted things for me."

My spine tingles and I can't help wondering how close we're skating to the truth. I turn slightly, to check I've not missed anything of the room and to cover the flush of my cheeks. "And when did you decide to propose?"

"I didn't like the fact you were going back to America so quickly. I realized I wasn't *ever* going to like you going back to America."

He sounds so earnest in his explanation that even I'm starting to believe what he's saying. I guess people believe what they want to believe, and the idea that someone like Ben could be in love with me? That's something I wouldn't mind being the truth.

I turn to him. "You're good at this game."

His eyes search mine. For once, I'm not waiting for a witty come-back, just looking at him, enjoying him looking at me.

Ben clears his throat, then turns and heads back into the hallway. I follow. He pads upstairs, and I'm faced with his perfect ass flexing beneath his soft gray joggers. Is there a possibility this is a Melanie setup? Maybe she and my dad got together and devised a way to send me overseas, and they've hired the perfect man to help erase Jed from my brain.

In one of his first on-screen appearances, Daniel De Luca had a supporting role in a Sean Penn movie where the main character's life had been turned into a disaster by his best friend because he was getting bored. I can't think of another explanation for why I'd be in this beau-tiful house, with this beautiful man, getting thirty thousand dollars to pretend to be in love with him. This isn't a hard gig.

There's only one sticking point to my theory: Neither Melanie nor my dad has thirty grand. It can't be them. This must be real life, but I've never come so close to living out my fantasies.

"Lower ground floor is a screening room, gym, hot tub—that kind of thing."

"Pool?" I ask.

"Nope. Seemed a waste to put it in just for me."

"Whereas living in a ten-thousand-square-foot home on your own is just fine."

"It's nine and a half thousand. We all have different lines in the sand."

"For future reference, I would have liked a pool. I mean, if you can, why not?"

"We can discuss it once we're married."

My heart somersaults at his statement. I know he's joking, but just the thought is . . . almost too much. "It cost you thirty thousand just to get me to wear the ring for a week. Getting me to the altar is going to be expensive, let me tell you."

"This is the master bedroom," he says, ignoring me. "The designer insisted on two bathrooms and two wardrobes for resale value. So I suppose this is yours." He leads me through the simple but large bedroom into a bright-white marble bathroom. "It's never been used. Obviously."

"What a waste," I say, running my fingers along the book-matched marble. "You mentioned the designer. They've done a tremendous job, and you have a beautiful house, but how much of it is you? You've said yourself your background is humble, which this place isn't. Does it feel like home?"

He shoves his hands in his pockets again, and the corner of his mouth twitches. "I've grown into it."

That doesn't tell me much. I cross my arms and transfer my weight from one hip to the other, waiting for him to elaborate. Two can play the brooding wordless hero—I've seen enough Daniel De Luca films to get the part down pat.

Ben knows instantly I want more and emits a small sigh. "It was slightly uncomfortable at first. But the designer did a good job interpreting what I wanted. It's not too bright or . . . zany."

I can't stop my laugh. "No, it's definitely not zany. It's moody and—"

"Vampirish?"

"Yes. And no. The feel is intense and atmospheric and . . . kind of just like you. But it's also comforting and warm and . . ."

"And you can't reconcile comfort and warmth with me." It's not a question. "Got it." He turns and heads out of the bathroom.

I scurry after him. "I wasn't saying that," I call. But wasn't I? If I'm being honest, I haven't seen the side of him that's all comfort and warmth. There have been hints—him talking to me about my mother and his parents. It would have made much more sense if the house were full of rooms that were stiff and formal and a little clinical. "It's just that I could live here. Like, without a question, I could move in tomorrow and feel completely at home."

"I don't see how that's a bad thing."

"It's not. Not at all. It's just . . . unexpected." I've never seen this side of Ben. I've found traces of his kindness and generosity; he's obviously not a monster. But I haven't had a chance to see all of him yet. The man who likes to walk around barefoot. The guy who lounges around in gray sweats, reading books about taxidermy and performing bears. The one who hides his humor so deep I can't help but wonder what else is buried there.

"I'm sorry," I say, and I reach for his arm as I catch up to him in the hallway. He's all warmth and hardness and my hand fits against him, slotting into place—a key to a lock.

He tries to shrug me off. "It's fine."

I hold tight. "It's not fine. I was saying it really badly. It's just . . . I feel really at home here, yet it's so grand and you're almost a stranger. It shouldn't make sense that I feel so comfortable. That's what I was trying to say." I pause and he meets my gaze. "And I feel I know you so much better now that I've been here."

His stare heats me from the inside out. After a few tense moments, when I can practically hear his brain whirring to compute everything I've just said, he nods. I have to release his arm and look away before I go up in flames.

He shows me a couple of guest rooms that look like they're from an exclusive, high-end hotel before we take the elevator down to the basement. I can't help but think how someone's home communicates something about their personality. Melanie's home is crammed full of things she's collected from her travels across America. It partly reflects the fact that space is at such a premium in New York City, but it also shows how sentimental she is, and how she's a wanderer.

My dad is still living in a house that's barely been touched since my mom died. He likes it that way, just like Melanie likes her disorganized chaos.

And then there's Jed and me. I walked out of our apartment with two suitcases and some boxes. Ninety-five percent of the things that surrounded us were rented. We lived in the short term, and I guess we loved in it too. I should have seen earlier that we were never going to work. We weren't living the dream; we only leased it.

"Gym area. Space for the pool we can start construction on when we're married, and then changing areas."

I know he's joking, but it doesn't stop my heart from racing in my chest at him mentioning us being married. I take a breath and try to get a grip. This is a job, not a date.

"Infrared sauna," he continues. "Lera has a bedroom and kitchen through there." He points at a door I hadn't noticed before.

"It's a beautiful house," I say. "Or more accurately, mansion. Ken Dream House. Whatever the technical term is."

He doesn't react, and we head to the stairs. "What would I see if I saw your place in New York?" he asks.

"I actually moved out of my place before I came to London," I say. "I'm not sure where I'll go when I go back."

"Jed kept your apartment? Broke the engagement and then threw *you* out?" He lets out a huff, and it kind of feels nice that he's so obviously Team Tuesday.

"No, he moved to Iowa. Out of nowhere. Quit his job and ran off with a ballerina."

"Jesus, Tuesday. How long were you two together?" He leads us upstairs and out into the hall where Lera showed me in, and I turn a full three hundred and sixty degrees to try to get my bearings. This place is huge.

"Nearly ten years. We were college sweethearts." I'm staring at the chandelier, wondering how in all holy hell the thing stays in place. It looks like it's floating in midair. "This is really pretty."

"Are you upset?" he asks, and I turn to look at him.

"Am I upset my fiancé cheated on me, nursed a secret desire to move back to his hometown, broke our engagement, and split? I'm fine about it," I say sarcastically. "Wouldn't you be?"

"It's just . . . You don't seem that cut up."

"You want me to cry on your shoulder?"

He rolls his eyes and leads me through a door I'm fairly certain we haven't been through yet. Somehow we end up back in the kitchen.

"You're right," I add. "I'm not as *cut up* about it as I thought I would be either. Maybe it's because I don't want someone who doesn't want me," I explain.

"And now you can focus on your real love, Daniel De Luca?" he asks.

I laugh. "My *first* love. I forgot about him for a while there. Being in England has brought the fairy tale back."

Our gazes slide together, and it's like he's pulled me into his arms—I can feel his warmth all around me. He's not Dracula, after all. Not even close.

He clears his throat and looks away. "Lera has prepared some food."

Since we were last in here, bowls and plates have appeared on one of the two islands, filled with every type of food imaginable. A literal banquet has been laid out, including what looks suspiciously like shrimp curry, which is one hundred percent my favorite dish, as noted in my questionnaire. It's like he's expecting twenty guests to appear.

"You know, I might need to move in," I say, surveying all the food and deciding what to try first. "Sample Lera's cooking on a daily basis. Make sure the gym works. That sort of thing." I look up at him. "For preparation purposes only, obviously."

He grins, and it's so boyish and open, for a second I forget about his buttoned-up, gruff side and smile right back.

"I thought we could just help ourselves," he says.

"As opposed to getting your footman to serve us?"

"Just fill your plate, Monday Morning." He hands me a dish, and we both dig into the feast in front of us.

"So you're having dinner with a woman," I say as I take a seat at the kitchen table. It's positioned by the window and has been laid with place mats, silverware, wineglasses, and a vase of white roses. I'm guessing we have Lera to thank for that. "How does it feel?"

"I have dinner with women. Just not women I date."

"Because you don't date," I add for him.

"Right. But I've had dinner with women for work."

"And you never get asked out?" I ask. He'd get hit on all the time if he was in New York.

He finishes the mouthful of food he's chewing. "Women make it known they're interested, if that's what you mean."

"I bet they do."

He raises his eyebrows in a flirty pulse.

"And you say"—I pause, only continuing once I've pitched my voice low and adopted a remarkably bad British accent—"'I'll fuck you, but I'm not paying for you to eat a meal beforehand'?"

He half chokes on his lobster and reaches for a glass of water. "Jesus, Tuesday. You think it's better if I take them to dinner, pretend I want a relationship, fuck them, and never see them again?"

I think about it. "I suppose not."

"I don't promise what I can't deliver."

"It's good, I guess. You don't promise them cake and serve them spaghetti. They want your spaghetti, they can have your spaghetti, but you're not giving them cake." The words hang in the air, and I can almost hear the clink and hiss of our brains catching up to what I just said.

"Interesting euphemism," he says. "If you're implying I'm a selfish . . . lover—"

He stops as my jaw hits the table and my eyes pop out on springs. "I wasn't talking about your sexual technique."

"I've never had any complaints," he says, silencing me. "For the record, I like to give cake. Lots of cake. Cake is a favorite of mine, as you know. And further, for the record, there's nothing . . . noodle-y about me."

My face heats like someone's holding a blowtorch to my cheeks. Ben laughs as I slowly turn puce, but I can't look away from him. I'm a thousand times dead and also incredibly turned on. I'm officially a horny zombie with a staring problem.

We manage to get through the rest of dinner without further euphemisms or any more moments where I'm too embarrassed to breathe. We talk about where we went to college, what our favorite TV shows are—not surprisingly, he doesn't watch much of anything other than the news. He asks me lots of questions and patiently listens, which I realize isn't something I'm used to. Jed used to talk a lot. It suited me to let him, I think. But it's nice to have Ben listen. Another quality to add to the growing list.

"What about you? I had Daniel De Luca as my fantasy guy growing up. Who was yours?" I ask.

"I don't remember having a celebrity crush, if that's what you mean."

"Were you always so focused on work? You didn't have a Scarlett Johansson poster taped on your bedroom wall along with your copy of the *Financial Times*?"

He rolls his eyes and stands. We both take our plates back to the counter, where he flips down the dishwasher door and loads his plate and silverware into the machine. It's oddly endearing to watch a man who's clearly so wealthy do something I'm sure Lera would be more than happy to do. He reaches for the plate I'm holding, and our fingers brush and electricity sparks between us.

His eyes dart to mine. "Sorry," he mutters as he places my plate in the dishwasher.

"Yeah, you can't apologize for touching me when we're at the duke's pad," I say.

He laughs. "Yeah, probably not." He straightens, and I step toward him.

"We should . . . practice," I say.

"Practice what?" he asks. "Accidentally touching each other?"

I shrug. "Yeah. I should give you a pat-down or something."

We stand opposite each other, and I shift my weight from one leg to the other.

"This is hopelessly awkward. Engaged couples aren't this . . . unco-ordinated." I hold out my hand as if I'm going to shake his. "Take my hand. We haven't even—"

He slides his hand into mine. I lift my gaze as his warm palm envelops mine, his fingers tangling around my wrist. I hold up my free palm. "Your hands are *huge*."

He releases my hand and puts his palm to mine. I look like I'm Alice in Wonderland and just took the Drink Me potion. I breathe in his musky scent that reminds me of an open fire and toasted marshmallows.

He brings his other hand up, moving the wisps of hair around my face, winding them around my ear.

"Yeah," I breathe out, a little dizzy. "We need to be comfortable being physical with each other."

He releases my hand, and I catch his wrist and place his hand on my hip. "Like this." I look up to him, and his eyes are wide, following my every move. "Now, you put *my* hand where—"

He takes my hand in his and places it on his chest, over his heart.

My fingers press against his solid pectoral muscles, and I pull in a breath. "Yes. Good." I reach for his other hand and place it on my other hip. His hands are firm and hold me in place. I wrap a hand around the back of his neck, rising up to my tiptoes and pressing against him for balance.

He pulls me even closer, his hands sliding around my waist and up my back. Every part of me is throbbing. My head, my heart, between my legs.

I'm needy for more of him.

His gaze flits between my eyes and my mouth. There's a deep ache in the core of me, echoing, begging to be soothed.

He leans forward and I lift my chin, ready to sink into his kiss, but his kiss doesn't make it to my lips. Instead, he presses his lips to my forehead. I can't help but wonder if he's ever done that to any of the women he's not-dated before.

He doesn't move away quickly. We stand, pressed against each other, so close I can feel the pulse under his skin. He takes his lips from my forehead and then dips his head down until our cheeks graze one another. I feel his breath on my skin. My body is buzzing and I sweep my hands over his shoulders.

This time, he presses a kiss on my cheek. So chaste but so *anything but* chaste. I want him to strip me naked, spin me around, and bend me over the kitchen counter.

When my fingers find the back of his neck, he groans, then quickly steps away. I miss his warmth immediately.

"Maybe that's where our preparation should end for tonight," he says.

The distance between us helps me regain my composure. I remember which way is up, where I am, and what I'm doing.

This isn't real.

I fold my arms, trying to cover my body, not wanting to give away how much I'm drawn to him. As much as part of me might want to, I don't ask him if he's serving cake for dessert.

CHAPTER THIRTEEN

For days, I've been poring over the spreadsheets and graphs that relate to Ben's investments at the bank. It's not the first time I've done work like this, but it's the first time I've done the work for someone whose house I've visited, and definitely the first time I've worked on an account for someone I'm going to spend the weekend with while pretending to be his fiancée.

It probably shouldn't, but it makes a difference to know the person who will be on the receiving end of all the data. I've seen Ben barefoot in his kitchen, and apparently, that impacts how I look at a spreadsheet. I really want to do a good job for a thousand reasons. Obviously I want Mr. Jenkins to be happy with the job I'm doing, as he holds my career in his hands. I also want Ben to keep his investments at the bank because we're good at what we do—not merely because he's got history with "James." And not only because it's part of the deal he's made with me.

So far, I've spotted a few minor errors in the data, which probably would have been picked up at some point anyway. But Mr. Jenkins wants me there as a safety net, coordinating departments and making sure everything runs smoothly. And he's the boss, so he gets to decide how I spend my time.

As part of Ben's annual health check, Mr. Jenkins wants to pitch him a real estate investment in South America the bank is handling. Apparently an entire city is being developed, including homes and retail units, leisure facilities, schools, and businesses. It's tipped to have tremendous upside for those investing in the early stages, and the only way UK investors can get in on the investment is if they go through the bank. Mr. Jenkins wants me to put together a proposal that's personalized to Ben.

It would be a huge coup if Ben extended his investments beyond UK assets. It would be the cherry on the cake if he chose to invest more because he thought the bank was the right place to put his money, and not because I'd agreed to pretend to be his fiancée.

"I just want to pop to the loo," Gail says from where she sits opposite me. "But James usually comes out right around now, wanting a coffee. Can you tell him I'll bring one in for him?"

"Of course," I say. I can do even better than that. I'll make his coffee myself right now, anticipating his needs. I know Mr. Jenkins likes his coffee black and hot, because I've been paying attention to how Gail has been making his drink from day one. I'll make one now, and if he comes out of his office while Gail is in the restroom, I can give it to him right away. If he doesn't, I can drink it—albeit after adding in a gallon of milk.

I round my desk and head to the small kitchen at the end of the corridor. I work quickly to put the coffee machine on, then take a step back and lean out of the kitchen so I can keep an eye on Mr. Jenkins's office door. The machine grunts and complains but finally spits out some coffee into the white cup and saucer I've noticed Gail always uses for his coffee.

Some bosses are laid-back about everything that doesn't matter— Mr. Jenkins is not one of those bosses. He seems to care about everything. He likes his trash can emptied twice a day. He doesn't take any calls directly, and he likes everyone who works for him in the office before he is. He's a boss who would have thrived in the fifties. In fact, I'm surprised he doesn't slap Gail on the ass every morning when he passes her desk while smoking a cigarette.

I set the cup on the saucer with a satisfying *clink* and head back down the corridor to my desk. I'm just a few yards away when Mr.

Jenkins opens his door, his eyes wide and blinking like he's experiencing daylight for the first time. He scans Gail's desk and, seeing it empty, his eyes narrow.

"I've made you a coffee, Mr. Jenkins," I say, holding out the cup like I'm presenting him with a prize.

"You have? Don't be telling HR."

"Of course not," I reply. I turn at the ping of the elevator, expecting to see Gail. Instead, Ben strides down the corridor. My heart lifts in my chest, and I'm not quite sure if it's because it will put Mr. Jenkins in a good mood, or if it's for my own, more selfish reasons.

I push my lips together, trying to dissuade the grin threatening to unfurl. He just looks so different in his suit from the last time I saw him padding around his Ken Dream House, but my, he wears his suit even better than he wears his sweats.

He sees me, and we lock eyes as he walks toward the two of us. My heart rate picks up speed, and I shift my balance from one foot to another. I should look away. I don't want Mr. Jenkins to pick up on the fact Ben and I are spending time together outside the office. But somehow, I can't, and he doesn't seem to be able to either. It's like we're magnets; however hard we try to look away, basic physics means it's impossible.

As he approaches, I back away slightly, as if I'm expecting him to grab me and kiss me right there in front of my boss. But when he's a few feet away, Ben manages to shift his focus to Mr. Jenkins. I slip back to safety behind my desk.

"Thought it was only fair to come and congratulate you," Ben says.

A bubble of anxiety or guilt or something fizzes in my stomach as I wonder what Mr. Jenkins needs congratulating over, when I realize they must be talking about soccer. I make a mental note to do an internet search about when Mr. Jenkins's team plays. I flick back a page on my notepad: Chelsea.

"Very gracious of you, I must say," Mr. Jenkins says.

"It was a good win," Ben replies. "There's no doubt about it."

"Agreed. And Arsenal only lost by a fraction. Bad decision by the ref if you ask me."

Ben nods. "Maybe." He glances at me, and I try my best not to meet his gaze . . . and fail as my eyes slide to meet his. His pupils flare, and he clears his throat before returning his focus to Mr. Jenkins. "But we have to take bad luck on the chin and focus on playing well."

"Very good," Mr. Jenkins says. "Very good." He pauses and turns his attention to me. I keep my focus on the computer screen and pretend I'm not listening. "You've met our new project manager, haven't you?" He narrows his eyes as if he's trying to remember.

"Last time I was here."

I look up at them both.

"She's looking over some very exciting opportunities for investment in South America. I thought I might take you through them during our annual review."

Ben nods carefully. "I'm happy to review that investment." The way the words come out are uncomfortable. It's as if he's being asked a question in court and needs to be careful with every syllable. I pull out a pen and scribble a note in my notepad. There's something about his expression I need to understand further. Just below my scribble from the first day of how Mr. Jenkins likes his coffee, I write: *Ben. South America. Investments.*

Ben and Mr. Jenkins trade a few more remarks about soccer, then Ben leaves without another glance at me. I'm half relieved and half disappointed.

"Was that Ben I just saw again?" Gail says as she arrives back at her desk.

"Came to congratulate me on the Chelsea game," Mr. Jenkins says, sipping his coffee. "He's a good man, that one."

"We don't normally see him so often," she says. "Are you sure he's not measuring the place up, getting ready to sell?"

Mr. Jenkins laughs and then stops himself. "Don't say things like that. He gives us a good rent. We don't want anything changing."

Gail takes in Mr. Jenkins's coffee cup and frowns. "Did you make your own coffee?"

"Tuesday did. Very nice too."

I know it's just coffee, but getting it right for him feels good. Maybe it's not a guaranteed place on the fast track, but it can't hurt.

Mr. Jenkins goes back to his office, and Gail returns to her desk.

"Thank you for making James's coffee," Gail says.

I beam at her. "It was my pleasure."

She returns my smile, but it's a little forced. "How are you finding London?" she asks.

"Interesting. It's my first time abroad, so everything is so different."

Gail nods, but I can tell it's half-hearted. I just don't know why. "Can I give you some advice?" she asks.

"Of course," I say.

"If you were a male in your position, over from the New York office, trying to prove himself worthy of a place on this newly consolidated fast track . . ." She pauses, as if she's trying to figure out how to word the end of the sentence. "Well, he wouldn't be making James's coffee."

Was she mad? "I'm sorry, I never meant to overstep—"

She holds up a hand. "That's not what I meant. I don't mind if you make the coffee. Saves me a job. I'm saying, as a woman, you have to be careful how you're perceived. And as someone trying to get ahead, don't present yourself as someone who makes the coffee. It's okay for me. I'm not looking to get ahead. I have the job I want."

"I suppose I just want to be helpful."

"I know," she says. "But protect yourself. Like most banks, senior management here is dominated by men. I want that to change. You want that to change. Leave the coffee to me, focus on Brazil, and get your place on the fast track. That's what you're here for." She sends me a smile that says, *I know it's tough love, but you need to listen to me.* And she's right.

"Thank you," I say.

"You're welcome."

I type into my browser bar, "South America, Ben Kelley." I scroll through the results. Nothing much comes up. Then I decide to do a search on Ben more widely. What are his businesses and how exactly has he made his fortune from nothing? I remember I have that file listing all the companies he's associated with, and I dig it out from my bag.

Over the next couple of hours, I piece together Ben's extraordinary rise to billionaire business mogul. What almost every article mentions is how private he is. Some call it unassuming. Others secretive. Some publications clearly feel he should be courting them more than he does. No one mentions Ben's desire to own the Castles and Palaces Hotel Group he so desperately wants.

I then start a deep dive on his businesses, which is when I finally make the connection between one of Ben's subsidiary companies and South America. It's the operating company that manages the development of the new city in Paraguay Mr. Jenkins wants to pitch to Ben.

Mr. Jenkins wants to try to sell Ben his own investment.

Luckily, Mr. Jenkins didn't tell Ben exactly *which* South American investment he wanted to pitch. I'll just have to find something else we can mention in the meeting so Mr. Jenkins will be spared any embarrassment.

Mr. Jenkins emerges from his office and rumbles over to my desk.

"Have you finished the Paraguay presentation for Kelley? I want to make sure it's properly tailored to his portfolio of assets, to the extent we know what they are."

"Actually, I've uncovered some pertinent information about that." I slide the article I printed off earlier.

"What's this?" Mr. Jenkins asks, picking up the paper.

I don't say anything and just let him read.

He looks up from the paper. "You're sure about this?"

"Completely sure." I didn't just rely on that article. "There's corroboration on the website, if you look closely."

"Show me," he says.

I pull up the website devoted to the development and investment into Paraguay. There, buried in fine print at the bottom of the site map, is the name of the company that owns the city. "The shareholder in that company is Ben's main holding company."

Mr. Jenkins nods. "Good work, Tuesday."

A warm glow fills my chest, and I smile at his back as he returns to his office.

I glance over at Gail, who's grinning at me.

"That's what he'll remember when he makes his decision about you. That you saved him from having egg all over his face. That you're detail oriented and see things others don't. We all want our boss to think we're doing a good job. But that's how you do it. Not with coffee."

Gail's right. I just want people around me to be happy; I'll do everything it takes. Too much, sometimes. Ben's noticed my tendency to put the feelings of others first too. In his particular, subtle, *Ben* way, he tries to help—ordering the starters when I didn't like the cod. Saying no to the dress in Ralph Lauren. When it comes to my work in the bank, I need to be more strategic with where I put my energy. When it comes to everyday life . . . that's another story.

CHAPTER FOURTEEN

I know we've done everything we can in the time available, but that doesn't stop the nerves battling in my chest as we turn into the entrance to the stately home of the Duke and Duchess of Brandon. Luckily my anxiety about being discovered has overridden my nerves about being in the close confines of a car with Ben. Our almost-make-out-slash-practice-touching has long been forgotten, and we're focused on our objective.

I spent every working hour of the last week trawling through paperwork regarding Ben's finances. Every hour *out* of the office I spent revising Ben's completed—very personal—questionnaire, interspersed with me frantically firing off even more personal questions by text and receiving calm responses and reassurances that everything was going to be fine. My entire life has become about Ben in the last few days. I've thrown myself into the role of Ben's fiancée, and I'm certain I couldn't have done anything more, but I'm far from confident about pulling off our charade. My anxiety skyrockets as we pass through the gates to the estate.

"It's going to be fine," Ben says as we pull up in front of the house. I don't even need to say anything. My nerves are boomeranging around the car.

"What happens if it isn't fine?"

"We get thrown in a Thai prison for the rest of our lives and have to come to terms with the fact that life will never be the same." He speaks in the same tone of voice he always does. Serious and studied, except I know him well enough now to know he's joking.

My mind flits to our almost-kiss in the kitchen, and I shiver.

"I'm serious, Ben. What happens if they see through our . . . act?"

He pulls in a breath. "I'm going to tell you what I've told you the last ten times you've asked that question: People aren't looking for holes in other people's stories; they're looking for things to make sense. We're prepared. They're not going to see through anything."

I go to object, but he silences me as he raises his eyebrows and adds, "Worst-case scenario, we leave in a couple of days, and the duke doesn't want to sell me his hotels. And that's exactly the position we're in now. You'll be thirty thousand dollars richer. You have nothing to lose. Just try and enjoy yourself."

He opens the driver's door and then comes around to the passenger side, scooping up my hand in his. Our eyes lock at the physical contact, but I look away. Somehow, him touching me neutralizes some of my anxiety. It's like he's my shield, my protector, the man who has my back. Like someone's taking some of the load from me.

It's such an unusual feeling, it throws me off guard. Before I know it, I'm standing in front of the Duke and Duchess of Brandon, being introduced as Ben's fiancée.

"Your Grace," I say as I shake hands with the duke. When Ben explained how I should address the duke and the duchess, I laughed. I didn't think he was serious, but now I'm here, standing on the steps of this enormous house, it feels entirely natural. Like I'm in a real-life *Bridgerton* novel or something.

The duke is one of those tall, very thin men who always looks like they're in need of a sandwich. The duchess is slight and impossibly beautiful, with an elegance that can't be taught, but she's not haughty or at all standoffish.

"Oh, good, an American," the duchess says without explanation. "Do call me Verity. And my husband's George." She has a kind smile and tiny, tiny wrists. I shake her hand very gently. I do not want to break the duchess's bones before we're even through the front door.

I half expected the duke and duchess to greet us wearing tailcoats and tiaras, but both of them are dressed in jeans and blazers. However, the duchess's hazelnut-size diamond studs give away a little of who she is. Our introduction is short, and I glance over my shoulder to see another couple coming through the front doors behind us. It's as if the duke and duchess are a stop on a conveyor belt, and we've moved past them.

Ben doesn't let go of my hand as another man, Grant, introduces himself as the butler and guides us upstairs. We're all meeting in the drawing room for cocktails at six, followed by dinner. The grandfather clock we just passed says it's a little before four. I wonder if I can chill the hell out between now and then.

"This is your room," Grant says as he opens the door, stepping aside to allow us in first.

"It's beautiful," I say, before I've even had a chance to take it in. But as I glance around, it's clear I was right. Spacious and bright, with duck-egg-blue walls and dual-aspect windows overlooking the undulating grounds of the house. A sumptuous-looking four-poster bed occupies one side of the room, opposite a couch between two long windows, and on the other side, another two large couches sit opposite each other, either side of a fireplace. A bathroom is on the left.

One bed.

"Please let me know if there's anything you require," Grant says before giving a little bow and gliding out of the room.

"This is good," Ben says once the door closes and Grant's footsteps fade. He doesn't drop my hand right away, and I don't slide mine from his. It feels too nice having him close. "A sofa will suit me fine."

All week Ben has been preempting any anxiety I might be feeling and trying to chase it away. He doesn't make it obvious; he doesn't say, "Don't worry, I'll take the sofa." He just constantly walks a little way ahead, clearing my fears just as they start to develop. I'm not sure if it's conscious or a coincidence. It feels like we're in sync. I don't have to ask for reassurance; it's offered just before it's needed. Another quality to add to the list that grows hourly.

"It's a beautiful house," I say. "It looks familiar. Probably seen it on a Jane Austen adaptation or something."

"I doubt it," Ben replies, finally dropping my hand and moving to the window. "The duke doesn't need the money they'd get from hiring the place out."

I bend to unzip my suitcase. Maybe one stately home looks a lot like another, but there's something about the stone steps up to the grand entrance that seemed familiar. "So cocktails and then dinner. You have a preference about what I should wear?"

Ben is facing the window that looks out onto the gardens, his hands in his pockets, his profile lit up like he's the president. He isn't just handsome. He's commanding.

In New York, I can spot a really powerful man by their intangible presence. Ben's one of those guys.

"Wear whatever will make you feel comfortable," he says, staring straight ahead. What's he thinking about? How to approach the duke about buying the hotels? Whether or not he thinks we can pull off being fake-engaged? Maybe he feels out of his depth. Just like me.

"So a thong and nipple tassels are okay with you?"

He keeps staring out of the window. "Let's keep the nipple tassels for behind closed doors, shall we?"

A shiver snakes down my spine at the thought of things being kept private between us. But that's not what he meant. He was just being funny.

I finish hanging up evidence I'm sponsored by Ralph Lauren, then grab my makeup and toiletries and head to the bathroom.

"You mind if I take the left side of the sink?" I call to Ben.

He doesn't respond, so I take it as permission to do as I like.

When I finish unpacking in the bathroom, I go back to the bedroom to find Ben hasn't moved.

"You want me to unpack for you?" I ask.

Ben frowns, then glances away from the window and meets my gaze. "You're not my servant, Tuesday."

I tilt my head. "Depends on your definition, I suppose." He's paying me to be here, after all. "If I was your fiancée in real life, maybe that's what I'd do." I would have unpacked for Jed.

Ben shakes his head. "If this was real life, you definitely wouldn't be unpacking for me. We have plenty of time." He turns back to the window.

"Right. Time. I might as well keep busy. Otherwise, what else are we going to do?"

"You mentioned nipple tassels . . ." he says, like he's just asked me if I remembered my phone charger.

I roll my eyes, but can't conceal my smile. He's so much funnier than I could have thought. I bet most people don't see that side of him.

"Why don't you take a bath," he suggests. "It might help you relax. I can run it for you, if you like."

"Run me a bath?" I ask, incredulous. I look up to check his expression to try to figure out if he's being serious, but he doesn't turn around.

"Isn't that what engaged couples do for each other?"

I can tell by his tone, he's entirely serious.

"Not in my experience," I scoff. "I'm going to . . ." He glances away from the window to look at me when I don't finish my sentence. His gaze presses into me like fingertips on my hips. "Fix my migrating mascara."

"As long as we're not late," he says. "I'm not sure how long migration issues take."

I nod. "Not long." Maybe when I'm wearing something more formal, I might *feel* more like the fiancée of a man like Ben. A man who's gorgeous and rich and powerful, and on top of all that, funny.

After my bath, I fix my makeup, run a brush through my hair, and squirt on some perfume before getting dressed. I've gone for the gray silk skirt-and-shirt combo tonight. It's the kind of outfit that perfectly occupies the underpopulated ground between formal and casual.

I step out of the bathroom. "Ready?" I ask Ben.

He doesn't look like he's moved; he's still standing, looking out the window. Except he's changed into a blue suit and white shirt with a . . . I do a double take when I see his tie. It's exactly the same pink-and-blue polka-dot tie I bought Jed for Christmas, which he returned. He said it wasn't *him*. But it looks great on Ben. I glance up at his face, and he's staring back at me.

"You look—"

"No need for compliments when there's no one to overhear," I interrupt, crossing the room. I need to remind myself that we're not actually a real couple. But the closer I get to Ben, the thicker the air seems. I stand in front of him, lift my hands, and adjust his tie slightly.

"You look beautiful," he says, his voice low. The timbre vibrates across my skin. I feel a blush blooming on my cheeks.

I brush my fingertips across his jaw because I can't *not* touch him. His Adam's apple bobs when he swallows. "Thank you," I reply. "I like your suit."

There isn't an item of clothing in existence that would stop Ben looking like a god, so giving him any kind of compliment is almost ridiculous—an understatement. Nothing could convey quite how incredible he looks. It's like saying there are seven days in a week. It's true, but it doesn't say *enough*. It doesn't mention that those days are stuffed full of sunshine and sapphire-blue skies. That they're spent splayed on a blanket, watching boats go by and making daisy chains, dreaming about who you might become when you're grown.

"My tie straight?" he asks, his eyebrow raised.

I reach up to his hair and push a stray strand back. "I think you'll do."

He grins that boyish grin I've only seen from him once before. "Let's go." He holds out his hand.

I slide my palm against his, and the buzz is unmistakable. Does he feel it too? I glance up, and his brows are knitted together like he's trying to work out a complex math problem.

"If we get a question we haven't rehearsed, then we stick as closely to the truth as possible," he says. "Just like you suggested. Okay?"

I exhale. "Agreed. I just hope the discussion is about hotels and business and not our relationship."

"It seems the two are inextricably linked." Almost like a yogi's chant, the guttural vibrations of his grumbling somehow relax me.

We meet Nick at the top of the stairs.

"You're here," he says, stating the obvious. "How are things going?"

"We met the duke and duchess briefly."

Nick nods. "Excellent." He turns and watches an elegant woman come toward us. "Here's Elizabeth, my wife." Her hair is swept up and she's wearing flat shoes and a bright-red lip. She looks like she lives here and doesn't seem to have any of my nerves, but then again, I suppose I'm hiding more than she is.

Ben and Elizabeth obviously know each other, but Nick introduces us and we exchange air kisses.

"How are you feeling?" He glances at our joined hands. "Good? You make a handsome couple, if I do say so myself."

"Stop," Ben says. He tugs my hand and we take the sweeping staircase down. Grant appears from nowhere to meet us at the bottom with a tray of champagne.

We didn't live in a mansion and have holidays in Europe when I was young, but we weren't poor—or I never felt it until right now. Even being toured around Ben's house didn't intimidate me. But the kind of life that involves a butler who appears out of nowhere with drinks is slightly intimidating.

"His Grace is out on the terrace," Grant says. "At the end of the corridor, on your right."

The terrace is covered in roses of every color and size, growing over the pergola at one end and in pots and raised beds at the other. We're not the first to arrive. There are three other couples standing on the far end, the duke and duchess waiting by the door for people to arrive.

The duchess is wearing a soft-pink skater-style dress with a string of pearls and her hair up in a chignon. At least I feel like I'm suitably dressed. The duke's in a navy suit that looks like Ben's, so that's another tick in the box, although Ben's sartorial suitability was never really in question.

We're all so dressed up for dinner, and we're not even going out. But this is obviously normal for them. I can't help but wonder if this is normal for Ben too. He says he doesn't come from money, but is this a life he's become comfortable with? Does he throw lavish dinner parties or go hunting for the weekend often? He doesn't seem the type, but I don't know him very well.

"Tuesday is such a beautiful name," the duchess says as Ben drops my hand.

My knees fizz with nerves at the loss of his support. Even if I were actually engaged to Ben, I'd still be a little nervous. Life with Jed in New York was incredibly glamorous at times, but I've never had dinner in a stately home with actual nobility.

"It's so unusual." Her eyes are sparkling and full of interest.

My name gets me plenty of attention and not always in a good way. There are a lot of snobs in New York—mainly Jed's friends and work colleagues—who used to love to make snide put-downs about my name. I'm fully attuned to backhanded compliments, but this isn't one. The duchess is being completely authentic.

"Thank you," I say. "I love it. It was my mother's choice. Ben loves to tease me about it."

"I don't know what you mean, Sunday," he says, quick as a flash.

Smiling, I roll my eyes, like I'm well used to his jibes. Which I kind of am.

"So how long have you two been together?" the duchess asks.

"Less than a year," I say—technically, not a lie. "It's been a whirlwind."

Ben isn't a talker. Anyone who's ever met him knows that. He can't start gushing over our fairy-tale romance because it'll sound fake. Most of the relationship questions have to be answered by me.

"It's a cliché, but when you know, you *really* know," I say.

The duchess is smiling like she knows exactly what I mean. "I agree. I see couples together for four and five years and then they split up, and I think, 'What were you doing? If you knew it wasn't right, why did you waste all that time?'"

I can't help but think about Jed. We'd been together nearly a decade and hadn't made it down the aisle. I always made the excuse that we were young and had plenty of time. But maybe he'd been dragging his feet a long time because he didn't believe in us. Or maybe *I'd* been the one with doubts. Maybe on some level, we knew we weren't each other's forever.

"You're right," I say. "Though I guess sometimes you can be happy enough to stay in a relationship, but not happy enough to turn it into forever." I lay a hand on Ben's upper arm and squeeze.

"Absolutely," he says.

I laugh because he's clearly so uncomfortable, and it has nothing to do with me being his fake fiancée. Even if I was the love of his life, the woman he was going to marry, he'd be just as uncomfortable. It's just who he is.

The duchess laughs as well. "I know how that feels," she says, nodding to Ben's rigid demeanor. "I can count the number of times George has told me he loves me on one hand. It's the British stiff upper lip you'll have to get used to."

"I don't see the need to remind you," the duke says. "You're an intelligent woman. It's not likely you're going to forget. Excuse me." He moves away to greet another couple who have appeared in the doorway. I never thought to ask how many people were coming this weekend. So far it's six couples and the duke and duchess.

I expect the duchess to make her excuses too, but she just shakes her head in a way that says she loves her husband but can find him completely hopeless. "Do you have a date in mind for the wedding?"

"We're mid-discussions. Ben would have us elope tomorrow." I shrug. "It's not like I want something really huge, but I think it would be nice for our friends and family to share the day with us."

"Are your parents excited?" she asks.

"Nothing much excites my dad. As long as I'm happy. My mom died when I was young, so—" I get a sudden and unexpected lump in my throat, which silences me for a couple of seconds.

The duchess puts her hand over mine and mouths, *I'm sorry.*

I'm used to talking about my mom and it rarely gets me emotional when I mention her in passing, but she would be excited for me if Ben and I were getting married. No doubt, she'd be making plans for her and Dad to move to England for at least part of the year, and she'd be helping me with preparations. One day, when it finally happens for me, I'm going to find it tough without her. Dad's input alone isn't going to cut it.

"As long as we don't wait too long," Ben says, rescuing me from having to form a sentence. The duke rejoins us as Ben says, "I don't see the point in protracted engagements. We know we're getting married, so let's get on with it."

The duke gives a firm nod of his head. "My thoughts exactly."

I take a steadying breath and smile. "Your home is quite lovely," I say, keen to steer the conversation away from our relationship. "Has it been in the family long?"

"Since 1679," the duke replies. "The year construction was completed. The seventh Duke of Brandon commissioned it, and it's been in the family ever since."

"That's wonderful," I reply. "I love the idea of creating and maintaining history that can be passed down through the generations."

"Yes, the title shall pass to my cousin or his son," the duke says in a clipped tone. "Do you have a big family?"

"Not yet," I say. "I've always wanted lots of children, though. Ben agrees."

"*Define* 'lots of,'" he growls, and I laugh because it's exactly how I'd expect him to react if we were actually engaged and talking about children. The duchess laughs, too, and I like her for it. I don't really know her, and she's British aristocracy, but somehow I feel like we have lots in common in the way we react to the grumpy men in our lives.

"But seriously," I say, "one would be a blessing. If I could convince him to have three or four, that would be even better."

"Let's just take it day by day," Ben says, gazing at me like he thinks I'm the most wonderful woman he's ever seen. He's such a great actor. "We both agree we're going to try once we're married."

"Sounds like we need to get you married as soon as possible," the duchess says.

She's so sweet and kind, I feel a little bad for lying to her. But she'll never know. Engagements are broken all the time. I've got evidence of that.

We talk a little more about her wedding to the duke and about how her niece is newly engaged. The duchess is charming, and I can't imagine anyone meeting her not falling a little bit in love.

From out of nowhere a gong sounds. No one says anything, but people start filing inside through a different door from the one we came out of, straight into an elaborately set dining room. I try not to come across too awed, but I can't not notice the gold leaf on the ceiling and the elaborate candelabras on the long table set with a crisp white table-cloth. It looks like we're in a movie. I wish Daniel De Luca had more of a back catalog in costume drama. I feel a binge coming on when I return to London.

I find myself sitting opposite the duchess, with Ben to my left and Nick to my right. Ben's opposite the duke.

"You're going to settle in England?" The duke looks between Ben and me.

Panic slithers down my spine. Somehow, this issue didn't make it onto our questionnaires, despite it being a major lifestyle choice. Just about now, I'm thinking we're both idiots for overlooking such an obvious issue.

"Yes," I say. "It's much easier to move my career than Ben's. And anyway, ever since I first touched down in this country, it's kind of felt like home."

It's not a lie. I don't know whether it's because I've had a thing for British movie stars since forever, or because I've watched every Daniel De Luca film a thousand times over, but this country feels a bit like my home away from home. I feel a kinship I never expected.

"I love all the history, but more than that, Ben's here. And I would follow him anywhere."

That's how it's supposed to be when you're in love, right? Jed once mentioned the possibility of moving to Iowa a couple of years ago. His parents are there, along with his older brother and his wife. Even though he was trying to be funny at the time, I remember feeling like he'd sucker-punched me with the idea. Jed and I were inextricably linked with New York—at least, I thought we were. I couldn't picture us anywhere but the city where we'd spent our twenties together. He never brought it up again, and I'd forgotten about it until he ended things.

"What work do you do?" the duke asks.

"At a bank," I say. "Since college. It was the first job I got. My father encouraged me to take it." Actually, my dad just wanted me to be happy with whatever career choice I made. Jed pushed for me to take on a role at the bank.

The duke stops chewing, and I feel like I've dropped a bomb. "You follow a lot of your father's advice?"

My heart is spluttering. Did I mess everything up? My father would say, when in doubt, tell the truth. "Yes. He's such a brilliant and kind man and . . . He gives the best advice."

The duke nods and resumes chewing. I hold my breath as he swallows and then replies, "I was always the same with my father. I always went to him with my struggles. I wanted to be just like him." I allow myself to exhale. However impossible it might seem, the duke and I seem to have something in common. "When he passed the estate down to me, I could only imagine being as successful as he was."

The duchess reaches over and presses her hand over her husband's. "You've been the most successful Duke of Brandon by far. Your father would be proud."

The duke nods, his expression solemn. "And that's all any of us want: for our parents to be proud of us."

The tablecloth pulls beside me, and I move my glass before it topples over. I look down and realize Ben is gripping the edge of the linen. I glance up at him, and his expression is the same as ever, totally belying the tension in his body. I slide my hand onto his thigh, and he clasps it as if he'd been waiting for it. My heart clenches.

The duke clears his throat. "Nick here tells me you still want to buy my hotels." I hold my breath, desperate to know how Ben is going to react. But the duchess lowers her voice to talk to just me, and I give her my full attention. I keep my hand on Ben's thigh.

"Have you ever seen the film *A Duchess for a Duke?*" she asks.

I can't stop the grin from spreading across my face at her mention of the Daniel De Luca movie. "One of my favorites," I confess in the same almost-whisper.

"I'm so pleased to hear that." Her eyes seem to dance like she's about to reveal a secret. "Much of it was filmed here."

My lungs stop functioning and I have to consciously breathe. "Here?" I lean closer to her, point my finger in the air and circle it.

"The entire house and gardens. I convinced George to go to the Chelsea house for three weeks while I stayed here during filming. He wasn't happy about it, but a friend of a friend is a producer, and she thought Fairfield House would be the perfect location for the duke's country residence in the film."

"It was—*is*—perfect," I reply. "So beautiful." I shake my head. "I can't believe the coincidence, but Ben and I met when I was visiting the spot in Green Park where Daniel and Julia Alice meet for the very first time. In fact, I mistook him for Daniel and made a complete fool out of myself."

She laughs. "Yes, he does look rather like him. I thought that when we met this afternoon. It gave me flashbacks to when they were here filming."

"What are you two talking about so conspiratorially over there?" the duke asks.

"Oh, nothing," the duchess says, her eyes twinkling.

"I bet you're talking about that stupid film," he huffs.

I can't help but laugh. The duke isn't quite as grumpy as Ben, but he's not far off.

"We're having more fun than you lot over there, talking about hotels," the duchess says.

The duke grumbles under his breath but goes back to his conversation with Ben.

"Was filming very disruptive?" I ask. How exciting to have movie stars wandering about your house.

"The duke would have thought so, but I enjoyed it. There were certain rooms they weren't allowed into—our bedroom, George's study, the afternoon parlor, the morning room."

I scan the room around me, thinking back to the movie. I haven't seen it for a while, but I don't remember this room as a setting.

"Your bedroom is the room where the duke and duchess first kiss," the duchess says.

I sit back in my chair. The excitement is almost overwhelming. I wish my mom were here—she would freaking *love* to hear this. "The duck-egg-blue silk walls. Of course. I should have remembered. That scene was so beautiful."

"So romantic."

"The *most* romantic. Up until that scene, I wasn't certain he would ever make his move. I mean, all those brooding looks! I suspected he loved her, but that scene . . ." I sigh, remembering how he spluttered over his declaration of love.

"I think she was in love with him from the start," the duchess says. "I know they were strangers when they first got engaged, but it was like she always saw a different side of him than anyone else."

"I think it might be my favorite movie of his. I wasn't expecting to like it; I didn't think I'd appreciate Daniel De Luca in britches. But he can make anything look good."

The duchess laughs a full, throaty laugh, and I catch the duke smiling to himself as he watches her. "Some men are like that. I always tell George he should buy his suits from Marks & Spencer because he could make them look just as good as the suits he has made on Jermyn Street."

I shrug. "You're right. Some men can look good in a garbage bag." I squeeze Ben's hand. There's not a bone in my body faking anything at that moment.

"You know they had to move the bed in your room to get the shots of the kiss. They built a camera track in a circle."

"It must have been so awesome to get to see it all. Did you get to talk to the actors?"

"Absolutely," she says. "Both Daniel and Avani have come to stay with us since, and we occasionally meet up with Daniel in town. He's a lovely man. Very thoughtful."

I'm sitting opposite a person who has sat opposite Daniel De Luca. Maybe Melanie was right and the duchess will introduce us, and we'll fall wildly in love and get married.

"I'm such a huge fan," I say. "Tomorrow, could I take some pictures of the places where they filmed?"

"Of course. I can give you the full film tour."

If the ladies attending the convention back at my hotel could only see me now. Who'd have thought that pretending to be an almost-stranger's fiancée would have led me on another journey closer to Daniel De Luca?

Sometimes, you just can't escape fate.

CHAPTER FIFTEEN

Sitting on the bed while I wait for Ben to finish in the bathroom, I take in the blue silk wallpaper. I can't believe I get to sleep in the bedroom where Daniel De Luca kissed Avani Tudor in *A Duchess for a Duke*. It was such an iconic scene because it was the first time the duke let his cold exterior thaw a little. The thaw quickly became a flood, and he kissed her.

Daniel De Luca and Avani Tudor's chemistry was electric in that movie, and there were lots of rumors swirling during filming that the two of them were having a torrid affair. If they weren't, they should have been. I love to imagine the sparks between the actors on screen spilling over to real life; it makes watching so much more exciting. I'm still convinced Josh Lucas and Reese Witherspoon are destined to be together.

The bathroom door opens. My gaze falls on it like I'm lost and Ben is a homing beacon, but he doesn't come out right away.

My stomach flips in anticipation.

I really didn't think this through. Wearing a white tank top and white sleep shorts, I feel entirely naked. I hop into bed and sit up against the headboard, but I pull the covers over my bare legs just as Ben comes out of the bathroom. He definitely planned better for this moment, because he's fully covered in navy PJ bottoms and a tight white T-shirt, which I'm appreciating the hell out of. Any stranger seeing Ben in street clothes could tell his chest is broad, but seeing it like this is a treat. He's gorgeous.

"You've been making use of that home gym, I see," I say, and then immediately want to die. I've basically just told him I'm ogling him.

The corner of his mouth lifts. I'm not sure if he's pleased at the compliment or trying to cover a cringe. Maybe both.

I just can't stop digging. "We had a gym in the basement of the apartment complex, but I was convinced it was a home for serial killers and therefore, quite logically, refused to go." I need to get off the subject before he starts checking out my lack of abs. "Anyway, how was dinner?"

"We?" he says, pulling a couple of the pillows from the bed and a comforter that's arranged across the end of the mattress and tossing them onto the couch.

"What?" Not for the first time, I'm not following his train of thought.

"You said, *we* had a gym. You and Jed?"

I sigh. "Yeah, me and Jed." When I left New York, the breakup was so fresh it felt like a big gaping wound that would never heal. Now, the pain has subsided quicker than I expected. What's weirder is my memories of him and us and our life together are . . . blurry. Like one of the watercolors that line the walls of this very grand house. Maybe it's the ocean between us.

"Do you miss being a *we*?" he asks, and even though he's asking me about my feelings, it's like we're studying facts on our questionnaires. He's so focused on the answer.

"Not here in England," I say. "You're my *we* here." My heartbeat trips in my chest at what I'm saying, not because I'm embarrassed but because it's true. Ben and I feel like a *we*. "I should be asking you if it's weird *being* a *we*. I know you don't typically like a girlfriend cramping your style."

I don't expect him to answer the question, but he does. "It's not as weird as I thought it might be." He sits on the couch, his legs apart, his arm draped across the cushions on the back. I follow his movements, unable to look away from the lean, long lines of him.

"I'm going to take that as a compliment," I say, and I tilt my head, wondering what his lips would feel like on my neck.

He nods but doesn't say anything. I wish, not for the first time, that I could read this man's mind. He has such a physical effect on my body, like I'm a firework waiting to light up whenever he's around. I'm drawn to him—the sea pulled toward the moon. I want to know if he experiences the same reaction to me.

"Do you think you'll go back to the US?" he asks.

I let out a small, nervous laugh. "Of course. The position at the bank here is just for five weeks. It's an opportunity to impress the CEO. Besides, where else would I go?" My friends are there. It's the city I call home. "Anyway, I want to know what happened with the duke when I was gossiping to the duchess about Daniel De Luca."

"Right." He pulls back the comforter and settles down on the couch.

"So?" I ask.

"Ray?" he responds, and I'm flummoxed for a second until I realize he's trying to make a joke.

"Nope." I clear my throat in preparation to sing—or make the noise that, for me, approximates singing. I'm a horrible singer. "*La, a note to follow So, Ti, a drink with jam and bread. That will bring us back—*"

"Please stop that." He winces in a brooding, hot way.

"Only if you tell me what happened with the duke. Is he going to sell?"

He tucks an arm behind his head, and I try not to swoon at his flexed muscles. He's not one of those gym types who train twice a day and have a weakness for steroids. He's not bulky, just tall and broad and . . . I need a cold shower. I look away, afraid he'll be able to see what I'm thinking in my expression.

"Too early to say. He likes you." He glances at me and his mouth curls up slightly in an almost-smile.

I pause, wondering if Ben likes me too. Because I'm beginning to *really* like him. "He's more charming than I expected," I continue. "He definitely has some grump to his personality—maybe that's a nationwide British thing—but he's . . . less formal than I was anticipating. Lighter than—"

"Than me."

It's an unspoken question he's not looking to have answered, but I give him one anyway. "I don't think you're heavy."

He raises his eyebrows in silent accusation.

"I'm serious. You're not heavy. You're . . . taciturn, certainly. But when we were at your house, you . . . I don't know how to put it." I think for a while, aware he's watching me as I stare out the window, waiting for my words to come. "You don't let the world see all of you. There's a layer underneath the surface you don't reveal very often."

He looks away as I turn back to him, like I've caught him doing something he shouldn't. It's all the confirmation I need that I'm right.

"You seemed a little upset at the dinner table at one point. What was that about?" I ask.

He shrugs. "I don't remember."

"The duke was talking about his father," I press. "About wanting to make him proud. Do you feel the need to make your dad proud?"

"I know he's proud of me. Can we drop this?"

His expression isn't harsh, but I can see pain in his eyes. Whatever upset him is firmly embedded in that layer he doesn't want to show me. I don't push any harder. There's no need to upset him or remind him of his pain.

"There's darkness in everyone. But there's also plenty of lightness in you," I say. "I've poked a few holes in that armor of yours. I've seen it."

He lets out a half laugh. "You might be right."

"I've seen you without a tie already. Give me a couple of months and I'll have you lip-synching to Taylor Swift songs and driving with the windows down."

He growls as he stares at the ceiling. "I'm focused on the end goal."

"Sometimes you have to have fun on the way."

"So they say. *My* fun is achieving what I set out to do."

He's so driven. So focused. I try to think about whether Jed was like that. He was certainly ambitious, but he never seemed so . . . determined.

"I get that. But do you ever just kick back and relax? Do you ever call in sick and stay in bed and eat popcorn and watch movies all day?"

"Who would I be calling in sick to?"

"Hmm, I suppose that doesn't make much sense when you're the boss. But doesn't it just mean you can do it more often? We should try it when we get back to London. I'll tie you to the bed and force-feed you hot buttered popcorn and Daniel De Luca."

"Not my kink," he replies dryly.

Tiny explosions start going off in my shorts because I can't help but wonder what his kink is. Does he want me to ask? It's like he's left a door ajar, and I can't tell if he's being deliberate or oblivious.

"Hmm. Maybe more of a Timothée Chalamet fan?"

Ben chuckles. "Definitely not."

He's not giving much away, but now I can't help myself. "So what do you like?"

"I don't watch many films," he says, and I don't respond because I know this already. It was on the form. I want him to give me more without being pushed. I'm not sure what I'm asking for. I don't want to know his favorite sexual position—or maybe I do—but I want to know him better. I want to know all of him. "I like to work out and make myself cheese on toast when Lera is off."

"Toast in bed could create a crumb catastrophe."

He smirks. "Every now and then, I've been known to watch a little . . . *Strictly Come Dancing*."

I'm mentally deep diving into my Anglo-American dictionary, trying to figure out what he's saying. "The show? Like *Dancing with the Stars*?"

"My mum was a dancer. When I was a kid, I used to take Latin and ballroom classes."

My ovaries switch into hypersonic overdrive. "You can *dance*?"

"A little."

All I can focus on is the thought of his hand on my back and hips pressed against me, his thigh sliding against mine. "Holy shit." It's the only appropriate response. A man like Ben should be strictly a dad dancer. There's no way the women of the world are ready for this man being able to dance.

"Well, that's settled. Cheese on toast—whatever the hell that is— plus *Dancing with the Strictly Stars*. In bed. You deserve a day off when we get back from here."

"You've decided that's what I need?" he asks. "You've diagnosed my problem, and high-fat foods and shit TV shows while bedridden is the prescription."

I sigh and flop back onto the bed, propping my head up with my hand so I can still see him. "It's pretty much the solution for every problem I can think of. I swear, all international diplomatic relations should be conducted from bed. The UN should rip out the seats from the Assembly Hall and replace them with beds with a built-in widescreen. The world would be a better place for it."

"You'll have to police me," he says. "I'm not sure I've got the staying power to last a day in bed."

"Police you? Not my kink."

He chuckles, reaches for the eye mask on the table, then turns off the lamp next to the couch, sending the room into darkness. "No costumes required. Just a partner in crime."

"Maybe you haven't had the right incentive to spend the day in bed before?" I suggest.

"You're right," he says. "Maybe you're what I've been missing."

I pause, waiting for a sarcastic follow-up, but it doesn't come.

"I need to state for the record, I'm entirely onboard if you're offering snacks and trashy TV." *And a day in bed with you,* I don't add.

"Good night, Tuesday," he says.

It's one of the few times he's used my real name, and the sound winds around my body like one of his large hands sliding around my back, readying us for a waltz.

CHAPTER SIXTEEN

I'm dressed in jeans, a cream cashmere sweater, and a navy quilted jacket. I feel underdressed, considering I'm staying at the stately home of a duke and duchess, but everyone I've seen so far today is in more or less the same. We've gathered in the "morning room" to start our day. I'd like to see the afternoon room, to see how it's different. Why do they have different rooms for different parts of the day? Maybe it has to do with the position of the sun, or maybe if you're a duke and duchess, life can get tedious with just one room for the entire day.

The day's itinerary has all guests meeting in the morning room before we go shooting, but Ben and I are the only ones here. Did we miss a memo?

"I'm so sorry, the duke's not here and hunting is canceled," the duchess says as she enters the room. "The gamekeeper has been taken ill. It's a dreadful shame. The duke is stuck on a call with some Indian business associates. We're not having the best morning. Again, I apologize."

"It's no problem," Ben replies. I'm sure he's disappointed not to be seeing the duke this morning, but he doesn't let it show. "I also understand that Nick's caught up in a crisis, and I believe he's drafted Elizabeth to help."

Hunting with the duke would have been great for Ben, because he would have had the duke in a guaranteed good mood. By all accounts, the man loves to hunt. On the other hand, I'm delighted by the change in plans. Shooting wasn't open to first-timers, so we would have been separated—leaving more opportunity for slipups in our cover story.

"I think most people are going into the village to look around," the duchess says. "It's terribly pretty. We could join them or . . . I thought I could give you a tour of where they filmed *A Duchess for a Duke*." She laughs. "It's completely self-indulgent. I love to relive it, and George isn't interested at all. It's rare I find a kindred spirit."

Just when I thought the day couldn't get any better. "That would be great," I say. "You're happy to do our Daniel De Luca tour of the house and grounds, aren't you?" I say to Ben, slipping my hand into his. I savor the increasingly familiar strength and warmth that comes with the contact, alongside the buzz I feel whenever we touch.

Ben narrows his eyes. "Define happy."

I laugh and the corner of Ben's mouth lifts, which is pretty much a full-on guffaw in Ben language.

When I glance back at the duchess, she's smiling, like we're a couple of kids amusing her.

"You don't have to join us, Ben," she says. "Feel free to make use of the library or go into the village."

"He wouldn't miss it," I say before Ben can pick something else. Much safer to have him by my side.

"Excellent," the duchess says. "First stop, the orchard."

"Oh, yes, where he stumbles across her after she's run out on their kiss." I don't squeal, but it's not because I don't want to.

The duchess smiles as she leads us out of the front door. "Have you seen the film?" she asks Ben.

"I confess I haven't, but I shall make sure I do when I get back to London." He squeezes my hand. It's unnecessary but a nice touch. Something engaged couples do, right? I can't remember the last time Jed and I held hands. We were always getting in and out of cabs, walking through crowded bars and restaurants . . . but I can't remember him ever grabbing my hand to ensure we wouldn't be separated.

"It's quite charming, really," she says. "The duke wasn't keen when I told him I wanted to let them film, but he agrees the house and grounds look their best on film."

"It *does* look incredible in the movie," I say. "But having had the honor of visiting, I prefer it in real life. It's more of a home than I could have possibly expected."

"That's very sweet of you to say," the duchess replies, her eyes kind of . . . twinkling.

We cross the huge gravel driveway and head west toward some trees. "We'll come back through the walled garden," she says, gesturing to her right.

"Oh, yes! The walled garden where she retraced the steps of the dance they had together. That's one of my favorites. It's so lovely." I tug on Ben's hand, half expecting him to share in my excitement. Of course, he's stoic as always.

"Until he finds her there, reliving their moment together," the duchess continues. "I always shout at the screen and tell him to walk in the other direction. It's so embarrassing for her."

"Yes, it's humiliating," I reply. "But I don't think things between them would have progressed if he hadn't found her. It was clear she liked him, and I don't think he would have let himself believe it if he hadn't seen it with his own eyes."

"You're right," the duchess says. "It gives him confirmation that she's developed real feelings for him."

"I wonder if that happened in real life ever," I say. "Marriages were arranged for financial reasons, right?" I've watched my fair share of Jane Austen adaptations. I know the score.

"Absolutely," the duchess says. "Even back when George and I married, many of my friends were paired off to whoever was the best strategic match, rather than who they were in love with."

"That's so sad," I reply.

"It is, but some of them definitely fell in love with their husbands *after* they were married. I think that's just as romantic." The duchess is leading the way, and I can see the orchard more clearly behind her. Wizened trunks poke from the long grass, and lush leaves create a canopy of green umbrellas studded with red fruits.

"If not more so," I say. "Imagine thinking you were going to have to spend the rest of your life alone, even though you were married, and then it turns out your soulmate is right by your side all along."

"You're quite the romantic, aren't you?" Ben says under his breath, while the duchess deals with a message on her phone.

"Do you think?" I ask. It's not how I would describe myself. My mom was the romantic in the family.

"I do. Maybe you've buried it in a layer you don't want to show anyone," he says, and I know it's a pointed echo of my words from last night.

"I'm an open book," I say.

"We all have layers, Tuesday."

My heart booms in my chest as he says my name. I don't know why, but hearing it from him feels like a revelation every time.

"You think I have secret layers?" I ask.

"Maybe. Or maybe they've been buried awhile so you've . . . forgotten them."

He looks through me, right into my soul, and I entertain the notion that he's right. Maybe I've suppressed a romantic side of myself—the side I got from my mom. After she died, I wanted so desperately to move on from the pain of losing her, I pushed away things that reminded me of her. Maybe I pushed away more than I realized.

London is bringing out the romantic, sunset-seeking, Daniel-De-Luca-loving part of me. The me I was before I lost my mom. Ben sees it—that version of me. The wholeness of me, the parts that have been dormant for a very long time.

The duchess finishes the messages she's sending and turns back to us. "Right, let me show you the exact spot they had all the cameras set up," the duchess says. "I used to bring everyone Battenburg and homemade digestives just so I had an excuse to see what was going on. By the end, I had my own chair. They even had my name put on it." She lets out a throaty laugh. "It was such fun. Although I'm not sure the duke has ever forgiven me for spending so much time away from him. He likes me close by."

Her phone rings and she pulls it from her pocket. We all come to a stop. "Speaking of. I have to get this, but it's just over there—by the tree with the stone at the base."

I pull Ben over to the pear tree the duchess indicated. "They left it." I drop his hand and crouch down to read the inscription. It's exactly the same as the one in the movie. "It's a dedication to his beloved sister who died in childbirth, who loved the orchard when she was alive. When Avani Tudor first moves into the house as duchess, she finds it. The love the duke has for his sister makes the duchess finally see he isn't the monster everyone thinks he is. Oh, Ben, it's like it's real."

It's beautiful. A smooth stone, weathered with lichen and time. The words have started to fade. It's just a name and the dedication, *She loved it here, so I love it here.*

In a second, I'm transported back to a fall afternoon with my mom. We'd stopped for gas, and someone mentioned the trees over by Trent's farm were looking pretty. We drove over and kept following the fall colors until we were fifty miles away, then watched the sun go down, eating gas-station beef jerky and sitting on the hood of the car. It's stupid, but this trip has brought every memory of my mom racing back in a kaleidoscope of color. I miss her so much.

She would have loved to be here. I would give anything to have her back, just for this moment. And maybe a few moments more. Even though it's been years, it feels like I need her more than ever.

She'd be able to reassure me I could find plenty of joy in life without knowing what my future holds, without the job or Jed or the fancy apartment. None of that stuff would have mattered to her. She'd hold me and tell me everything is going to be okay. Right now, that's all I need.

"We're talking about the duke and duchess in the film?" he asks.

I pull the corner of my sweater over my thumb and dab at my eyes. "Yes."

"Are you okay?" Ben pulls at my elbow, but I shake him off.

"I just need a minute."

But instead of pretending I'm not crying and backing off, he crouches down beside me. "Are you upset about the sister dying?"

I shake my head. "I'm fine."

"Oh, you've found it. Good." The duchess rushes over, and we both get to our feet. "I'm so sorry, but I'm going to have to leave you. George has got himself into a tizzy, and I need to go back to the house."

"No problem at all. Is there anything we can do to help?" Ben asks, saving me from having to speak.

She waves her hand in the air. "Nothing at all. See you inside for lunch at twelve thirty. Make sure you visit the walled garden. It's on the other side of the house."

We stand side by side in silence as we watch the duchess head back to the house.

I pull in a breath and steady myself, refocusing on the here and now. "This is a bit of a wasted morning for you," I say. "No duke or duchess to impress. We can go back to the house if you want to catch up on emails or something?"

"Are you okay?" he asks, ignoring my deflection completely. "Is it your mum?"

"I'm fine," I say with a shrug. "I just . . . I just miss her sometimes."

His large hand smooths up my back even though there's no one to notice. "I'm sorry."

"She died a long time ago, but she would have gotten such a kick out of me being here. Even the bit where I'm fake-engaged to a hot, moody Brit. She'd think it was a huge adventure." My voice wobbles as I finish my sentence. Ben steps in front of me and envelops me in a hug. Instead of pushing him away and telling him I'm fine, I sink into him and just let myself breathe.

He smells delicious, like wet pine forests and cinnamon. He feels safe, like a big old oak tree that's been here for three hundred years. How can I feel so comfortable with him when I've known him just a few days?

"I'm usually stronger than this," I say, needing him to know I'm not always such a crybaby.

He just pulls me tighter, and I burrow deeper into his jacket, laying my face on his chest. He doesn't move, doesn't try to pull away. We stand like that for what seems like hours. I flick through the various expressions my mother would have if I told her I met a duke and duchess, if I described staying in a place like Fairfield, if she saw the ring on my left hand. If I told her I was sharing a bedroom with a man like Ben.

When I let myself surface from all the *wishes* and *should-have-beens*, I press my palms against Ben's chest and step back.

"Sorry," I say.

"No need to apologize. You've been going through a lot recently."

I can't help it—I start to laugh. From the outside, I might look like I'm bouncing from one extreme emotion to the next. Maybe my laugh is an expression of complete terror. "What, because my career is on the brink, I have nowhere to live, and my real fiancé dumped me?" I shake my head. "Things could be worse. I'm in a wonderful country, staying at the very fancy house of a real-life duke and duchess. And I get to hang out with you."

He cups my face, sweeping his thumbs across my cheeks. It's as if he's using his body to say, *It's okay, I've got you,* and I feel it in my bones. "Is hanging out with me in the plus category or the minus category?" He gives me a half smile and raises his eyebrow as he releases me.

I nudge him. "Oh, you're in a swing seat. Depends on the hour."

We start to wander back toward the house. I really hope we're heading to the walled garden. The scene filmed there lives rent-free in my brain, and I must see it.

"You're going to be thirty thousand dollars richer by the end of the weekend," he adds. "That has to be in the plus category."

I'd almost forgotten about the money. "You see? Life's so good that didn't even feature in my Top Three at the moment," I say.

"Good to know." He looks at me for a beat too long, and I can't decide whether he's feeling sorry for me or if it's something else. "Shall we head to this walled garden you're so excited to see?"

Without thinking about it, and without anyone watching, I slip my hand into his. He squeezes like he's been waiting for it.

I wasn't sure what I was expecting from a walled garden, but I'm not disappointed. It might be the prettiest place I've ever seen. The crumbling, redbrick walls are covered in climbing roses in pink and white and yellow and red, like daubs of paint in a toddler's artwork. Down the middle of the oblong-shaped garden, there's a runway of grass three or four yards wide, stretching from the pretty wrought-iron gate we've just come through right to the other end about one hundred yards away. On either side are large borders of flowers—more roses and other blooms I don't recognize. There are so many it looks like a bouquet in a vase, like they're growing together in a floral rainbow.

It might be September, but this garden seems to be at its peak— overflowing with color. Every now and then, grass walkways run at right angles to the main stretch of grass, leading through the beds and to the side of the garden so visitors can see the blooms from every angle. Despite never having been here before, it looks entirely familiar. It looks just like it did in the movie.

"It's so pretty," I say. "Really breathtaking."

"It helps that the sun is shining," Ben says. "The upkeep on this place must be astronomical."

I can't help but smile to myself at the typically practical lens through which he sees the world. He's right about the sun, though— the bright-blue, cloudless sky helps bring the place to life. The light reflecting off the brickwork makes the walls almost sparkle and injects an air of magic to the place. I'm so lucky to have gotten to come here—not only because of the Daniel De Luca connection but also because it's just so special. I'm genuinely having a great time.

"It's worth every penny," I reply. "It's the most beautiful house and grounds. Completely magical."

"You like it? I thought you were a city girl?"

"I love the city, but I grew up in the country. I have both in me. The duke and duchess have the perfect balance, what with a town house in London and then this place to retreat to whenever they wish. If only I had millions in the bank. That's exactly how I'd live my life." I let out a laugh at the idea.

He nods but doesn't say anything.

"It seems heartbreaking for the place to go to someone else eventually, after being in their family for so long. What will happen to it if they don't have any children?"

"No idea. I suppose it will get sold by whoever inherits it."

"You should buy it," I say. "You seem to have more money than God. If you promise to keep it and not make it into a hotel or something, the duke might sell the hotels to you as well. Like a package deal or something."

"It's a good idea, except if he won't sell the hotels, he's not going to part with the house they both have such affection for."

Grumpiness notwithstanding, Ben has an uncanny ability to understand people.

"True," I say. "What is it about the hotels that makes you want them so badly? Surely there are other things to invest in."

"I have my reasons," he says.

Another thing I like about Ben: I ask him a question he doesn't want to answer, and he doesn't lie to me. He doesn't even skirt the question and give me a nonanswer. He just tells me he's not going to tell me. My dad would answer the exact same way. It would be so easy to make something up—*It's a great investment* or *I suspect there's oil in the grounds*—but he doesn't. I haven't known him long, but I suppose it's one of the reasons it feels like I can trust him. One of the reasons I feel so safe around him.

"Aha," I say. "I'll have to dig deeper if I want my answer."

But I don't dig. He's not in the mood to share, and I respect that. Instead, I twirl an entire three hundred and sixty degrees, taking it all in. "I'm going to make you watch the movie when we get back to London. It's so romantic. They've married under pressure from their families and have no time for one another in the beginning; they're both resolved to endure their lives rather than enjoy their marriage. The night before the scene in the garden, they've hosted a ball, and when they dance together in the ballroom, she realizes she's fallen hopelessly in love with him. She comes to the garden and relives their dance, going through the steps and even mimicking the conversation they had. And then he finds her. He watches for a while from the gate, and then as she spins, she sees him."

He arches an eyebrow. "Embarrassing for her if he's not feeling it."

I let out a small laugh. "Except he *is* feeling it. He pulls her to him for a waltz around the roses."

"Like this?" He grabs my hand, hooking his thumb around mine, and holds our arms up like we're about to dance.

I suck in a breath, trying to will away the blush I know is coming from being so close to him. After lifting my other hand to his shoulder, he presses his palm to my back. Suddenly there's no space between us, his hard stomach pressing against my rib cage. My heart thumps in my chest so loudly, I'm sure he can hear it. We're two strangers, pretending to be lovers, standing body to body, like we're actually lovers. I try to control my breathing because I don't know how to act. I don't know what to do.

"Ben." I can barely say his name because I have no air in my lungs.

"Just relax and let me lead you." He inhales and seems to grow another two or three inches before stepping forward, taking me backward.

Suddenly we're dancing. He leads me in small, rhythmic steps, almost like we can both hear music. I can feel every muscle in his body, his thigh is against mine, and I have to bend backward to look up at him. I'm no virgin, but I don't think I've ever felt so intimate with a guy. Despite feeling exposed, Ben's so unfazed, like our closeness is no big deal, that I do what he says and relax. I let him lead us up and down the pathway between the rose bushes. He guides us so I'm floating. My feet barely touch the ground. Maybe I missed my calling and I should have been a dancer all these years. But of course, it's all Ben making me feel so good.

All of a sudden, he twirls us around, and this time, my feet actually do hover in the air. I squeal and close my eyes.

He sets me down and I look up at him, willing him to keep moving because I'm not ready for this to be over. We sway left, then right, and then he begins to move his feet. The pace is slower than before, and it's easier to keep up. He drops his frame, and it's like he's unzipped his old ballroom costume, stepped out of it, and Ben's back—except we're still dancing. It's just a little more equal this time. It's how we might move if we were dancing at a wedding or something. We're just an engaged couple in a garden who have decided on an impromptu waltz.

Because that happens all the time.

I smooth my hand over his shoulder and look up at him, pulling in a breath as I take in his sharp jaw, his full lips, and how close he is to me. He'd only have to move his head a little, and we'd be kissing. I fight the urge to burrow under the soft wool of his jacket, to feel more of him, to be even closer than we are.

I don't know what it is, but something has shifted between us this morning. There's an easiness, a *knowing* between us that wasn't there before.

"You're a fabulous dancer," I say. Of all the talents I could imagine Ben having, ballroom dancing wasn't one of them.

"You've got good rhythm," he replies, looking away and over my shoulder as our movements get smaller and smaller. "And now you've reenacted one of your favorite scenes."

"Day made. No—life made." More and more, Ben's featuring in my favorite parts of this trip. And it's not just because of how much time we're spending together.

A grin unfurls on his face, revealing his rarely seen dimple.

"How many people know you can dance?"

He narrows his eyes like he's looking into my soul. "It's my secret superpower."

I laugh. "I bet there's a small club of women who know the truth. It's got to be the world's easiest way to get someone into bed with you." If I didn't think Ben was the most attractive man I'd ever laid eyes on before today, I certainly do now.

He doesn't say anything; we just dance in silence. The smell and feel of him is solid, familiar. Almost like he belongs to me. I could stay like this, in this weird filmlike reality, forever.

We've drifted apart a little and he pulls me closer. I lean my head on his chest, enjoying the warmth of his hand on my back. He seems in no hurry to go back to the house, and neither am I. I can't think of anyplace better to be other than swaying in my fake fiancé's arms. For a few minutes, maybe real life can ebb away, and I can pretend the fantasy is all there is.

CHAPTER SEVENTEEN

Ben comes out of the bathroom just like he did last night, but things have changed. The shift between us today at the tree, in the walled garden, hasn't reset as I thought it might. There's a closeness between us now that's more than just physical. We're connected in a way that's hard to explain.

Today at lunch, he was so attentive he seemed to know exactly what I was thinking and feeling. Just before I realized I needed his reassurance, his hand would find its way to my leg for a couple of seconds. During dinner, a look or a shift of his chair toward me suggested that his mind was as occupied with me as mine was with him. Maybe it's been growing since we arrived here—maybe since we met—but it feels like we're inching toward the peak of a mountain and we're about to get to enjoy the view.

I hope we're not in a bubble that will pop with the slightest pressure.

"Hey," he says as he comes through the bathroom door and sees me sitting on the bed.

"Hey," I reply. It seems ridiculous that he's taking the couch when I have this enormous bed. "You're sure you're okay on the couch? There's plenty of room in this bed."

"I'm fine," he says, much to my disappointment.

He heads to the window and peeks through the curtains. "It's raining," he says.

"How is that possible?" I ask. "It was bright sunshine a few hours ago."

"A sign autumn is on its way." He takes the pillows and comforter from the bed and arranges them just like he did last night, then slips under the blanket, eye mask in hand.

"I had a really nice time today," I say.

It seems ludicrous that I'm getting paid to be here. I'm having a better time than I would have in London on my own. I'm getting to experience more of the country I'm visiting, meeting more people, even seeing more Daniel De Luca film locations.

"Good," he says as he tucks an arm behind his head. I flop back onto the bed, restless and not ready to sleep.

"How did snooker go with the duke?" As shooting was abandoned, the duke joined us for lunch and then invited Ben, Nick, and some of the other men to play snooker with him. The duchess arranged in-room massages for wives and girlfriends, or pedicures in the morning room. She and I spent the afternoon going through the house, and she regaled me with more stories from the filming of *A Duchess for a Duke*. Most excitingly, she confirmed the affair between Daniel and Avani. I'd had a lovely afternoon, but it was strange to be separated from Ben. I doubt the feeling was mutual. Ben got what he wanted, which was time with the duke.

He sucks in a breath. "Really bloody well actually."

"Really? Tell me."

"Apparently the duchess is trying to convince him he needs to take control of his legacy. He doesn't want distant relatives inheriting, so he's considering liquidating some assets and creating a foundation to support worthy causes."

I sit bolt upright and crawl to the end of the bed to see his expression. How is this guy not punching the air with excitement? "What's the catch?"

He glances over at me. "Well, there's nothing certain. He's not entirely convinced, and from what I know of him, the hotels won't be the first assets to go."

I swing my legs over the end of the bed. "Okay, so you're telling me the duke has gone from the mindset of never selling the hotels to maybe selling the hotels, and you're lying there like you've still got the weight of the world on your shoulders? Why aren't we cracking open the champagne?"

"There's still a long way to go."

I shake my head and slide off the bed. "You've got to celebrate the small wins."

He pulls himself into a sitting position and nods. "So far so good. But it's a delicate situation. I don't want to fuck anything up."

I spring up and take a seat next to him and immediately regret it, because I feel I've overstepped a physical boundary.

"How could you? He clearly likes you, and he must be considering you as a potential buyer or he wouldn't be telling you about his plans." I'm thrilled for him and proud I might have had a hand in making this happen. It's like I'm on Team Ben, sharing in the victory.

He pushes his hands through his hair. "I know. I just want to tread carefully. I don't want to push too hard. He needs to make this decision in his own time."

"You've told him you're still interested, though?"

"He knows."

"But does he? You should make sure he does. You don't want any misunderstandings between you."

Ben turns to meet my eyes, and we stare at each other for a few minutes. I'm waiting for him to say something. And it's like he's waiting for me to say something.

He sits back, pulls in a breath, and exhales very slowly. I can't take my eyes off his rising and falling chest. His T-shirt is rumpled above his hips but doesn't quite give me a glimpse of skin underneath. I know how that flat, hard chest feels. I've just not seen it.

"I'm very single-minded about things. Sometimes that's my best asset and sometimes my biggest weakness." He's staring at the ceiling, and I take the opportunity to watch him. I want to memorize this moment, and every part of him. There's something very attractive about a man who accepts his weaknesses as well as his strengths. Jed always viewed personal foibles as fatal flaws, which I realize now put a ton of pressure on me to be infallible. How did I ever think I was happy before?

"But he should know if you're interested," I say.

"I said, he knows."

"Okay," I say. "If you're sure."

We sit side by side in silence, neither one of us moving. What's he thinking about? Maybe he wants his bed back. I should stand and go back to bed. But something is stopping me.

Finally, he speaks. "I think you're lovely."

His words hang in the air and then dissolve on my skin. I don't think I've ever had such a beautiful compliment.

He doesn't move and neither do I. I'm unsure how to respond. "You do?" It's a ridiculous response to the sweetest words, but he has emptied my brain and set my heart waltzing around my chest.

"I do."

Still, neither of us moves. I scramble for something to say. He's just told me what he thinks about me. Surely, I should do the same in return. "I think you're . . . wonderful."

Truly wonderful.

More than wonderful.

Completely wonderful.

He blows out a breath and slides his hand into mine. My pulse is racing, impatient, like a horse before the gate opens. Sitting here with him, hand in hand, feels so right. Like he's someone I've known for years, not days; like here is exactly where I'm meant to be.

Like I'm with the person I'm meant to be with.

He stands and pulls me up to face him. He pushes the hair from my eyes and cups my face. I'm so weak with anticipation, with these feelings of desire and need, I'm not sure I'm going to be able to stay upright.

"I can't stop touching you." The timbre of his voice has taken on a gravelly edge that sends a shiver from the top of my head down my spine. But I'm not nervous. I'm wanting.

He presses his lips against mine. All I can think is, *Finally, finally, finally.*

It would have been so easy to have missed this moment. I might not have spotted him that day in the park. He might not have been standing behind me in the coffee shop. I might not have accepted Nick's dinner invitation. Hell, I could have not left New York. I could still be with Jed. The images of what might have been flicker in my brain like the surface of a pond being disturbed by a gentle breeze—there, then gone—and all I can think about, all I can feel, is Ben.

I slide my fingers up Ben's arms, and he deepens the kiss. My skin heats everywhere he touches: my face, my lips, my stomach pressed against his hips as he snakes a hand around my back. I'm hot and so weak, as if his desire has stolen my resolve. His tongue presses against mine, and I can't help but let out a small moan of relief that I finally get more from him. My nipples pinch against my tank, and I don't know if he feels them, but he groans. The vibration bounces around in my chest. Did I just make Ben *groan?*

His palm at my back pushes us closer together, but it's not close enough. It's like the pan of hot water is about to break into a boil, it just needs a few. More. Seconds.

His hand rounds my ass, and I'm about to wrap my legs around his waist when a knock at the door interrupts us. We jump apart like we're teenagers on the verge of being discovered by parents.

He shoots me a look I can't quite read and stalks over to the door. It's just the housekeeper with two hot water bottles.

"Not sure we need those," he mutters and discards them on the bed.

I stand rooted to the spot, vibrating with need for him, willing him to come back to me, hold me, kiss me. I want to feel him everywhere.

Instead he collapses on the sofa, grabbing my hand as he goes down and bringing me with him so we're back to sitting where we were before our kiss. Except this time we're hip to hip, and the heat is almost overwhelming.

He doesn't let go of my hand, and instead begins to circle his thumb over my palm. I try to focus on breathing. I'm not used to navigating a man other than Jed. I feel like a teenager. The last time Jed and I kissed with tongue, without being naked and one of us trying to get to orgasm—because it never happened at the same time—we were probably still in college.

I don't know where I want this to go next. I really like this guy. But my life is at such a crossroads right now, do I need to complicate it any further?

"You're overthinking," he says.

"Always," I reply.

He huffs out a laugh, and I smile because I know how hard it is to amuse him. "Same here. There are lots of moving parts. For both of us. If logic were to prevail, we wouldn't . . ."

"Right," I say, agreeing with him, although logic isn't prevailing anywhere in my body right now. "You don't date."

"And I need to stay focused," he adds.

"I'm fresh out of a ten-year relationship."

"I'm paying you to be here," he says. "I assured you . . . nothing physical was part of the bargain."

"I know that, Ben. I don't feel pressured to accept your kisses."

He turns to look at me, as if seeking out visual confirmation I'm telling the truth.

"I promise," I say. I tilt my head, and he drops his gaze to my neck as if he's wondering how it would taste.

But it's complicated. We both know it.

I also know I want him to kiss me again, and if he wanted to peel off my clothes and lick me from neck to ankle, right at this moment I'm unlikely to say no. At the same time, we're guests in someone else's house, he's trying to focus on achieving something that, for whatever reason, is incredibly important to him, and I just got out of a serious relationship. "There are lots of reasons not to act on—"

I don't get to finish my sentence, because Ben slides his large hands around my waist and pulls me onto his lap. He cups the back of my head.

"I have this urge to touch you all the time," he growls out, coiling his fingers around my bare thigh. His skin against mine is so electrifying I'm frightened to move in case I burst into flames. Yes, we've held hands and touched in small, intimate ways, but somehow in this room tonight, everything feels different. Bigger.

I turn toward him and place my palms carefully on his chest, slowly, in case he has the urge to stop me or I change my mind.

But he doesn't. I don't.

I feel the heat through the white cotton of his top, but it's not enough. I want to feel his skin. I skim my fingers down, down, down, dipping my fingertips under the hem of his T-shirt to his hard warmth.

"I know. I feel it too." My voice is fractured and strained, like I'm six thousand feet above sea level and can't catch my breath.

Finally, he gives me the oxygen I need, pressing a kiss to my mouth. As our lips join, I melt beneath him, like ice against his flames. His touch burns every other kiss I've ever had from my memory, and I know from now on, I'll only remember him. I'll only *want* to remember him.

He pulls at me, maneuvering me on his lap so my legs are either side of his hips, his hardness beneath me. I sigh and my muscles unlock. We're not pretending anymore. This feels so perfect, so right, like I've been waiting to come home to him and now I'm right where I'm meant to be. He tucks my bottom closer to him, and we slot together, our hips and chests pressing against each other. The thin cotton between us acts as the final barrier, and although it's flimsy, it's the only thing stopping Ben from owning me completely.

His hands drift up to the sides of my breasts, and I tip my head back, my entire body throbbing. Desperate.

I gasp. Because this—just this, the kissing and the closeness—is almost too much. We're still fully clothed, and while things might seem pretty PG from the outside, on the inside? On the inside, we're three seconds away from a nuclear explosion. My hands on his chest, I twist in his lap, circling my hips. He cups my breasts, his thumb grazing my nipple under the cotton.

"Ben," I choke out, almost overwhelmed with sensation.

He lifts his hands, holding them out like he's surrendering. I'm endlessly grateful and heavy with disappointment at the same time.

We press our foreheads together as if we're trying to take a beat before exploring each other. Except we're connected everywhere.

"This needs to . . . We should . . . We can't do this here," he says, finally finding his words. "Not now."

I get it. He's making the right decision, but I'm not quite sure how I'll survive around him for another second without wanting more and more and more. And if not now, when?

CHAPTER EIGHTEEN

I fold the note Ben left me on the nightstand, put it in my wallet, and then head out. I've slept in and it's nearly nine. In his note, he said he would come and wake me if I needed to be up, but I feel terrible lazing away the morning in bed. I'm getting paid to be here. The least I can do is be awake. When I think back to last night, I can't help but smile at the memory of his lips, his hands, his body against mine and the unspoken promise that we'll pick up where we left off another time.

I see Grant coming toward me as I reach the bottom of the stairs. "They're in the breakfast room," he says with a smile. "Just down on your right."

Moving down the hall, I glance at the wall opposite, covered in paintings. There's a gold label attached to some of them, and I lean in to read *Duke of Brandon*. The painting is clearly hundreds of years old. I can't imagine what it must be like to fill the shoes of your predecessor, to grow up knowing exactly what life has planned for you.

I have to call my dad as soon as I'm back at the hotel tonight.

Farther down the hall, I hear chatter behind a closed door. I twist the brass doorknob and open it an inch so I can see whether I'm in the right place. Someone pulls the door wide. It's the duke. "Good morning, my dear. Welcome, welcome. We're still waiting on my wife, but we're not standing on ceremony. Let's get you some tea."

I catch Ben's eye; he smiles and heads over. It's the same smile as yesterday—the one with the dimple—and it's completely infectious.

"Good morning," he says as he approaches. I grin back at him reflexively, like I'm under his spell. I've spent enough time with Ben to know he's not this good of an actor—he's pleased to see me. And the tingling in my body that travels from every corner of me and heads right to my core tells me I'm pleased to see him too.

"I didn't want to wake you." He lowers his voice so he speaks just to me, and it feels so intimate I could be standing there in my bra and panties. He places his hand on my shoulder, and the heat from last night roars back to life. We lock eyes and I know he feels it too. He presses a kiss to the top of my head like it's the most natural thing in the world. I slip my hand to his waist and hook my thumb over his hip bone.

Boundaries have begun to blur. I can't tell what's for show and what's real. I can almost believe we're a newly engaged couple, come to stay with friends for the weekend.

Except I know I'm being paid.

He takes me by the hand and leads me around the table. Covered in a bright-white linen tablecloth, it's set like we're in a gigantic Victorian doll house, complete with a large fruit display in the middle, silverware I suspect is *actually* silver, and plates decorated with blousy flowers and gold accents.

I say good morning to those we pass. When we reach Nick and Elizabeth, Nick gives me a nod and a grin like he's in on some kind of secret. Ben pulls out my chair and I take a seat. Immediately a waiter appears, offering me a choice of teas. I glance up at Ben, looking for him to guide me. I'm a little dazed from our greeting, and I'm not sure if there's an appropriate tea I should be drinking.

"Green or . . . nettle maybe?" he suggests, like the most attentive fiancé on the planet.

I nod. "Yes, nettle would be lovely."

"And what can I get you for breakfast?" a man, younger than Grant, wearing a suit asks.

The duke has asked Ben a question, which takes his attention. I'm not quite sure what someone orders for breakfast in a stranger's house. Yesterday, everything was brought to the table.

"Can I suggest eggs benedict and fruit?" the waiter says. "That seems to be a popular choice this morning."

"Sounds great," I say.

Everyone sits and then we all leap to our feet again as the door opens and the duchess arrives.

"Good morning, everyone," she says, smiling and nodding at us all. Then she exchanges words with the waiter and we all sit. "Another beautiful September day," the duchess says. "I'm just sorry you're leaving us today. I've really enjoyed having you all stay."

"I've had a really wonderful time," I say, and the sentiment is completely genuine. It's surprising how easy it's been. I guess it's not hard to fake being in love with a man like Ben Kelley. "Thank you so much for your incredible hospitality. Getting to see the English countryside from the viewpoint of this magnificent house . . ." I shake my head. "It's been an honor."

The duke and duchess exchange a look, and my stomach roils. Was I too effusive? Did I seem insincere? I glance at Ben, but he's looking at the duke.

"My husband and I have had a discussion," the duchess starts. "We would like to host part of your wedding celebrations if you'd let us. We'd love to have the wedding breakfast here or, if you don't feel comfortable, perhaps the engagement party?"

My heart inches higher in my chest. What a wonderfully generous offer. This can only be good news for Ben, right? The duke must like him if he's prepared to host his wedding. I glance at Ben, and my heart swoops and crashes into my stomach. There's just one problem—I'm not actually marrying the man next to me.

"That's incredibly generous," Ben says, his voice a little tighter than I've heard since we got here. I can tell he feels awkward. I need to be a good wingman here.

"It's beyond generous," I say. "I can't think of a more magical place to celebrate our marriage than Fairfield House, can you, Ben?"

He shakes his head. "Absolutely not."

The duchess smiles. "I knew, when I saw you dancing in the walled garden, you'd felt the magic of the place." She saw us? I thought she had returned to the house while we lingered in the garden. "Some people come and appreciate the landscape and the history of the place, but since you walked in, I feel you see the soul of this wonderful estate."

It's such a huge compliment, and she's not wrong.

"You two remind us of us when we were newly engaged. You're so in tune with each other. I see young couples all the time, and I can tell the ones that are going to last from the ones who are getting married for all the wrong reasons."

My stomach churns with guilt and regret. I'm so desperately sorry to be misleading her.

Ben slips his hand onto my thigh like he can hear what I'm thinking and wants to comfort me.

"That's lovely to hear," I say. "Ben is . . . such a wonderful man. There's not a better foundation for a partner, I think."

The duke and duchess share another look. I glance at Ben to find him already looking at me, just like he did last night before our kiss. It's a look that says, *I think you're lovely*, and it melts me from the inside out.

"We're just in the early stages of planning," I say, pulling my gaze from Ben's. "I'm not sure if Ben is going to win the elopement argument—"

"There's no obligation," the duchess says. "I just wanted to offer. If you decide to go a different way, then of course you must. Don't think you'll offend us."

"Oh, I'm sure I can offend you," I say. "I'm American, after all." Everyone laughs, and thankfully the course of the conversation changes.

"Whatever happens, you all must come and stay again. The estate is quite marvelous in the autumn. The colors are astonishing, aren't they, darling?" The duchess turns to the duke, who nods and takes a mouthful of the eggs that were just placed in front of him. "All year round. And especially wonderful at Christmas."

"We would love that," I say, genuinely excited, as if I'm actually going to be able to come back and see the changes to the landscape and holiday lights sparkling in the trees lining the driveway. "I can't wait for a Christmas in England."

"Ben, let's see if we can set up a meeting this week at The Fairfield." The duke dabs his mouth with his napkin. "I want to go through a few things with you."

The Fairfield? I'm not sure what that is, but I try not to stare at either Ben or the duke. This has to be good news for Ben, right? Maybe the duchess has convinced her husband to sell the hotels. Surely, this is progress?

"Absolutely. I'll call your office and get something set up."

"Very good," the duke replies.

"When I'm in town, we should have tea at The Fairfield," the duchess says to Elizabeth and me. "Then we can pop to Fortnum's for some shopping. I'm sure Ben and Nick are all work, just like my husband. I'd be happy to show you some of my favorite places, Tuesday."

"Absolutely." Taking tea with the duchess, followed by shopping, sounds like what daydreams are made of. At first, I couldn't think of anything worse than pretending to be someone's fiancée. Now, I don't want to think about calling things off between us. I like the sound of our life together, where I dine with duchesses, spend Christmas in London, and hang out with Ben every day. I also like the idea of sinking into Ben's touch every evening, his lips on mine every morning and in between. We've been here less than forty-eight hours, and I want to stretch it out for as long as possible.

But in just a few hours, we're going to get in the car and return to real life. Everything about this weekend is going to evaporate.

The feelings of loss and sadness are even more profound than when Jed and I split. I'm unsure how that's possible. Maybe it's the realization that real life—the one where I'm fighting for my job and still in the shadows of my breakup—isn't the life I want anymore. I want to be a woman who waltzes around rose gardens and who Ben thinks is lovely. I want the fairy tale.

But fairy tales are fiction—lies we tell children to make them feel better about the harsh, real world. Given my reality, maybe I've been trying to make myself feel better by letting myself believe this weekend was real. Only now, I'm left with the unfortunate necessity to close this storybook once and for all—and it's not going to end with Happily Ever After.

CHAPTER NINETEEN

As we pull away from Fairfield House, it's like my edges blur, and I feel less like myself than when I was pretending to be Ben's fiancée. All I can think of is how sad I am to be leaving. Maybe it's the anticlimax, now that the adrenaline is seeping away. Or maybe it's more than that. Maybe this weekend has shown me who I want to be.

"So I guess that's it," I say as we turn out the large gates that felt so imposing when we arrived. I'd been so nervous, but I needn't have been.

"Tell me about your life in New York," Ben says as if he hasn't heard me.

"We've just told a web of lies and semi-committed to getting married at Fairfield House, and you want to chitchat about my life in New York?" *And we made out!* I don't add. Part of our charade turned into something real. Didn't it?

"Are you over your ex?" he asks.

"What?" Not only are Ben and I not on the same page in this conversation, I don't even think we're in the same book.

"Your fiancé. Do you think you'll get back together?" Ben stares straight ahead, seemingly focused on the road.

"No, we're not getting back together. He moved to Iowa with a ballerina from SoHo. I told you that."

"Would you want to get back together if he left the ballerina?"

"What? I haven't even . . ." Jed is many things, but he isn't a flip-flopper. When he said we were over, I knew he wouldn't change his mind. It hadn't been an overnight decision for him. "He won't."

Ben lets out an exasperated breath.

It hadn't even occurred to me to think about what would happen if Jed came back, begging for my forgiveness, because it would never happen. "Life doesn't move backward," I say. "We were together a decade. I thought I knew what he was thinking before he did. I was wrong about so much. But I know one thing: Jed won't come back. He's made his decision."

Silence twists between us. What's Ben thinking? Does he want to kiss me again? Because I really want to kiss him.

"Are you deliberately not answering my question?" he asks.

I fold my arms in front of me. Now I'm the one who's exasperated. I've answered Ben's question. I have nothing to hide.

"You told me what *he* would or wouldn't do," he says. "Not what *you* would do if he came back. I can't tell if this is just you being you, prioritizing everyone else's needs and desires over your own, or if there's a part of you that genuinely wants him back."

I uncross my arms and stare out the window. Ben's right. Since we broke up, I've only really considered Jed's side of our relationship. But if reality were turned on its head and Jed came crawling back to me, what would *I* do?

"No," I say, all my thoughts slotting into place. "I wouldn't take him back. But not because he cheated and lied." I laugh out loud because that should be enough of a reason not to take back a boyfriend. "I think I needed him when we met. I needed something or someone to take me away from the grief of losing my mom. Jed helped me hide from that, from the *me* before . . ."

Being with Jed helped me carry on when I could barely breathe, I missed my mom so much. I couldn't imagine a time when I wouldn't be so heavy with sadness; I could only just move from my bed to the couch. Dad had insisted I still go off to college, and looking back, it was the best decision I could have made in the aftermath of Mom's death. Then I met Jed and life just . . . moved forward.

"And now?" Ben asks.

"Things are different now," I say. I'm not sure how, exactly—they just are. Last time I was single, I'd been paralyzed by grief over my mother's death. Now I still miss her, but every action or inaction isn't driven by that grief. "I don't need a lifeline to pull myself through an ocean of sadness, and in all honesty, I haven't needed one for a long time. I think I hung on to Jed because part of me was afraid of what would happen if I let go. I don't want to hide anymore. I don't need to. I like the me I was when my mom was alive. Being in London . . . It's helped me reconnect with that part of myself, and I don't want to lose that. I'm not the same woman I was when I was with Jed. And I don't want to be."

Ben reaches for my hand and our fingers interlink. We travel in silence through the winding country roads. The colors of the trees remind me of home. Not New York City home, but Franklin, Madison County. The leaves on the trees are transforming from new and green to a rainbow of gold, red, rust, and orange. And they're all the more beautiful for it.

"I'm very aware I paid you to be here with me this weekend," Ben says out of nowhere. His tone suggests we're in the middle of a conversation, and I wonder how long he's been talking to himself in his head.

"Yeah, well, I can't take your money." It's a gut reaction. I didn't think before I spoke, but as soon as the words are out, I know they're true.

"You can and you will," Ben responds.

"You can't force me to take thirty thousand dollars from you. I had one of the best weekends of my life. I met incredible people, stayed in an amazing house. I even had a behind-the-scenes view of one of my favorite films. And then . . ." *There's been you,* I don't say. "There's no way I can take your money."

Ben swerves over to the side of the road, where there's a clearing in the hedgerow and a gate to a field. He cuts the engine and, without explanation, gets out of the car.

He can't be angry with me. Maybe he urgently needs to pee? Tentatively I open the door, poke my head out, and see him leaning against the trunk.

What is happening?

I climb out of the car and take in his body language—rigid, taut as a bowstring, and radiating energy like a nuclear reactor. "Are you . . . mad?"

He won't meet my eye. Instead he runs his fingers through his hair, staring at the road we've just come down. "I think I might be heading in that direction."

"So . . . just slightly irritated but it's building?" I ask, more than a little confused.

"I mean I think I'm . . ." He lowers his hands and turns to me. "I like you."

His words hit me in the chest with near-physical force. I can't help but lift the corners of my mouth into a smile. "And that makes you angry?"

His frown deepens. "Not that kind of mad. The kind of mad that has you wondering if you've lost your mind."

Warmth floods into my chest. He's conflicted. He's discombobulated. He doesn't know the next step, let alone the next ten. That must be deeply disorienting for a man like Ben.

I step toward him and hook my finger into the waist of his jeans, needing to touch him. I stare up at him, but he won't meet my eyes. "You like me, and therefore, you think you might be losing your mind?" I'm smiling even though I know part of me should be offended. I'm not. I understand that unexpected feelings could catch a man like Ben off guard. I'm just pleased he's having them. Because it's entirely mutual.

He slides his hands around my waist. "I think . . . It's just . . . I . . . I . . . I." He finally meets my eye. "I've paid you to be here . . ." He shakes his head.

"It's not just that. The money wouldn't do it because you said no to that. But when my connection to your boss was made clear . . ." He stops again like he's trying to pull lots of threads together to make a tapestry of the inner workings of my brain. "Did you kiss me because you wanted to please me or because you wanted to please you?"

There's a pressure in my forehead I'm not used to. Confusion or frustration—I can't be sure which. "Please you?" I ask.

He searches my face for answers, but there's nothing to find because I'm not quite sure what he means.

"I like clarity," he says. "And you and me? We're not clear." I see all the conflict within him laid out like a bowl of spaghetti spilled onto the floor.

I smooth my hands up his arms, enjoying the firm, safe feel of him. "Let me tell you something for free: I don't kiss men I don't want to kiss. Not even if they have an ass as good as yours. I don't tell men they're wonderful when I don't think they are. You didn't take advantage of me. And anyway, I told you, I'm not taking your money. Even if I did, thirty thousand dollars wouldn't make me kiss you. Three hundred million dollars wouldn't do it either. I like you. That's why I kissed you."

"And I told you, you absolutely are taking the money. You earned every penny. The duke and duchess were entirely charmed by you, and the duke has asked me to The Fairfield. Even in my wildest dreams, I couldn't have imagined making as much progress as I have over the last weekend." His energy changes as he talks about the duke. It's like he's shifted into business brain. While I'm pleased he looks less concerned, I'm slightly disappointed we've moved on from talking about kissing.

"It helps that the duchess wants him to sell."

"Yes, but now he sees me as a man he might want to sell to. A lot of that is down to you."

"I'm glad things are working out," I say. Ben is a wonderful man. He's just not great at *showing* everyone how wonderful he is.

"Are we off the clock?" he asks.

"There's a clock?"

He doesn't respond, leaving me to guess what he's really trying to ask.

I reach up to stroke my index finger over his cheekbone. "If I say yes, does it mean you'll kiss me again?"

"Promise me something," he says as his eyes close under my touch. I don't respond and he opens his eyes to check I've heard him. "When you're with me, don't say yes to anything you don't want."

I frown. "Why would I do that?"

"Tuesday," he whispers, and it's the only explanation he gives as he cups my jaw.

I lift myself up on my tiptoes and reach for him. His lips find mine and I feel my insides unfurling under his touch. If I spend the rest of the day by the side of a road, the intermittent zip of a car in the background while I kiss the man in front of me, it might turn out to be the best day I ever spent.

As we kiss, he flips us around so I have my back to the trunk. He presses his hips to mine, pinning me to the car, his urgency more evident today than it had been last night. I dig into his hair, my fingers exploring, and I have that same floating sensation as when we danced in the walled garden. He growls into my mouth, and the vibrations spread across my body, bringing the blood to the surface of my skin. Every inch of me wants him.

He pulls away suddenly and steps back. As he pushes his fingers through his ruffled hair, I scan his face for doubt. What I find is focus. "We need to get back in the car. Or we're going to get arrested."

"Do the British police arrest people for kissing?"

He moves around the driver's side, and I mirror him, opening the passenger door.

"No, but I'm afraid of what I might convince you to do if we keep going."

I have to press my lips together to stop myself from smiling. I like that he feels a little out of control with me. I can't imagine it happens a lot for Ben.

We slide into our seats and resume our journey in comfortable silence. The countryside is beautiful, but it creates an ache for home inside me I haven't felt for a long time. I glance across at Ben.

Ben. Ben. Ben.

When I was with Jed, I don't ever remember feeling as special as I do with Ben. The way he looks at me, like he's stunned he's lucky enough to be near me. The way he kisses me, like he just can't get enough. The way he holds me, like I'm precious. I've never felt that before.

Ben's words echo in my memory. *Don't say yes to anything you don't want.*

Did I ever *want* Jed? Or did he just want me?

One thing I know for sure is that I want Ben.

My phone beeps with a message and I open it.

"It's the duchess," I say, skimming the message. "She's inviting us to dinner with her and the duke on Saturday at their town house."

I glance across at Ben, but he's unreadable.

"I'd be happy to continue our . . . fake engagement if you want to go," I offer.

"I can't ask you to do that," he says. "I've already taken up too much of your time. You're meant to be focusing on work."

"For a start, you didn't ask, I offered. And second, I like the duke and duchess. If you didn't know already, I kinda like you too. An evening with the four of us sounds fun."

He shakes his head. "Always wanting to please someone."

My stomach sinks into my seat. It wasn't the reaction I was expecting.

"Is it what *you* want?" Ben asks.

"I just said so, didn't I? But if you want to take some other woman with a straightforward coffee order, then . . ." I shrug. "I guess that's life."

Ben's gaze stays on the road. "If you're sure you're happy to do dinner on Saturday as my fiancée, I would appreciate it. It's the last time I'll ask, I promise," he says.

"Happy as a clam," I say, ignoring the bit about the last time. I don't want to think about saying goodbye to Ben. "On one condition. You drop the idea of paying me for this weekend."

He growls, but nods. "And then what?" he says.

"Then what *what*?"

"When do you go back to New York?"

"Three weeks."

He pushes his hand through his hair and shakes his head. "So you have three weeks left in London, then you'll be in New York."

I laugh because he's repeating what I just said, and not because he doesn't understand. Then the penny drops. He's having trouble asking me out. "Do you want to hang out again? Just the two of us?" I ask. "Maybe . . . ask me to dinner?"

He meets my gaze and nods.

He might be the most adorable man in the history of adorable men. I slide my palm up to his cheek and grin at him. "Good," I say. "I'm going to say yes, because I want to hang out with you too."

I expect to see a flicker of a smile on his lips, but instead he stays focused on the road ahead of us, sliding his hand onto my thigh.

Eventually he nods as if he's been assimilating everything for the last few minutes. "Dinner," he says. "Good."

Adorable.

CHAPTER TWENTY

My phone rings, interrupting a delicious dream I'm having about a very naked Ben, which I'm hoping is prophetic given I'm seeing him tonight for the first time since we came back to London. Squinting, I find the button to answer and then shut my eyes again.

"Hey," I say, not knowing who I'm talking to.

"How's my favorite Anglophile?"

"Melanie?" I ask, and I open my eyes. I haven't spoken to her since before the weekend away, and we have so much to catch up on. "What time is it?"

"Time you were awake. There are sights to see, Daniel De Luca to track down. I have some intel. He's on location, filming in Central London and staying at a hotel. Do you have a pad and paper?"

I sit up and glance around. Hotels always have a pen and paper somewhere, don't they? "Hang on, let me find one." I grab the flimsy pad of paper and pencil from by my bed and scribble down the name of the hotel where Daniel De Luca is supposed to be staying.

"I've missed you." My old life comes tumbling back into focus. Sadness and relief mix in my stomach. "How are the girls?" I ask. "How were Friday night cocktails?"

"The same, and I don't want to talk about them. I want to talk about you. How was last weekend? Did you pull off being fake-engaged to a stranger? How have I not spoken to you in five days?"

I hadn't been deliberately dodging Melanie's calls. Not exactly. The time difference is definitely a factor, but I know in my heart of hearts if I'd wanted to speak to Melanie this week, I would have found a way. Part of me—a big part—wants to keep this past weekend to myself. At least until I can make more sense of it all.

I grin. "It was great. The duke and duchess were so nice and welcoming, and it wasn't as intimidating as I expected. I probably made a thousand faux pas, but everyone was kind enough not to mention them."

"You're hanging out with the British aristocracy, boo. If Jed could see you now, hey?"

I rarely thought about Jed over the weekend, other than how different Ben is from him. I was far more focused on Ben. There wasn't much space in my brain left for anyone else.

The truth is, I don't care what Jed would think of me here in England, or at all. "Catch me up on everyone. How's Callie?" Melanie's a part of me, but the other girls? I'm fond of them, they're fun, and it's always great to catch up with what's going on in their lives, but I can't say I've actually thought much about them since I've been here. It's like they got washed away by the ocean on the way over.

"Well, Ginger thinks Michael's about to propose."

I'm genuinely shocked. They've been together five years, and there'd been no talk of marriage. "Really?"

"She's just hit thirty and he's nearly thirty-two. If they want to have kids, they better get on with it."

"What, so you hit an arbitrary birthday and you have to settle down with whoever's around? Dating as musical chairs—the music stops and you grab whatever's left?"

Melanie pauses before she says, "It's not like that. They love each other. They're living together; they're practically married anyway."

"I guess. Except I was practically married to Jed, and look what happened there." Ginger and Michael are a great couple. Just because Jed and I didn't work out doesn't mean they won't. I'm not bitter either;

I just see things more clearly now. Jed and I were a great couple in lots of ways. But we weren't meant to spend the rest of our lives together.

"David spoke to Jed last week."

I'm sure I should feel some kind of pain at the idea of Jed calling my best friend's boyfriend, but I don't. I don't feel a certain way, but I'm not numb to it either. I'm certainly not in denial anymore.

"Do you want to talk about this?" she asks.

"Not really," I say honestly. Not because I don't want to dredge up old feelings, but because old feelings aren't relevant to my life now. Jed's gone. I might feel differently when I get back to New York, but honestly, it feels like I'm over him. It's better like this. "Jed leaving was a shock. But I think he did the right thing. Beyond history, I'm not sure what we shared. I'm realizing we weren't connected in the way a couple should be. The fact he could suddenly up and leave me and I didn't have the slightest inkling means something between us was missing."

"You think you grew apart? Became like . . . brother and sister?"

I shrug. All I can see is Ben at the moment. "I'm not sure we would have stayed together if it hadn't been for my mother's death."

"Tuesday, men don't stay because they feel sorry for women. Not for a decade anyway."

I didn't mean *Jed* stayed, more that I had. I was so afraid of losing someone again, I clung on well past the time I should have let go.

"Yeah, but we weren't right together." I think back to dancing with Ben in the walled garden—how in sync we were, how connected I felt to him physically and mentally. "I never felt Jed and I were a team. I could never read him like I can read—"

She's going to think I'm nuts if I start comparing Jed to a man I met just a few weeks ago, but when I put them side by side in my head, all I can think about is how much more I feel for Ben than I ever did for Jed. I like the way Ben doesn't pretend to be an open book like Jed always did, while really keeping all his true feelings secret. Ben is the opposite. He's private and zipped up and keeps it all in, but if you pay attention and gently nudge the closed doors open, it's all there to see. He's not pretending to be anyone he's not.

"I never felt like I saw one hundred percent of Jed. Yeah, he was easygoing and charming and super friendly. He was everyone's best friend within five minutes of meeting them. But that was only part of him. The rest he kept hidden. Even from me."

"You think he's a secret serial killer and the police are closing in, and that's why he ran back to Iowa?" She laughs heartily. But I can't. Not because I think Jed's got a trail of dead bodies in his wake, but because I think it's so sad he would have proposed marriage to me and not felt he could show me his whole self.

There's a knock on the door, and I spring to my feet. I don't want to talk about Jed anymore, and I'm grateful for the interruption. "Hang on, I have to get the door."

I open the door and am greeted with a huge bouquet of flowers. "Miss, can I bring them in? There are several vases."

"Several vases of what?" Melanie asks. "What's going on?"

I flatten myself against the wall as three porters bring in roses of every single color. I'm immediately transported back to the walled garden. There's only one person who could have sent me these.

"Someone sent me flowers," I say.

"Show me," she asks.

I turn our call to video and point the camera to where the porters have placed the flowers on the dressing table in front of the TV. They're wonderful. I scan the vases for a card before the porter hands me an envelope.

I tip him and they leave, the envelope growing hot in my hand.

"Who are they from?" she asks.

I open the envelope. I'm not sure I've ever seen his handwriting before. I love the way he exaggerates the "y" in my name, and in the word "lovely."

"Tuesday?!" Melanie splutters.

"Ben," I say as I read the note again to myself.

Lovely Tuesday
I'll pick you up at seven.
       B

My heart lifts up, up, up.

His first dinner with a woman, and my first first date in a very long time.

"Ben? The hotels guy? What, as a thank-you?"

"Maybe," I say. "He's taking me to dinner tonight." I flip the phone around so I can see her face. Her eyes are as wide as the Hudson.

"Oh, so you and he . . ." She pulls her mouth into a smile, sucks in a breath, and nods. "This is good." She pauses. "Tell me everything."

"There's nothing much to tell. I got to know him a little while we were away, and he asked me out and I said yes." I'm understating it, but that's all I want to share for now. I want to keep the rest between Ben and me.

"Don't go falling in love with him and moving to London."

I laugh along with her, but there's no humor in it—at least, not for me. I guess I'm feeling more . . . open to possibilities in a way I wasn't before coming here. I'm dating someone new. I'm in a different country. My future isn't mapped out anymore, but instead of feeling terrified about losing my job and apartment and fiancé, I'm excited about what's next.

But first, dinner.

CHAPTER TWENTY-ONE

Daniel De Luca's most successful film, *Dinner for Two*, takes place in a restaurant where he plays a chef. Julia Alice plays a waitress who comes to London to study at the Royal Academy of Music. Daniel is hot-tempered and foul-mouthed, and Julia hates him. Everyone does. But Julia isn't scared of him, even though he tries to intimidate her. When she dares to tell him the sauce he serves up with the duck is bland, plates fly. Literally. It's probably my favorite scene from any Daniel De Luca movie. I love it so much that for my fifteenth birthday, my mom and dad took me to a Greek restaurant in Albany just so we could smash plates. It was my favorite birthday ever.

There's no way Ben could know any of that. But still, here we are in front of the blue-and-white awnings of what looks like The French House, the restaurant in *Dinner for Two*.

"Do you recognize it?" he asks me. His brow is slightly furrowed.

"Of course I do," I say. "I just didn't think it was actually a restaurant. I assumed it was made up for the movie." My gaze catches on the sign above the door that says THE FRENCH HOUSE. I don't remember seeing the restaurant on the Daniel De Luca map. I would have definitely put it on my London to-do list.

Ben frowns and leads me inside.

The restaurant is empty.

I glance at Ben, but his expression gives nothing away.

The host greets us with a dramatic bow. "Mademoiselle, monsieur, let me show you to your table."

Doesn't he want to know our names? I know Ben has a Wikipedia page, but he's not Daniel De Luca himself.

The tables are set out just how they were in the movie. The host seats us at the table where Daniel De Luca and Julia Alice have their first date after they finally realize they don't actually hate each other. The only time they can both fit dinner in is after the restaurant closes. He cooks her duck à l'orange, and she says it's the best sauce she's ever tasted.

The host presents us with our menus, and when I open it to see duck à l'orange, I realize what's happening.

He's done this for me.

I dip my head and lean forward so no one can hear. "Did you hire out this entire restaurant?"

He stares at me for a beat, then says, "Sort of."

I narrow my eyes. "Sort of? What does that mean?"

"I kind of . . . bought the place. The owner didn't want to make the changes—you know, to the name and the awnings and the tables—"

My head is spinning. I can't make sense of what he's saying. He's going to need to break it down. "Wait, you bought the place?"

"I thought you'd like it. You know, because of the movie. It's from the Daniel De Lu—"

"I know the movie. It's a favorite of mine. Are you telling me the restaurant didn't actually exist before . . . you bought it?"

"There was a restaurant here. It just wasn't called The French House, and it didn't have these tables or"—he nods toward the staff—"the uniforms. And they did some decorating."

"Who did some decorating?"

"My people." He shrugs. "I wanted tonight to be . . . I wanted you to have fun. And I know how obsessed you are with all things Daniel De Luca. I thought you'd get a kick out of this."

I reach for him without thinking, pressing my palm against his cheek. Nothing about tonight's dinner is about Ben. It's all about me. He's just done everything he could to make me happy. "I'm getting a *huge* kick out of this. The biggest of all kicks." The corners of his mouth twitch.

Yes, it's amazing to be at a restaurant just like the one Daniel De Luca and Julia Alice had their first date in, but the biggest kick of all is that Ben would do so much just to make me happy for a single evening.

"So you finally watched a Daniel De Luca movie, huh?"

One of the waiters comes over with the house cocktail—the one from the movie, obviously. He takes our order. We both opt for the duck à l'orange.

"Yeah, I like to prepare for . . . important . . . things."

I laugh. "I know that about you," I say, thinking about the questionnaires. "Which movie is your favorite?"

He takes a breath. "I've not watched them all. Mr. De Luca has been rather prolific in his career. But . . . I have his complete collection back at the house set up in the screening room. Along with the popcorn you mentioned. I thought you might like the second half of this date to involve a movie."

"The classic date combo of dinner and a movie." There's nothing typical about this dinner. He bought the freaking restaurant and recreated a scene from my favorite movie. When do things like that happen outside of an actual Daniel De Luca film?

"I don't want you to think that if you come back and watch a movie, we have to—I mean, I don't expect . . . anything."

Awkward Ben is adorable. But the joke's on him, because I'm expecting it *all* when I go back to his place. In fact, I'm pretty sure I'll be ready to skip to the good part and miss the movie entirely.

He must see the desire in my eyes. He slides his leg between mine and takes my hand across the table.

I want to ask him whether it feels different between us, now that he's not paying me to be here, but I don't get a chance. Our food arrives and we're forced to drop our hands.

"I confirmed dinner with the duke and duchess tomorrow," he says. "I suggested taking them out. They've insisted on hosting us at their town house."

"They're such great hosts. What should I wear?"

"I'll send you something."

"No, there's no need." It's weird. When I was being paid for the weekend, going to Ralph Lauren was a little odd but okay because it felt like Ben was buying me a uniform for a job. But when I'm going to dinner with the guy I'm interested in, it's more than weird for him to buy me the dress I'm expected to wear. My phone buzzes with a notification, and I pull it out from my jacket pocket. "Sorry, I just want to get it in case it's my dad."

"Go ahead," Ben says.

It's not my dad. It's a message from my bank. Normally I'd ignore it, but something makes me swipe up.

There's been an unexpected deposit into your bank account. Please contact us immediately.

A feeling of dread circles my ankles like fog in a horror movie. He didn't, did he?

Quickly, I log into my banking app.

Oh, yes he did.

"Ben?" I say. "I didn't give you my bank account details because I told you I didn't want your money. I was really clear about that."

His frown is back. The dimple that's been on display all evening has disappeared. "You earned that money. We had a deal. I don't back down on a deal."

"It's too much money. I had fun."

"Compensation wasn't contingent on you being miserable."

"But it wasn't a job. I enjoyed myself. I had an experience I would never have dreamed of if you hadn't taken me there."

"Then that's a perk. You negotiated that money. It's yours."

"It was two nights at a fancy country house. It wasn't worth thirty thousand dollars."

"It was to me. You were perfect."

I groan. "I wasn't perfect. I don't know how I'm going to convince you to take that money back."

"I don't want you to convince me. That money is yours. You deserve it. If it makes you feel better, you can purchase your own dress for dinner tomorrow."

I pause, mulling over whether or not I could live with taking money from this man. It seems so wrong.

"I'm serious." I glance up at Ben. "I don't want your money."

"Then give it to charity. But we had a contract. I'm fulfilling my obligations the same way you did."

I groan. He's so freaking honorable. Why couldn't he take his money back when I offered it to him? I could like him a little less.

"It's very . . . charming that you offered." He fixes me with his gaze, and I'm out of arguments. He's not being weird about it, so why should I be?

"I'm buying my own outfit for tomorrow. Don't send me anything or I'll be mad."

"Not even underwear?" he asks.

A frisson of electricity sparks between us.

"Especially not underwear," I reply. I'd rather surprise him.

CHAPTER
TWENTY-TWO

If I'm honest, when Ben suggested a movie back at his place, I was expecting it to involve less silver screen and more nakedness. But warm buttered popcorn and *A Duchess for a Duke* will have to do. For now, at least.

"This is the bit in the rose garden," I say, nudging him with my elbow. We're sitting hip to hip on the oversize velvet sofa in his screening room. There's been no kissing, which is disappointing, but I hope that will happen before the credits roll. He probably thinks I want to watch the movie. Which I do . . . but I wouldn't choose it over kissing Ben. That must say something about the way my feelings for him seem to be blooming.

Watching this movie with me must be beyond irritating because I can't help but tell him what's about to happen.

"See how he watches her? He finally gets it." I roll my eyes. "Finally! Men are so dumb sometimes."

"Dumb?" he asks.

"Yeah." I say, exasperated. "Like, he *must* know how she feels. It's been building between them for so long."

"Maybe he has doubts," he says, taking the carton of popcorn and grabbing a handful. "Not about how he feels, but whether kissing her is the right thing to do."

Silence circles us and I can't help but wonder whether we're still talking about the film. I turn so I'm staring at the side of his face, then he turns and our gazes lock; it feels like each of us is waiting for the other to speak. The tension between us sparks, and my heart thrums in my chest, sending vibrations throughout my body.

How could he doubt that kissing me is the right thing to do?

"But he knows her," I say, my voice sounding throaty to my own ears. "Better than anyone. They're so connected."

"That's how *he* feels. But he doesn't know if she feels it too."

"Of course he knows."

He shakes his head, his gaze dropping to my lips and then back up to my eyes. "He wants to be sure. She's been through a lot and he has all the power. He doesn't want to fuck it up."

"He won't fuck it up," I whisper.

He smooths a strand of hair from my face. "Sure?"

I nod. "Kissing her is absolutely the right thing to do," I say breathlessly.

He tosses the popcorn bucket behind him and cups my face.

My nipples harden and graze against the lace of my bra, and I squeeze my thighs together. I nod and he sweeps his lips against my cheek.

"Here?" he asks.

"Everywhere," I say on a sigh.

He lets out a guttural moan and presses soft, slow kisses up my neck and along my jaw, each one eking out more and more sensation. He pulls away for a second and checks my expression.

"What?" I ask.

"You're beautiful," he says. "And I . . ." He frowns. I know that he has more to say, and I want to hear it all.

He moves to kiss me again and I stop him. "You, what?" I ask.

He doesn't reply for a second or two, his gaze flitting from my eyes to my lips, lower, then up again. "I really like you," he says finally.

I nod. "Yeah, I really like you too."

He swallows and I watch the bob of his throat. I reach for him, smoothing my fingers down his neck, wanting to be closer to him, desperate to feel him from the inside.

"Tuesday." He cups the back of my head with both hands and presses his lips to mine. I sink into him, half drowned in him, thankful that this is where we are right now.

Tentatively, I place my hands against his chest, and he pauses, just for a fraction of a second, like my touch has interrupted his circuitry, and it takes him a second to reconnect his brain to his body. His mouth pulls from mine, plowing a path along my jaw, his fingers pressing, his tongue more insistent.

He sweeps his hands down my arms and presses me down, flat on the sofa, so I'm on my back and he's over me. His eyes are hooded, and I can feel his need, his desire for me. It's coming off him in waves. I have to have him, or a part of me will be left empty for the rest of time.

"I've waited so long . . ." He trails off.

"I know," I say. "I want this too."

He shakes his head. "You can't possibly want me as much as I want you."

A smile tugs at the corner of my mouth. Feeling his yearning sends heat to my core. Like he's bringing me to life after years spent waiting. "You're wrong." I hold out my hand and he threads his fingers through it.

He slides over me, both of us fully clothed but our barriers abandoned. Our hips lock together and I can feel him against me, and I'm more aware of each part of me that he's touching. His body over mine magnifies every sensation, coaxing fire to life in places I've never felt it before. I worry I might combust if he stays here, on top of me, but I might wither and die if he doesn't. I need him. He shifts over me and I try to muffle the sound that echoes from me at the feel of him so close.

"I want to hear every sound you make, Tuesday," he says. "I want to know all of you."

I sigh as his lips resume their journey, pressing and pulling, licking and sucking. A coil inside me winds tighter and tighter, every touch tethering us closer together.

He pulls my shirt from the waist of my skirt and skims his teeth along my stomach. The connection leaves a trail of heat—he's a lit match and I'm a twist of paper. I roll my hips, trying to feel more and less at the same time. The buttons of my shirt are undone, but I'm so dazed I don't remember how they got that way. Ben is licking and pressing and my blood dances in my veins, my heartbeat throbbing . . . everywhere.

He sweeps his hands up my thighs and under my skirt, then hooks his fingers into my underwear and tugs them down, just enough that he can slide his palm over me. He groans as he feels how warm I am.

How wet.

How completely ready.

My hand winds in his hair and we stare at each other, understanding where we are: at the point of no return.

But I don't want to go back.

"More," I whisper. "I want everything."

His hand rocks over me, his fingers finding more of my wetness. I arch my spine as sensation washes through me. Such a small touch . . . How will I handle more?

He dips and scrapes his teeth over my nipple. Even through the fabric of my bra, it sends sparks across my vision.

"Ben!" I cry out. He's pulled me to the event horizon in just a few seconds; any further, and I will fall and fall and fall.

I'm not ready.

And he knows.

His mouth moves to my collarbone, but his hand stays, his fingers smoothing and dipping . . . It's just a step away from too much.

I reach for the buttons of his shirt with trembling fingers. I pull at them, finally freeing the fabric. I grasp him, pulling at his shoulders and waist, impatient for more, eager to quench this thirst I have for him.

He takes his hand from my underwear, sucks in a breath and pulls off his shirt, then slips the rest of mine off, tossing both onto the floor beside us. As he kisses me, our tongues entwined, I splay my hands across his hot, hard back, trying to feel as much of him as I can. His pulse hammers against mine, like they're competing against each other in a wild race both are guaranteed to win.

Now skin against skin, his weight on me, his heat all around me, I begin to melt underneath him. I wrap my legs around him and he groans.

I can't help but smile. I want to collect all his sounds and put them in a jar that I can open when I need a little more of him. When I need to feel him raw.

"Fuck, Tuesday," he hisses.

"I know," I say.

"Will we survive?" he asks, and I laugh, even though I know he's entirely serious. The same question has crossed my mind too.

"I think so," I say. "And if not, so be it."

His hand slides behind my ass, and he tilts me up, toward him, so I'm as close to him as I can get.

But it's not enough.

I circle my hips, trying for more, but there's too much fabric in the way still. I reach for the waistband of his jeans and try to push down.

"I need you," I say and our eyes catch. "Now."

In seconds our clothes are gone, discarded somewhere, and we're finally where we need to be.

He has a condom from somewhere, and I watch him, my skin buzzing, my breathing shallow as he rolls it on.

Our eyes meet. It's like he's waiting for me to say no, to change my mind. Doesn't he know that's never going to happen? He nudges between my legs, and I splay my thighs wide, desperate for him. Our gazes are locked as he presses into me, and I'm full with his heat.

He pauses, his jaw tight. I watch the pulse in his neck, reach and press a finger against it, then pull him closer so I can feel it with my tongue.

He starts to move. I bring my hips up to meet his with every thrust so it goes deeper and harder and *more* than I ever thought possible. I see the understanding on his face, and it's exactly how it feels in my chest—like this is exactly how we were meant to be. This is how it was always meant to be. His movements feel more desperate; he pushes harder and harder, and everything is black and white and bursts of light. I can't think about anything but this and him and us.

I grip his shoulders, digging my nails into him because I don't want him to be able to ever get away.

"Fuck!" he calls out and I know it's not a complaint. I know he's feeling what I'm feeling, and the thought makes me tighten.

He shifts, moving to sit back on his heels, bringing me with him so I'm sloped away from him. He pulls me deeper onto him, pushing his hips against mine, connecting over and over.

He reaches for me, pinching my nipples, pulling slightly, and I groan, throwing my hands over my head. He shifts again, pulling me up so I'm sitting astride him. My head tips back as he lifts and lowers my hips, each time sinking lower, feeling fuller.

"So deep," I say—to myself, to him? I've lost control. All I can do is feel.

We're face-to-face, our bodies pressed together, our lips connecting every few seconds in clumsy half kisses as our orgasms rattle in the distance, threatening to thunder after us and break this spell of sensation we've cast.

"Tuesday, Tuesday, Tuesday," he whispers. My name on his lips breaks the last thread of control I hold.

I'm not sure what day it is, let alone what time. When my alarm goes off, at first I think it's a fire alarm. Then I have to remind myself where I am.

In bed.

With Ben.

Our bodies are intertwined, and as I pull my limbs from his to reach for my phone, he grumbles in his sleep and pulls me closer. Eventually, I manage to grab the phone and silence the alarm.

And then I realize why it's going off. It's not morning. Not a decent hour anyway. I'm meant to go on a Daniel De Luca stalking mission at his hotel as arranged with Melanie. This is my one opportunity to see my previous obsession in the flesh.

"I have to go," I whisper as I watch Ben, his expression no less stern because he's sleeping.

He doesn't say anything, just reaches for me and pulls me toward him so my back is against his front. We're side by side, spooning. His hand skates up and down my thigh, and it's only when it dips between my legs that I realize he must be conscious.

"Ben, I have to leave."

"Don't," he says, as he brings my leg back to rest on his thigh, opening me wide.

"Stay." He presses a kiss to my shoulder and his hardness nudges my entrance. My brain is frazzled.

"For just a few minutes."

He chuckles into my neck. "You're never going to want to leave when I'm done with you."

He's probably right. I'm not sure anything—not even Daniel De Luca—could make me want to leave Ben's bed.

CHAPTER
TWENTY-THREE

Melanie has never been as into Daniel De Luca as me, but she insists on staying up late in New York while I loiter outside the Soho Hotel waiting for him to emerge. It's not even light yet, but I finally managed to escape Ben's persuasive techniques for getting me to stay with him. I better get to see Daniel De Luca this morning. I've given up a lot.

Melanie didn't want me to do it on my own. But honestly, if we hadn't arranged this call, I probably wouldn't be here. Every part of me aches, and not because Ben and I were up most of the night, but because I'm not in his bed now. Every time I blink, I feel his teeth on my neck, his fingers on my skin, his tongue . . . everywhere.

"Hold me straight!" Melanie squawks from the video call, pulling me back to the moment.

"Whoops, sorry. There's nothing much to see."

Security has set up a small barricade, but I'm the only one here. And it's pouring rain.

"It's no wonder you're in love with him. I mean, he's hot as all holy hell," she says.

"I don't think I'm actually in love with him. Back in the day, maybe, but I was a teenager. I just like his movies, and I've enjoyed visiting the locations; it all brings back memories of my mom."

"I don't mean you're in love with Daniel De Luca," Melanie replies. "I'm talking about Ben."

The rain is coming down harder now. Ten minutes ago, it was just drizzling. Now the rain is falling in full-on sheets. The sound against my rickety tourist umbrella must have made me mishear. She can't have just said I'm in love with Ben. "Say that again? I didn't hear you."

Melanie laughs. "I said, I'm not surprised you're in love with Ben. He's hot. And he's obviously a romantic. The flowers? That date? He bought a goddamn restaurant for you, for crying out loud. He's got it bad too."

She doesn't even know about the sex. This morning it feels like all the cells in my body have been rearranged and I'm biologically different now. But that's not love.

I roll my eyes, but she can't see because I have the phone screen pointing toward the hotel doors. She doesn't know what she's saying. Maybe she needs an explanation of why I'm not more upset about Jed. The more time that goes by, the more I think I was over Jed before he ended things between us. Melanie can believe it's because of Ben if she wants. "I've known Ben a little over two weeks. I'm not in love with him." I can't mention the sex or she'll definitely tell me it's love. Because it wasn't just sex. It was something more than that.

"Two weeks is long enough to fall in love," she says.

We fall silent as the hotel door opens revealing two women dressed in puffer jackets, neither of whom are Daniel De Luca.

"Love happens at first sight, remember," Melanie continues. "When you compare that with how long you've known Ben, two weeks to fall in love with him is actually a very long time. You've spent a lot of time together."

"*Lust* happens at first sight." The lust fairy definitely waved her magic wand at me when I first saw Ben. What isn't to like? He's tall, dark, and handsome. But he looked like he wanted to murder me. I hadn't fallen in love with him that afternoon in Green Park. There was no way. And I'm still not in love with him. That's completely impossible.

Even if he did things to me last night that make me wonder if he should carry a special license for his skills. "Attraction. Not love. That takes . . ."

"How long? A month?" Melanie asks. "Do you have to pass a test? Maybe if you can stand each other for two years, then you can be deemed to be in love?"

I fall silent again and Melanie copies me. I hold up the phone as someone else comes out of the hotel. It's five a.m. Why on earth are people coming out of their hotel so early? If they're on vacation, shouldn't they be enjoying the comfort of their *made by someone else* bed? If they're on business, what kind of company needs you up so early?

This time it's a man, but it's not Daniel De Luca. It's a balding guy in his sixties.

"Maybe he checked out," I say.

"Or perhaps his call time is later today," Melanie counters.

"I'm the only person waiting. That should tell me something. I might head back to my hotel and nap."

"Didn't get enough sleep last night?" Melanie asks.

I don't answer. Melanie always spills the tea about sex with her boyfriends, but I want to keep last night to myself for a while. Like if I tell her, I might use up some of my memories and feelings by talking about it.

"I need coffee," I say.

"You mean you want to go to the coffee shop where you ran into Ben again. You want to swap your Daniel De Luca quest for a Benjamin Whatever-His-Name-Is quest. If Ben trumps Daniel De Luca, it's all the evidence I need that you're in love with him."

"More evidence? You haven't provided any so far other than he's good looking. If that were the only criteria, I would be in love with Mario Lopez."

"*Ewww.*" She looks at me like I've just thrown a cup of cat pee all over her.

"I said what I said and I don't regret it."

"That's not the only evidence I have," she says. "I hear it in your voice. In the way you talk about him, but also how much . . . lighter you seem."

I do feel lighter. Happier. I feel free.

I don't know if it's being free of Jed or of the life I had back in New York. Maybe it's freedom from the grief I thought would come with thinking about my mom so much. Maybe it's just because I've connected to the girl I was before my mom died—her joy and enthusiasm, her hope for the future.

"You must admit that Ben has helped you get over Jed."

I shrug. "No more so than Daniel De Luca has. He's provided a distraction." I pause. "No, that's not entirely true. Spending time with another man has provided a contrast I didn't know I needed. Seeing the kind of man Ben is has made more obvious to me the fact that Jed and I weren't meant to be together. I've spent a lot of the last ten years not noticing stuff I should have focused on. Glossing over incompatibilities I should have faced."

It's not until I listen to Melanie talking about Jed that I realize just how much of our relationship was about what *he* wanted. I didn't want to live on the Upper East Side. I certainly didn't want the rent there. But I never told him. I'd been happy to go along with it, because I wanted Jed to be happy, even at the cost of my own happiness.

Don't say yes to anything you don't want.

Ben's words circle my brain like a breaking news ticker.

I think I said yes to a lot I didn't want during my time with Jed.

"Everyone's perfect when they're as good looking as Ben and you haven't known them long enough to know they always leave the toilet seat up or their orgasm face is a real turn-off."

"You still haven't had the conversation with David?"

She shakes her head. "I just focus on his shoulder for the last few minutes. We've been doing more doggy, which makes it easier."

Apparently, I'm not the only one with a tendency to gloss over things in her relationship.

"I'm sure he'd switch it up if you just told him he looks like he's sitting on the toilet when he climaxes."

"You're trying to distract me from my argument that you. Are. In. Love. With. Ben."

"I promise I'm not. It's just . . . Do you think I say yes to things when I . . . just because I want to keep the other person happy?"

For a second I think I've lost the connection because she doesn't answer right away. After a few beats, she says, "I don't know. Do you think that?"

I think about it. "I don't want to move to Brooklyn." I fist my hands, bracing myself for . . . something.

"Brooklyn might be our only option," she replies.

I *really* don't want to live in Brooklyn.

The doorman, dressed in a long black coat and top hat with a gold band around it, gets a message on his radio, and I freeze. Melanie goes silent.

"Copy that" is the only thing I hear carrying over the rain. A second later, a blacked-out sedan pulls up in front of the hotel. I try to peer in the window, but there's absolutely nothing to see.

"You think this could be it?" Melanie asks.

My heart rate switches from a relaxed stroll to a trot. I crane my neck to try to see around the sculpted, twisty bushes that flank the entrance to the hotel. I'm only about five yards from the entrance, but because I'm on the same side of the street as the door, it's impossible to see what's going on inside the hotel.

This might be it. It really might be happening.

A blond woman in sunglasses—despite complete darkness all around us—appears through the doors. She's wearing a white coat and is about the same height as me.

"Is it someone famous?"

"Either that or someone who thinks they *should* be famous."

The doorman opens the sedan's door and she slips inside.

"Maybe she's traveling with him," I speculate.

"Who's his costar in this film?"

"Sofia Flores. No way that's her."

The sedan pulls out and there's more chatter on the radio. A Range Rover with blacked-out windows appears.

"You should have taken a picture of that woman. I bet she turns out to be famous," Melanie says.

"I can't start snapping strangers. I'll get arrested."

The doorman mumbles into his radio and then catches my eye. He gives a subtle nod.

Goose bumps sprinkle my skin, and I put my umbrella down. There's no way I'm missing this. If I have to get soaked, so be it.

"What are you doing?" Melanie says as the phone is tucked under my arm while I figure out the umbrella.

"I don't want to miss this because I'm under an umbrella. I've waited my entire life for this moment." I'm not sure what I'm preparing myself for. Is Daniel De Luca going to look at me and fall in love instantly? Will he catch my eye and realize I'm the woman he's been missing all these years? No, but I'm not wrestling with an umbrella while I try to get a picture with him, even if I look like I've just been pulled out of the Thames.

A huge guy gets out of the passenger side of the Range Rover and pulls the door open, just as the hotel door opens. I stand on tiptoes. Whoever it is has a baseball cap on and their head bowed as they come out, their coat collar pulled up. I can barely see anything.

"I think it's him," Melanie says in a loud whisper.

"Daniel!" I yell. I want him to lift his head. I want him to look at me.

Daniel doesn't face me, just raises his hand in a half wave before ducking into the car.

I've finally laid my own two eyes on Daniel De Luca.

I sigh. Gosh darn it. Was that it?

As the car passes us, I can't even make out his silhouette in the back seat. The windows are like a concrete wall.

"It's the same every morning," the doorman says. "He never stops for the fans."

"He's a dick," Melanie shouts from the phone. "We just wanted a photo."

"I guess he's not feeling his best at five a.m.," I say.

"Or he's just a dick," Melanie says. "Maybe you can stalk him in the bar. Or at night when he comes back. What time does he come back?" she asks, and I point the phone at the doorman, but he just shrugs. "If I was there," she continues, "I would have dived into the car or clung on to the exhaust pipe. You need a picture with him. You *deserve* more than a hand raise."

I don't need to see him again, have a picture with him, or get more than a hand raise. I've seen him in person. That's more than I expected, even when I was fifteen years old. Melanie thinks I should be disappointed, but honestly, I'm not. Maybe seeing him, however briefly, means my teenage obsession is complete. Maybe I've just got other men to think about.

One man in particular.

CHAPTER
TWENTY-FOUR

As I press the bell on Ben's town house, nerves start to tumble in my stomach. Flashes of last night flip through my brain, and my hands start to shake with the anticipation of seeing him again. It almost feels like another version of myself was with Ben last night. A more *me* version of myself. He stripped me of more than my clothes and found a Tuesday I'd forgotten about, or maybe I never knew existed.

He opens the door and the first thing I see is that dimple. Part of me likes to think it only comes out for me. I know it can't be true, but I also know not everyone gets to see it. At least I'm part of an exclusive members-only club.

"You look incredible," he says, not breaking our gaze as I step over the threshold. I'm not sure he's even seen what I'm wearing.

"You happy with it? It's suitable for tonight?" I twirl and my skirt lifts. When I meet his gaze again, his expression is difficult to place. It's soft and kind and filled with gratitude, and it makes my heart inch higher in my chest. The time away from him, however short, increased my longing for him.

"More than." He reaches for my face, cupping his hand around my jaw. Heat radiates everywhere—the base of my spine, between my legs, across my collarbones. He presses me against him and I gasp as our bodies meet. He feels so . . . safe. He fixes me with a magnetic glare, and

I lean into him, wanting to be closer. His lips graze mine and I have to hold back a groan, I want him so badly.

"Thank you for my flowers," I say. After half seeing Daniel De Luca, I went back to my hotel to find more flowers waiting for me.

"I wanted you to have something that reminded you of me today."

"They're beautiful. But I'm not sure how you think I'd forget."

"You're beautiful."

A staccato knock at the door makes me jump, but Ben holds me in place with his hand and his stare. "My driver," he says.

"We should go," I reply, my voice weak from our proximity.

His chest lifts and lowers. I sweep my palm up his shirt.

He nods, takes my hand, and moves back toward the exit.

"One second," I say, seeing the mirror by the doorway. I pull my lipstick from my bag.

When I'm done, I turn to him, and he's looking at me, a question in his eyes.

"I was hoping you'd kiss me, so I didn't put my lipstick on," I say in explanation. The cherry red is a contrast to my black silk dress, and it stops the outfit from feeling funereal. If it smudges, I'm in trouble. I'll look like I have a shellfish allergy and just made out with a crab.

"You wanted me to kiss you," he says—not a question, just an observation.

"Of course," I reply.

He holds the door open.

"Is there anything you want me to say or bring up tonight?" I ask as I exit the house.

"About what?"

"I don't know. What do you think you need to get him to agree to sell the hotels to you?"

He blinks once, then twice; it's like he's trying to say something but can't quite find the words. "Leave me to worry about that." He holds the car door open for me. Maybe I'm imagining it, but it feels like the atmosphere turned a little frosty. I'm not quite sure if it's because he's nervous, because I wanted him to kiss me, or something else.

"You'll never guess what I did this morning." We get into the car and I tell him about my morning stalking Daniel De Luca with Melanie on speaker, and how I got completely soaked.

He doesn't say or do anything.

I slip my hand into his and squeeze. "Are you okay?"

"Yes. Just a lot on my mind. How's Melanie?"

I almost tell him she's deranged because she thinks I'm in love with him, but I decide against it. I don't want him to think I'm not only Daniel De Luca's groupie but his too. "She's fine. Keeping New York warm for me."

"New York. You'll be back there soon." His gaze is fixed ahead as if he's driving. He looks a little solemn.

"Hey." I drop my hand and stroke my fingers over his cheekbone. "You want to talk about it?"

He glances at me and my stomach flips. Just from a look. I might not be in love with him, but that damn lust fairy is working overtime.

"How can I cheer you up?" I ask. "You seem tense."

"Just be yourself. I'm better now you're here."

The idea I could lift whatever burden he carries warms me. "What else can I do?" I push my hand back into his and curl my fingers, locking them together.

"I hate that I've had to ask you to do this. I sort of hate that we have to go through this pretense again. I'm not sure . . ."

"I offered, remember? I'm happy to come along. I'll have a wonderful time." I don't say it, but I can't help thinking that we're not pretending. Okay, so we're not engaged, but we're romantically linked. Even if it's only for the last few days of me being here in London.

"But you should be enjoying London. And I . . ." He doesn't finish his sentence. He releases his seat belt and for a moment I think he's going to pull me onto his lap or something, but I realize the car has stopped.

"We're here," he says.

He undoes my seat belt for me and we get out of the car.

"It's this one," he says, nodding at the grand town house in front of us. The imposing black double doors are flanked by white columns, and the stoop is covered in pretty black-and-white tiles. Because it's a town house, it's not clear where the house begins and ends, but I can see it goes up about four or five floors. It surprises me a little that it's right on the street. Surely anyone could knock on the door.

Grant opens the door and we're shown into a huge formal living room. I can see the duchess's influence in the room's pretty feminine details: walls of duck-egg blue with gold-framed paintings hung close together; two huge chandeliers drip with light, emphasizing the elaborate crown molding and intricate plasterwork on the ceiling. As we're being offered drinks, the duchess arrives. Her hair is swept up in an elegant chignon, and she's wearing a black, knee-length cocktail dress. What I'm wearing looks like it could have come from the same person's wardrobe, and I relax slightly. The first part of my role is complete; at least I look the part.

"Let's have champagne," she says. "We can celebrate your engagement." She puts up her hand. "I'm not pressuring you to decide, but I just want to tell you that our offer to host the engagement party or reception still stands."

My stomach roils for all the wrong reasons. She's so kind and generous, and both she and the duke have already been so lovely to us I hate lying to them. It was bad enough for the weekend, but somehow it feels worse the second time around. I thought the fact Ben and I have slept together would make it easier, but somehow it makes it worse because the lie feels less necessary. Or maybe the reality of what I'm feeling for Ben and how much I like spending time with him also feels like a lie. I don't know what's the truth and what's for show.

"Thank you," Ben says. "Honestly, as long as she becomes my wife, I don't really mind about the wedding."

Tiny flutters explode in my heart. From his expression and tone, there's no way anyone could tell he's lying. He's entirely convincing. Even to me. But of course, he *is* lying. If he was telling the truth, it would be absurd. We've known each other a few weeks, and I'm going back to New York. But there's a part of me that *wants* him to be telling the truth. The flutters turn to churning. Living a lie—even for a few more hours—is more stressful than I anticipated.

"You always say the right thing," I say, pulling my mouth into a tight smile.

"Long may that continue," the duchess says. "It's exactly the opposite affliction my husband suffers from. Speak of the devil."

The duke comes through the door, dressed smartly in a gray suit, white shirt, and pink tie. "My apologies," he says. "That call took longer than it should have done."

"You've got to slow down, darling. I keep saying it to you."

"How are you two?" the duke asks, ignoring his wife.

"I was just reminding Tuesday and Ben that our invitation to host the engagement party still stands," the duchess says. "I always say to the duke, us not being able to have more children was such a waste. I would have been a wonderful interfering mother."

The duke squeezes her arm, and I realize I've never seen him touch her before.

"I'm so sorry," I say, then wonder if I should have pretended she hadn't mentioned her lack of children. Sometimes it's difficult to know with the British whether they want to talk about something.

The duchess smiles. "I've had a lot of time to come to terms with it. But it is a huge regret in our lives, isn't it, George? We love to spend time with and support young couples. I suppose that's how I've channeled my mothering."

"We're blessed in many ways, my dear."

"We are." The duchess puts on a bright smile and nods toward us. "We get to host lovely young couples like you at Fairfield House."

"I absolutely fell in love with the place," I say. It's the truth but I'm also relieved we're on safer conversational ground. "It has a magical feel. The house, the grounds—it's all so very special."

"You must come to our place in France in the summer. We have a number of friends of all ages who will be joining us." Another generous invitation. I know I should feel grateful, but my gut fills with guilt like a rain barrel in a storm. We're tricking two lovely people. This isn't just business. This is personal. "I'm there on and off between June and September, flying to and fro. We're not far outside Cannes. It's absolutely gorgeous and more restful than London, which is all go-go-go."

Grant comes in to tell us dinner is ready, and we make our way into the dining room. It's a gorgeous room that manages to balance coziness and formality. Dark-blue velvet drapes frame the three huge windows, and a massive chandelier hangs from the tall ceiling over the polished mahogany dining table.

"I know it's only the four of us tonight," she says, nodding at the huge table that must be large enough for twenty. "But I love this room. We'll have plenty of space to spread out."

"The table looks beautiful," I reply.

There are five or six wineglasses at each place setting. The light from the crystal chandeliers rebounds onto the silverware and lights up the flower arrangement in the middle. It looks like we're on the set of a movie. We could be in a scene from *A Duchess for a Duke*.

"The flowers are stunning," I say as we take our seats. "The roses are exactly the same as the ones you sent me this morning," I say to Ben.

"He sends you flowers even when you're with him? Or do you two not live together yet?" the duchess asks.

My stomach falls through my chair when I realize what I've said. Why would Ben send me flowers if I was living at his place? And what engaged couple *doesn't* live together these days? *Shit, shit, a thousand shits.*

"I suppose it's rather lazy," Ben says, his breezy tone not giving away we've just been caught in our lie. "Perhaps I should go and get them myself and then bring them home with me, rather than call a florist."

The quarter second before the duchess speaks feels like an hour, like we're both on trial awaiting the foreman of the jury to read the verdict to the courtroom.

"I think it's lovely you're still giving her flowers, however they come. George could take a leaf out of your book."

I try to cover my exhale of relief. Under the table, Ben squeezes my knee.

Though we got away with my slip, the moment settles resolve in my gut. I can't do this again. I won't spend another evening with the duke and duchess before I leave London. I can't lie to them anymore.

"We are never short of flowers, either here or at Fairfield," the duke says.

"I know, but it's only because I order them for the house. Not because you buy them for me. Anyway, what were we talking about?" She frowns slightly and then answers her own question. "Oh, yes, Cannes. The duke comes out to France when work allows. If I have my way and he retires, this summer we'll get to spend more time together than ever."

"Retires?" The duke sounds completely horrified.

I keep silent, determined not to say anything that might make him veer off course. I'm sure Ben is desperate to hear what his plans are. "Never! Letting go here and there is one thing. Retiring is quite another. I shall never fully retire. Fairfield House will see to that. One never retires when living in a place like Fairfield. There's always far too much to do."

"Exactly," the duchess says. "There's far too much to do without you having to worry yourself running thirteen separate businesses."

"You can't count each hotel. That's ludicrous. There are four businesses, including the hotels."

"Ben," the duchess says. I smell trouble brewing. "Running that many hotels is a huge undertaking, isn't it?" She turns back to the duke. "You get offers all the time. I don't understand why—"

"Enough!" the duke snaps. "I don't want to discuss this anymore. We're off on holiday next week, for goodness' sake. There's only so many times a year a man can sit around doing nothing, isn't that right, Ben?"

"I do struggle to spend time away from my desk, sir."

The duke shoots the duchess a look, but she won't be silenced. "All that tells me is you both have a problem. Not that it's right." She takes a sip of her champagne. "You should come with us. We're off to Scotland for a couple of weeks. Now the midges have gone, it's quite beautiful up in the Highlands. Have you ever been, Tuesday?"

I shake my head. "Never. I've heard the scenery is astonishing." Astonishing? When did I start using words like that? My brain is starting to think like a Brit.

"It absolutely is. Our place up there is in the middle of nowhere. It's so peaceful."

"The Wi-Fi is terrible," says the duke. "Absolutely shocking. No amount of complaining from me changes anything. It's infuriating. I have to do everything on the phone and get documents couriered. It's like we're in the late nineties."

I can't help but laugh. I would have expected the duke to be something of a Luddite, but obviously the opposite is true.

"Unfortunately, I have some immoveable obligations next week. Thank you very much for the invitation," Ben says.

"Maybe Tuesday can come on her own." The duchess shakes her head. "At your age, newly engaged, you probably don't want to be away from each other. Never mind. Another time. It's such a shame it's empty for so much of the year. It would be nice to see it used more." She sighs. "When the duke retires, or even semi-retires, we might make it up there a little more often. You know my mother was Scottish."

"Beautiful woman," the duke mumbles, and the duchess smiles.

"She was. I'd spend summers up there, just outside Loch Lomond. Very happy times. Where did you grow up, Tuesday?"

"Upstate New York in Madison County. We spent a lot of time outside when my father wasn't working. I want the same for my children." I say it without thinking because I'm relaxed, just having a nice conversation with three people I'm fond of, but it fits in perfectly with the narrative Ben and I have established.

Even though I'm telling the truth, my mouth takes on a tinny feel, like I shouldn't have said it. I just hate lying to these people. Ben and I won't spend our summers in Scotland. I haven't got long left in England. I'm not going home engaged . . . Hell, I'm not even sure I'm going to fly home with a job. I'm going to get on that plane, sad to be leaving, and . . . I'm going to miss Ben.

Really miss him.

The idea pinches at my gut, and I put my hand to my stomach to soothe myself. We've spent most of our time together studying each other—getting to know each other because we have to—but whatever the motivation, I do know him now. And I like what I know.

Maybe Melanie had a point.

My net has been open, catching feelings without me realizing. I glance at Ben as he chats with the duke, the duchess chipping in here and there as they talk about their most recent trip to the US. I smile and nod and say all the right things, but I'm barely taking it all in. It's like I'm hovering over them, watching them participate in this dinner. All I can focus on is how I might be falling in love with the man who's pretending to be my fiancé, and it all feels wrong on so many levels.

Maybe I'm blinded by the magic of this vacation, being in the land of Daniel De Luca, because I can't be in love with Ben. It doesn't seem logical. Then again, logic is what I had with Jed, and we all know how that turned out.

Even if I have fallen for Ben, does it matter? Does it change anything? It's not like there's a future for us. All we have is now . . . and now will just have to be enough.

CHAPTER
TWENTY-FIVE

I don't know how to tell Ben I'm about to ruin his life. Probably the same way Jed told me he was in love with a ballerina and going to live in Iowa. Quickly. And without mercy.

"Things have gotten out of control," I say to him as he slides into the car next to me. "The duke and duchess are lovely people, but I feel . . ."

"Like they want to adopt us?" Ben shoots me an amused look, instantly popping the balloon of anxiety that's been building in me all evening.

"Exactly." I glance out the window, back to the duke and duchess's town house.

I don't know if Ben told his driver to go back to his place or to my hotel. And I'm not sure where I'd prefer to be. I need to focus on my future and my career, not getting naked with a man who I won't see again after I take off for New York. Don't I? Ben is going to be an ocean away in just a couple of weeks. I'm already in up to my neck in emotions . . . Why make things worse?

At the same time, the pull toward Ben is so intense. I want him. Maybe it was the sex. Maybe it was the half-truths we just told at dinner that had me imagining I could actually be Ben's fiancée. But that's a fantasy, and holding on to Ben when I know it's going to be over so quickly seems like drawn-out torture. Isn't it better to rip the Band-Aid off and go our separate ways?

"I hate lying to them."

"I know," he says. His tone turns somber. "I hate lying to them too. They're good people." His frown has returned.

"I'm leaving for New York in just over two weeks. They're going to find out we're not engaged."

Ben pulls in a breath, and I try not to focus on the rise of his chest and what's underneath his shirt. Things have gotten so messy. I don't need to make things worse. Better we have a clean break. Okay, so we gave in and had sex, but it was a one-off, right?

"I know. I knew I was going to have to put a stop to things when the duchess mentioned staying with them in Cannes."

"Frankly, that's almost worth getting married for."

Ben almost smiles. *Oh, dimple, how I love thee.* "I'm going to have to explain."

"Two weeks is going to fly by."

Ben clenches his jaw and I pretend for a second that it's because he'll be sad to see me go, and not because my departure means his plans are going up in flames.

"Even if I was staying the year—"

"It's not right," he says. Then rushes to add, "The lying. Not the bit about you staying the year." He pauses. "Have you thought about extending your trip?"

"I'm here for work, Ben." I let out a small laugh of panic. So much has happened in London that I've been able to avoid the wreckage of the life I left in New York. But the second that plane touches down, I won't be able to dodge reality any longer.

"Right," he says. "I'll tell them."

"Are you sure?" I ask. "You never told me why the hotels were so important to you. Was it just about the money?"

"No," he says simply. "I have a personal connection. I—I don't want to talk about it."

My limbs feel heavy. I feel terrible that Ben won't get the hotels he obviously wants so badly. "I'm so sorry," I say. I wish I could speak to the duke and duchess, convince them Ben is a really good guy.

"Don't be. You've done more than I asked of you." He sounds so sad. I wish I could take it away.

"I could talk to them," I offer. "I could explain—"

"You don't need to think about it. I'll figure this out. It isn't your burden."

I turn and place my hand on his, trying to ignore the spark of electricity I feel every time we touch—even now. "Let them down gently."

"I'll say we're taking some time apart. I may wait until you're back in the US. Say you went home to care for"—he glances at me—"someone. And then maybe the distance takes its toll?"

"You'll have to maintain the facade without me for a few weeks, then."

He groans. "You're right. But I'm not sure I'm capable. Better to come clean straightaway. I'll say we've decided to call off the engagement. The reality of wedding planning showed us we were . . . incompatible."

The hairs on the back of my neck stand to attention at the idea I could be incompatible with Ben. I've never felt so completely compatible with anyone. But it's a good explanation. "We've had some disagreements over the long hours you work and how it wouldn't be compatible with family life," I suggest, my fingers tapping against his knuckles as I think to myself.

Ben's frown deepens. I swear I can see the faces of at least four presidents carved into the crevices of his forehead. "You think I work too much?"

"No," I say, surprised he wants my opinion.

"Because if I were married, I probably wouldn't work such long hours."

"Ben, I almost married a corporate lawyer. The fact you leave the office to sleep in your own bed makes me think you're practically unemployed."

He nods but it's not convincing. "And if I were a father, I would want to . . . you know, really spend time with my kid."

He's so adorable and perfect and wonderful. I want to squeeze him. "You gotta work harder on your *I'm a ruthless uncaring businessman* persona. It doesn't take too much to scratch the surface and get to the goo underneath."

He growls, and I pretend not to feel it in my vagina. "There's no goo in me. I just want to take an active role in my kids' lives."

I pull my hand away. "Code red, code red." I make to open the car door. "Red-blooded, rich, handsome man wants kids. I gotta go or my ovaries are going to make me do things to you that would make you blush."

The dimple is back with a vengeance. "You'd be surprised what I can cope with without any embarrassment whatsoever."

And then it's me who has to worry about covering my blush.

I clear my throat dramatically in an effort to neutralize the bubbling chemistry between us. Rip. The. Band-Aid. Off. "So, the duke and duchess. You're going to say we're splitsville. Planning the wedding for people on two continents made me realize I couldn't cope with being so far from my family."

He sinks back into his seat like a boxer who's ten rounds in and knows he's going to lose. "Sounds like a plan." His voice is dull and flat, his dismay palpable. I wish he'd tell me why the duke's hotels were so important to him, but maybe it's better he doesn't. He'll probably have to kiss that dream goodbye forever.

Even though he's reassured me I can't do anything to help, guilt still clings to me. "If it makes you feel any better, I'm going to miss being your fake fiancée."

He looks at me, his expression is so soft it's like falling back onto a blanket of freshly fallen snow. "I'm going to miss that too."

"Maybe we should . . . catch up when you've had a chance to tell them," I say. Even though I know I shouldn't wade into waters that are already too deep, I can't leave London without seeing him again.

"Just so I'm fully aware of what you've said in case I run into them. I can . . . corroborate your story." The excuse is so flimsy, I'm surprised the words don't form a puddle at my feet. When would I run into the duke and duchess?

He starts to say something but stops himself and nods. "Drinks, maybe."

"Dinner even," I say. "My treat. I'm feeling pret-ty flush right now."

He bites back a smile, and I bask in the sunlight of his amusement.

The car arrives outside the hotel, and my heart dips with disappointment. But why? This is better, isn't it? I can't let the waters get too muddied.

"Great. Not great. I mean, okay."

He pauses and smooths his hands down his trousers several times. "I have a meeting scheduled with the duke on Friday. We could do dinner Saturday night. That is, if you're not out stalking someone."

"No stalking in my plans," I say. "I'll leave that to you. I know what you're like in coffee shops."

"I'm giving up stalking. No one could compare to my most colorful stalkee—a New Yorker with a penchant for Daniel De Luca."

I want our back-and-forth to continue, but I know it can't. Not for long, anyway.

I enjoy the space he leaves in our conversations for me.

I enjoy the way he's so considered and considerate in what he says.

I enjoy being with *him*.

But our fake fairy tale is over. And real life involves me leaving the country in two weeks.

I go to open the car door, but I don't want to leave. I don't want to walk away from him. I'm not ready.

I turn to him and he's staring at me, his eyes hooded and intense, like he wants to devour me. "Wanna see the flowers you sent me?" I ask, not quite sure how to ask a man up to my hotel room.

He shakes his head and doesn't offer any further explanation.

"Oh," I say. "You probably need a good night's sleep."

He shakes his head.

"You don't need sleep?"

"I'll sleep when I'm dead," he says. "But what do you need, Tuesday? Do you need sleep?"

It's my turn to shake my head this time. What I need is him. "I'd like some of this cake you like to give out so much."

A grin curls his mouth. In record time I'm in my hotel room, my back against the door, my skirt up around my waist, and Ben's face between my legs.

As my orgasm rockets through me, I crumple around him. He scoops me up and carries me the few steps to my bed.

"You give really good cake," I whisper. I'm exhausted already.

"I like making you come," he says matter-of-factly as he pulls my dress from my body. "And I think you like it too."

Flutters of longing scatter through my body. How can I keep wanting more of this man? It's like no matter how much of him I gulp down, it doesn't quench my thirst. Is it because time is running out for us? If I lived in London, would it still be like this?

"It's okay to ask for cake, if cake is what you want," he says as he lies down next to me on his side, fully clothed. His hand skates over my skin, between my breasts and down between my legs.

"What about you?" I ask. "I just got cake. What do you want?"

He shakes his head. "At this moment, Tuesday, I'll take anything you're offering."

And at the moment, I want to give him everything.

CHAPTER TWENTY-SIX

Tonight isn't a date. Ben and I are just meeting for a debrief, but it's all I've been able to think about today. I haven't seen him this week because he's been busy at work, and I'm trying to keep my head clear so I can think straight, but the abstinence hasn't ripped the Band-Aid off. It hasn't even lifted a corner.

I'm fully dressed and sitting on my bed, waiting for him. My phone buzzes and I jump to my feet like it's someone knocking on the door.

I slide my finger up the screen and see a message from the duchess saying she's heard our news and would like the two of us to meet for tea.

I close the message, just as another one arrives from Ben, telling me he's in the lobby.

A ripple of something radiates from my stomach, pushing out and up every limb, over every inch of skin. I don't know if it's nerves or excitement, but I bite back a smile and head out the door.

There's only me and one other couple in the elevator. They're American, and from her Valley girl twang, I'd say they're Californian. Tourists. They're going to love it here. I don't feel like I'm visiting anymore. I know my corner of London too well. Plus, I've been invited to tea with a duchess, and I've hooked up with a British guy. At this point, I'm a step away from trading in my American passport.

The elevator doors open on the lobby, and I lock eyes with Ben.

He stalks over to me and kisses me on the cheek. He does it with a little too much force, like he's been impatiently waiting the entire week to kiss me and overcompensates. I step back to steady myself, and he catches my elbow.

"You okay?"

I nod. "High shoes," I say, plus the giddiness I feel whenever he's near. "Too much time wearing sneakers."

He glances down at my footwear. I've worn dark jeans and a white shirt. I've tried to keep the vibe non-date-like. The only thing that dresses it up are the shoes. High and strappy, and by the look in Ben's eye, the right choice.

"They look good on you." His voice is so thick I can almost feel it wrap around my waist.

"Thanks." We're not pretending anymore; there's no one to overhear or impress. I appreciate the compliment. I know Ben well enough to understand he doesn't give them out easily.

We head to the bar and it's weird. I've only known the man next to me for a few weeks, yet to anyone watching, we probably look like we've known each other for years. That's how it feels too.

The waiter immediately appears and I order a glass of wine. Ben orders a martini. Even his drink order speaks volumes about who he is. He doesn't give a crap what anyone else thinks, he just knows what he wants.

"Before I forget," I say, "I have something for you."

I dig into my jeans pocket and pull out the ring box.

"Are you proposing?" he asks with a smile.

I tilt my head to one side. "This is yours."

His expression doesn't change and he doesn't say anything. He just picks the box up from the table where I placed it and tucks it into his breast pocket, almost like he doesn't want anyone to notice what he's doing.

My fingers trace the space on the table where the box was, and I'm not sure if it's deliberate, but as Ben reaches for his drink, his fingers scrape mine. Our eyes lock, and I want to ask him to come back upstairs with me and spend the night in my bed.

But I don't.

I wish I knew what he was thinking. I want to ask him what he's going to do with the ring. Will he keep it for the woman he actually proposes to? I feel a little queasy at the thought. I need to distract myself. "So what happened? You spoke to the duke?"

He nods. "Yes."

"How was that?"

He pauses. It's his thinking pause, and I sit back patiently while he decides what to say.

"Overdue." Most people would look at him and say he is unreadable, but I know him well enough now to catch the slight softness in his gaze, and the way those lips sit with a little dip on the left, to know he's disappointed.

I wish I could have helped him more. But we would have actually had to be engaged and gotten married for things to have worked out.

"I'm sorry."

"Don't say that again. I should never have asked you to be part of this ridiculous charade. I lost sight of what was important."

"But getting the hotels *is* important to you," I say, leaving room for him to tell me why.

Neither of us says anything as the waiter places our appetizers in front of us. But when we're alone again, without prompting, Ben says, "I lost sight of the end goal. Without my integrity I undo everything I've worked to achieve." I'm not quite sure what he means by "end goal," but before I get a chance to ask, he says, "He asked after you." He pauses again, and I know he's trying to find exactly the right thing to say. "They're good people."

"Wonderful people," I reply. "You might still have a chance at buying the hotels. The duchess is desperate for the duke to sell. Why not to you?"

"You were there for the conversation with Nick. He wants a family man."

Isn't it better to have a man of integrity? That's what Ben is.

"I got a message from the duchess earlier." I pull my phone from my bag to see if I missed something in her text that might help. "She wants to meet me for tea."

"I'm sure you can think of an appropriate excuse."

"Maybe I should go," I suggest.

"You don't need to," he says.

If I went, maybe I could persuade her that Ben is a good man who'd do a great job running the hotels. She might influence the duke to sell to him anyway. "I can sing your praises and tell her how wonderful you are." Because that would be the truth. "How you keep your word and do exactly what you say you're going to do."

He doesn't look convinced, but there's a chance. The only problem is, I'm not sure she'll believe I've walked away from Ben. He's the entire package. Good-looking and sexy, which are two entirely different things. Jed was good-looking, but I never found him sexy. Maybe it was because we'd been together for too long. Ben exudes a confidence, a self-assurance, that has nothing to do with how handsome he is. It just rings out to anyone who listens. He's got a core of steel. He's also kind and thoughtful and one hell of a dancer. No one would leave Ben if they didn't have to.

"Tell me about your work at the bank," he says out of nowhere. Does he not want to talk about this? Is he completely heartbroken about the hotels?

"What do you mean?"

He frowns and shakes his head. "Tell me how you started there, what you hope to achieve."

"What?" But what I mean is, *Why?* We've spent countless hours together over the past few weeks, and this is the first time Ben has asked for specifics about my job. I assumed he was avoiding the topic because of how painfully boring it is, but maybe he's looking for a quick exit from the subject of the hotels.

"I'm interested. How did you get the job in the first place?"

I sit back, trying to remember how it all began. It feels like forever ago. "I was an undergrad. I was thinking about teaching, or even going to law school. Then I went with Jed to the job and internship fair on campus. I think I just got caught up in it. He said if we both got good jobs right out of college, we could move to the city. I loved Sarah Lawrence, but it felt too much like home. I wanted to get away. New York City was new and so far removed from Madison County . . . I thought maybe I'd forget about my mom. No, not my mom—just my grief, I guess. I wanted to put it behind me finally."

The server takes our plates. Ben's silence suggests he wants me to go on.

"I applied for a few internships, a couple of jobs, and the bank said yes."

"They chose you."

I shrug.

"But you could have said no if you wanted to teach," he adds.

"It was a great opportunity," I say. That's what my guidance counselor at the time had said. "The entry-level salary was more than I'd have gotten teaching, even after years in the classroom. Jed got a great offer from a big law firm, and he was so excited we'd both be starting work and earning a good salary. It made sense."

"Were you excited?" he asks.

I twirl the stem of my wineglass. "Is anyone excited about starting work? Why do you want to know all this stuff anyway?"

"You like to please people," he says like it's the explanation I've been looking for. Except that's hardly a revelation to me. But does it make me so different?

"Everyone likes to please people." It comes out a little more defensive than I intend. I like people I'm with to be happy. I've seen too much sadness. If I can help turn the dial up on their joy, why wouldn't I do that?

"Maybe," he replies. "To some extent. But do *you* ever decide what you want, or do you get bundled along with everyone else's decisions?"

His question is harsh, but I know he's not trying to hurt me.

"I said no to you the first time you asked me to be your fiancée."

He nods. "You did." He smiles, and it's so warm and genuine, it confirms my instinct that this line of inquiry comes from a place of caring and kindness. "When a perfect stranger asked you to go away with him for a weekend, you said no."

"Why do you care that I don't have the job I thought I wanted out of college?"

He nods, considering his response. "It's a good question. And I'm sorry, I'm not meaning to cause offense."

I bite my cheek at his apology. It's unexpected and it gives him a vulnerability that makes me ache.

"You're a beautiful, clever, funny woman with a strange name, Tuesday." His gaze meets mine. I feel like he wants me to say something, but I'm not sure what. "I just want you to be happy. I want you to choose something, someone, who'll make you happy. I've . . . enjoyed our time together."

I swallow, finding it difficult to listen to him describe me, and even more difficult to hear about him describing someone else in my future who will make me happy.

"I've enjoyed our time together too," I say, hoping I've found the right words.

He nods as if he's disappointed, but I'm not quite sure why. My heart rate picks up, like I'm nearing the end of an exam and there's no way I'm going to get to the final questions. I want to slow down tonight, take him back to my room. Make the next eight hours last a month. Draw out these final moments together.

"When do you go back to the US?" he asks.

I blink, trying to hit "Reset" inside me so I can figure out what day I'm on. "A week. Your health check is on Monday. That's the last thing I have to finish before Mr. Jenkins makes his decision."

"His decision about whether or not you have a job at the bank."

I frown. "Yes. That's what this whole trip to London has been about. You know that." Is he talking in code? I'm clearly missing something. I sigh. "I feel like you want to say something but you're not saying it."

"That's fair," he says. "I have lots of conflicting thoughts in my head right now, and I'm trying to work through them."

"Why don't you, you know, say them? Then I can help you sort through them."

He holds my gaze for a second, then two. "I don't want to . . . influence you."

"Influence me how? I feel like you're building up to tell me something and it's making you nervous."

"It's actually very hard to *not* tell you everything. Generally, I'm a straight shooter, but with you . . . if I make the wrong move, you'll . . ."

"Break?" I suggest. "I just came out of a ten-year relationship, and I'm feeling anything but broken."

He shakes his head. "No, I don't think you're breakable. More that if I say the wrong thing, you might . . . flee."

"Does going back to New York on my prebooked ticket count as fleeing?" I ask.

"Okay, I'm going to lay it out straight for you."

"Please."

"I like you. Really like you. And I like what we've had, physically and emotionally."

Somebody call the fire department, because my cheeks are aflame. "You thought that would make me flee?"

"No, I thought it would influence you. That you'd feel some kind of pressure . . . to please me."

"Oh, you think I'd want to please you because you said you liked me. Because I'm so used to kinda going along with things other people want?"

"Right," he says. "But I'm also conflicted because . . . Say you like me back, not because you want to please me, but because you really want me . . ."

I want you.

I want you.

I want you.

The thought fills with helium and lifts me up, up, up.

"I'm not sure where that leaves us," he continues. "We live on different continents. You have a family and a job in New York. My business is here in London."

My bubble bursts. I land on my ass with a thud.

He's right. We like each other, but so what? I'm a week away from leaving for the other side of the ocean.

"I think we can remove the hypotheticals in this situation," I say, feeling bolder. He goes to speak and I silence him with a look. "I like you," I say. "It has nothing to do with pleasing you and nearly everything to do with your gorgeous ass."

He chuckles and I mentally give myself a high five for making him laugh.

"You're not bulldozing me by confessing your feelings," I reassure him. "I like hearing it. Because I feel the same way. But as you say, it's not like these feelings are going to lead anywhere. We live three thousand miles apart."

"Right," he says, clearing his throat.

"For a long time after my mom's death, I was . . . scared to be unhappy. I ran—fled, if you like—from my grief. I did everything I could to maintain the status quo. I'd do anything that wasn't going to take me back to the dark place after my mom died. You're right. Jed, my job, my entire life in New York . . . It's all been a reaction to my mom's death." I feel so far away from the life I had before London. "London

211

changed things." *You changed things,* I think but don't say. "It's forced me to reminisce, to think about her. And it's been anything but sad. It's been . . . joyful. I feel healed."

He reaches for my hand and squeezes.

"You're right. I'm headed back stateside all too soon. But I'd really like to see you as much as possible before I go. Even if that means I'll be even more sad to leave."

"I like the Tuesday who tells me what she wants." He stands and takes my hand, encouraging me to rise.

I smile and something settles deep inside me. Like things have slotted into place somehow. I'm more me. More complete. "I like her too."

He mumbles something to the waitress and apparently the bill is taken care of without so much as a signature. We head out of the restaurant.

We stand facing each other. Is this it? I don't want to say goodbye. He'll have to say it first.

He tips my head back, pressing his lips to mine in the way he does that makes me feel like I'm made of cotton candy and clouds.

He pulls away and gazes at me like I'm the most beautiful woman he's ever seen.

"You know what I want?" I ask him. One side of myself has lost the internal battle to keep some kind of distance from Ben. I'm not sure if it's the right side or the wrong side, but I'm done trying to say no to what I want.

"Tell me."

"I want you to come upstairs with me," I say.

"Well, that's a coincidence, because that's what I want too."

CHAPTER
TWENTY-SEVEN

I'm alternating between sitting and standing at my desk. Every time I manage to sit, I get the urge to run to the exit.

"You're sure I don't need to go up there?" I ask Gail, glancing at the elevators. "Mr. Jenkins was adamant I was going to be in the meeting. I've been working on this health check for weeks."

Gail shrugs. "All I know is Ben called him and changed the meeting, so James went to him rather than the other way around."

"And he moved the meeting up by an hour? I wouldn't have gone to get my lunch if I'd known."

I spent the entire weekend with Ben. We watched two and a half Daniel De Luca movies. We went out for brunch on Sunday, where we'd had two mimosas each and eaten a truckload of avocados. He'd run me a bath that smelled just like him and then refused to join me in the water despite the tub being big enough for a dozen people. Instead, he sat on the bathroom floor and we talked about whether he should get a dog and how much I don't want to live in Brooklyn. About how he felt when he first moved into his house, and the sunsets in Madison County. When the water had reached room temperature, he'd toweled me dry, applied lotion all over me, and combed my hair. I wondered if there was a chance I could bottle our final weekend together so I could take part of it back to New York.

At no time did he mention anything about changing the time of the health check.

"Don't worry," Gail says. "James isn't going to be angry with you. You had the presentation ready for him. You briefed him. If he'd have wanted you in the meeting, he would have told me to call you, and he definitely didn't."

I sigh and lean back on my desk. "He's been up there over an hour. Is that normal?"

"For most health checks, yes. But Ben is usually too busy to spend the time. Stop worrying."

Easy for her to say. If I went back to New York without a place on the management fast track, what would I be left with?

Precisely nothing. No fiancé, no home, no job.

The elevator doors ping open and I jump to attention as Mr. Jenkins bounds in our direction. He's smiling as he passes my desk. I hold my breath, waiting for him to give me some indication of how it went.

Just as he gets to the office door, he turns. "Good job, Tuesday. You covered every base. He was very happy. You've impressed me. I'm happy to put you on the fast track."

He doesn't wait for a response before heading into his office and shutting the door.

I turn, open-mouthed, and stare at Gail.

"See? I told you not to worry," she says.

My brain feels empty, like I don't know how I'm feeling or what I'm thinking. I've been waiting for months to hear those words from Mr. Jenkins. I should feel elated. It was what I'd dreamed of when I checked in at the Daniel De Luca hotel all those weeks ago. It was the entire reason for being in London.

Having a job means my career up to this point hasn't been a waste of time. It means I can build forward from now on. It's the bit of good news I needed so badly.

I jump at the sound of Mr. Jenkins's office door opening again. He leans out. "Take the rest of the day off, Tuesday. You earned it." Then before I can protest, he goes back inside and closes the door.

"Take the day off?" I ask.

Gail narrows her eyes, like she wants to ask me a question.

"He's joking, though, right?"

"I've only seen him do it once before," Gail says. "To me, actually. I ignored him, and he was furious when he found me still at my desk. If I were you, I'd get out of here."

This day is turning into one of the most surreal I've had since landing in London. And that's saying something, given the things that have happened to me on this trip.

That was it? Health check complete. Career salvaged. Half a day off.

Then back to New York? Or Brooklyn.

And then what?

"Can I make an observation, Tuesday?" Gail asks as I slip my half-eaten croissant left over from breakfast into my bag.

If Ben was here, he'd say Gail shouldn't ask if she should make an observation, she should just do so. I smile to myself, despite my insides feeling like wet sand. "Of course you can."

"You've worked really hard while you've been here," she says.

I check my bag for my headphones and wallet. "Thanks."

"I started off in client relations," she says, and I snap my head up to meet her gaze. She shrugs. "I liked it well enough, but I didn't love it. I always knew I wanted to *love* my job."

I nod, encouraging her to go on. She's clearly got more to say.

"And then James's secretary left to get married; that's what a lot of women did in those days. They asked me to step in—again, it would never happen now. I was lucky, because I love *this* job. I can see the impact I'm having on James every day. I lighten his load, keep unnecessary nonsense from crossing his desk, make sure he doesn't spend time doing things he shouldn't. I get a real kick out of seeing the fruits of my labor."

"I can see that," I reply. "You run his office with extreme efficiency."

She gives me a confident smile. "I know. I just wonder if you think you'll get a real kick out of the management fast track."

I glance at James's office door. I would hate for him to hear our conversation.

"You don't need to worry about James. I swear, I could be out here naked with a baby gorilla on my desk and he'd never notice."

I briefly close my eyes, wanting to unsee the image that just popped into my brain.

"I've only ever worked at the bank," I say. "I've been wanting onto this fast-track program for the last five years. The pay is good and the people I work with are smart and savvy. And the bank's reputation is excellent . . ." I trail off as I remember my conversation with Ben. The job with the bank wasn't anything I was looking for when I was in college. "I don't hate it," I conclude lamely.

Gail nods. "It's different as you get older, if you have kids and a mortgage to make. This is the time to strive to do something you love. Not that you *don't hate*."

"You're saying I should give up all the work I've put in at the bank?"

"Life is long, Tuesday. Do you want to be in a job you *don't hate* for the next forty years, when there's something out there that will make your heart sing? Now's not the time to settle."

It sounds like the exact thing my mom would say to me if she were here now. She'd be able to see that although getting on the fast track is important, it's not because I love my job. It's because I've never thought about what the alternative might be. My life has been packaged in a neat box and fixed with a bow since she died; I wanted it that way. It was safe and not sad. But *not sad* isn't enough anymore. The box is too small and the ribbon is untied. I just don't know what's next.

I've never been to the coffee shop at this time of day. Even though Mr. Jenkins told me to take the rest of the day off, it feels like I'm playing hooky. It's busier than it is in the mornings. It seems the entire population of London wants coffee today.

Except Ben.

I've been glancing back at the door while I wait in line, but of course he's not here. Why would he be? But he's all I want right now.

I open my phone and check my list of Daniel De Luca sightseeing spots. I've done most of them, but there's one where he proposes to Poppy Kent I haven't gotten to yet. The scene was filmed on location at the Beale Theatre. It's kind of difficult to visit a theater without seeing a show, but that scene? It's a moment in cinema that turns the hardest heart to mush. Childhood sweethearts getting a second chance at love after a tumultuous ten years that saw Daniel's character move to Hollywood and become a famous actor. He runs into Poppy Kent's character when he's back in London taking the West End by storm. She's hauling her cello onto a bus in the rain. He stops to help and they meet again. Just thinking about that scene can bring me to tears sometimes. What would have happened to Simon and Rose if they hadn't met again by chance? If it hadn't been raining or if the bus had left slightly earlier?

I bring up details of the theater and learn there's a musical on at the moment: a remake of *Sleeping Beauty*. There are tickets available, but I can't bring myself to go on my own. But there's always something to see in London and so much I haven't done yet. I'm going to take a walk and see what I run into.

I turn left onto the street and dodge a delivery van unloading a brown paper package the size and shape of a cow into an art gallery. I'm the only one who notices. Everyone else going this way and that is focused on their day. I'm the only one floating about with no direction. No place to go.

I pass by a stationery shop, then stop and turn back. The window is crammed with every office accoutrement you could think of.

Highlighters, pens, pencils, Sharpies in every color of the rainbow, and a thousand other colors too. Swatches of paper and cards are arranged at the back like multicolored flowers, and on the right there's a tower of staplers. Hanging from the ceiling like ornaments in a Christmas scene are pads of sticky notes in every size. In between are lines of paperclips, linked together like daisy chains, spinning a little in the draft so they look like rain.

A window like this deserves attention; the shop behind a window like this deserves a browse. It's the kind of shop my mother would have lost an afternoon in.

An old-fashioned brass bell attached to the door rings as I enter. A pretty blond woman with a pixie haircut looks up from behind the counter and smiles. There's no offer of help—this is London, after all. But I don't want help. I just want to look.

There's an entire wall dedicated to pens of every type and color. I can't help but wonder if there're enough people buying pens to keep the place going. I pick out a couple and keep going to the eraser section. This place would have been heaven to teenage me, and it's still pretty exciting now, as I round the corner on thirty. Who knew I needed an iguana-shaped eraser? But I do. I pick it up and feel bad I'm leaving such true artistry behind. Along with the beautiful but expected rainbows, hearts, and butterflies, there are llamas, avocados, and even cartons of milk jostling for real estate in Eraser World.

Toward the back of the shop, things start getting serious. I feel like I'm standing in a rainbow of paper and cardstock stacked in neat, sectioned trays that look like they've been specially made for the purpose. I consider asking the woman behind the cash register whether I can bring my things from the hotel and spend the rest of my stay in London here. There's something so calming about it. My gaze hits on the stack of mount boards, which remind me of the vision boards my mom and I used to create before she died. They had all our hopes and dreams of the future on them. Usually, a future where I'd be Mrs. Daniel De Luca.

My love of vision boards died with my mom. So had my hopes and dreams about my future—marital and otherwise. Things started to rearrange themselves in my mind. I stopped hoping for things when my mom died. I just knew what I didn't want—the sadness. The grief. The loneliness.

I'd had enough of people leaving me after my mom died. I clung to Melanie, forsaking new friendships in favor of hanging tight to the one I already had. I went to college because I wanted to make my dad happy so he wouldn't have a reason to leave me. Then I hung on to Jed long past the point any love between us died. It was all in the name of the status quo—protecting myself from loss. Keeping grief at bay.

I'd been desperate not to be on my own. Desperate not to be sad.

Daniel De Luca was the last man I wanted. Until Ben.

What else have I been clinging to simply because holding on feels easier than letting go?

I pull out one of the gigantic mount boards. I know how I'm spending the rest of my day. I'm going to put together my first vision board in nearly fifteen years, full of things I choose for me. Full of my hopes and dreams for here and now, not way back when.

Before I tear the first image from a magazine, I know it won't be Daniel De Luca I put up on that board. And it won't be a job at the bank either.

CHAPTER
TWENTY-EIGHT

There are plenty of great hotels in New York, but the London Savoy might be the nicest place I've ever been. As I descend the wide steps toward the Thames Foyer, ready for my first ever afternoon tea, I can't take my eyes from the glass-domed ceiling in the middle of the room.

"Good afternoon, miss." The hostess smiles.

"I'm meeting the Duchess of Brandon." I bet I'll never tell a hostess I'm meeting a duchess again. I need to remember this moment. I just wish it was under better circumstances. I couldn't say no to the duchess's invitation to meet with her, however hard the conversation might be.

"Certainly. Let me show you to your table." I'm glad I didn't find out I could have afternoon tea during my lunch hour before now. I would have spent far too much money and eaten way too many cucumber sandwiches.

The duchess smiles like I'm a long-lost friend. After exchanging kisses on each other's cheeks, she orders champagne and we sit. She's on a chair and I'm next to her on a pretty blue sofa.

"This is so gorgeous," I say, glancing around. "And a piano." I didn't notice the music before. "How lovely."

"Don't tell my husband, but *this*, rather than any of his hotels, is my favorite place for afternoon tea in the whole of London."

I laugh. "I promise your secret is safe with me."

She smiles and then her face drops. "Tell me what's going on. I was so devastated to hear about you and Ben."

My thumb strokes my ring finger. I only wore it for a few days, but my finger still feels his ring's absence. "He's a great guy. There are no bad feelings. It's just . . . logistics," I say honestly.

"It's such a shame," she says. "I'm a people person, Tuesday. And the chemistry between you . . ." She looks at me like she's waiting for me to fill in the silence, but what can I say? "It felt so solid. Cemented. The duke and I both said how you reminded us of *us* when we were young," she finally says. "I'm so sorry if anything I said or did put too much pressure on you both."

I shake my head. I really don't want to talk about this. If she's not careful, I'm going to end up confessing everything. I really don't want to do that.

"Do you remember me telling you about my girlfriends who were matched in marriages of convenience?" she asks. "Not all of them, but many of them fell in love with their husbands, just like Lucy Madison fell in love with Daniel De Luca in *'Til Death Do We Part*."

I listen carefully, not wanting to say anything in case I give something away I shouldn't. Does she know Ben and I weren't a real couple when we came to Fairfield House?

"Have you seen that one?" she asks.

It's the only Daniel De Luca film I haven't seen. It's R-rated, and although I'd been desperate to watch it when it had been released, I wasn't sitting in a movie theater with my mom, watching sex scenes. She'd obviously felt the same way, as she never suggested we go.

"Are you sure you can't work it out?" the duchess asks. "Ben must be able to work remotely. Can't you split your time between New York and London? I have a number of friends who've done that over the years."

I smile despite my discomfort. She's not going to make this easy for me.

"Ben and I . . . There are too many obstacles to overcome."

"Did you have a fight?" she asks. "Whatever it is . . . Is it really a deal-breaker?"

"Yes. I . . . We . . . I think I rushed into a new relationship after the breakdown of my previous one." Well, that's true, at least. I need to be focused on me and my future, not pour all my attention into a new relationship.

"Just because something's quick doesn't mean it's wrong. You two are soulmates, just like George and me."

A shiver runs across my shoulders. Did she see something between us that made her feel that way?

"I don't know."

"What don't you know?" she asks. "Don't do something you're going to regret. Mark my words. I nearly left the duke before we were married. I wasn't sure I was ready for the scrutiny of being a duchess— all that expectation and whispering behind your back. There were a lot of women after George, and I wasn't sure I was up for the fight. Wasn't sure he was worth it. But he was. We've had such a happy life together. It's not been without its obstacles, let me tell you. But don't let go of things you know will make you happy, Tuesday. Promise me."

I started my vision board on Monday afternoon, but the process proved more difficult than I remembered. I've fallen out of the habit of looking at my life and thinking about what *I* want.

After the initial rush of learning I had a place on the management fast track, I couldn't muster much enthusiasm for my position at the bank. The job and Jed had been mixed up together; they seemed to come as a package deal. The job with the bank made sense when Jed and I were working toward a life together. But without that future, how does the bank fit into *my* future? I don't see how it can.

Was Ben right? Maybe I took the job at the bank because they asked me, plain and simple. Working there fit with Jed's vision of our future, and I never found a reason to say no.

"I know Ben's probably difficult, just like George is. They're both so focused and driven it can be infuriating at times. I see that in Ben.

But I also see the same attentiveness. The same devotion and care that made me say yes to George all those years ago."

My heart begins to race at her mention of the word *devotion*. It's such an evocative word, and one I feel in my gut. The bath. The French House. The flowers.

"When you find a man who loves you like Ben loves you, think twice before you walk away."

Emotion rises in me and I struggle to keep it down. I'm being ridiculous. Ben and I were never a serious thing. Undoubtedly we had sexual chemistry, but that's not love. That's not devotion. Is it?

"Ben is a good guy. I trust him. But we're from opposite sides of the world."

Our tea arrives, necessarily pausing our discussion while the waiter explains everything he's just delivered—from crustless cucumber sandwiches to the dainty mini raspberry cakes decorated with shards of dark chocolate.

I've lost my appetite.

"If you two are in love, you can make it work. I truly believe when you meet the person you're meant to be with, you can overcome any obstacles in the way."

I take a bite of my sandwich and remember our conversation back at Fairfield House. The more time passes, the more I know Jed and I weren't right together. I think he probably proposed because we'd been together so long it was awkward not to. If I had said yes for the right reasons, I'd still be running from sadness.

"Do you think you don't trust how you're feeling about Ben because of the previous relationship you mentioned?"

It's like she's reading my mind. "Yes. To an extent. I came out of my last relationship not through choice, but now that it's over, it's so clear it should have ended sooner. There's definitely a part of me that worries I lost touch with how I was actually feeling. If he hadn't ended it, I would have spent my life with a man I didn't love."

Why am I saying this to the duchess? It's all true, but that's not why I'm here. I should never have come. I should have told her I was flying back to New York and I'd see her next time I was in London. Which would be years from now, if ever.

I suck in a breath. The idea of leaving this city and not coming back is like a slice of darkness plunged into my gut. I love it here.

She nods knowingly. "Maybe you're punishing yourself for that. For women like us, it can be difficult to believe it's possible to fall in love with someone so quickly after ending another relationship. Or"—she hesitates, choosing her words carefully—"that it's possible for someone like Ben to love you."

My stomach goes into free fall. The idea of Ben being in love with me is ludicrous. But the idea of *me* being in love with *Ben* hits me like a baseball bat to the chest.

"Don't overlook the little things," she continues as I try to focus on pulling in small breaths and letting them out. "Little moments that tell you he cares. You know how busy he is, but I bet he makes time for you in the smallest of ways. That's what counts. George hates entertaining. He really doesn't enjoy it, but I love being a hostess and showing off Fairfield. He indulges me. He let me have the film crew in. We entertain new people every quarter for the weekend, like the weekend you and Ben came. He does it for me. Between you and me, I think he enjoys it more than he lets on, but I know if it were up to him, he wouldn't do it."

"The duke sounds like a wonderful man."

She places her hand in mine. "Find a way. Don't have any regrets."

Regrets. The word hangs in the air like a sonorous chime that threatens to sound forever.

She's right. I don't want regrets. I want to start building a life I've chosen, rather than living one that's been chosen for me. I don't want to be a supporting cast member anymore. I'm ready to be a star in my own movie. I just wish Ben could be my costar.

CHAPTER
TWENTY-NINE

Despite the glass of champagne I had with the duchess, I head straight to the bar when I get back to my hotel. I need to think through all the thoughts bubbling through my brain. Most importantly, if I'm in love with Ben, I need to decide whether that changes anything.

Maybe it changes everything.

I slide onto the same barstool I was on when I ran into Ben for the third time, just before I shared dinner with him and Nick. I order a martini and pull out my phone. I'm going to list out all the evidence that I'm in love with Ben, then all the reasons why I couldn't possibly be. It's the advice my dad would give me in this situation. If my mom had made it to my dating years, she would probably tell me to go watch the sun go down from a rooftop somewhere, then take a cab to Ben's place. But the DNA that came from my dad, together with all the years of following someone else's plan, won't let me do anything quite so impulsive.

Someone slides onto the stool next to me. Out of the corner of my eye, I spot the edges of a navy wool suit. My heart begins to race.

It couldn't be, could it?

I snap my head around and break out into a smile. If Ben's here, I'm no longer going to say I don't believe in signs and fate, because what else could it be?

And then I realize I'm not looking at Ben, just someone who looks an awful lot like him.

"Hi," Daniel De Luca says, lifting his glass.

He might not be Ben, but this is definitely a sign. Or maybe a message from my mom. A message that says I should still be chasing my dreams.

"I'm sorry," I say, trying to explain why I'm grinning like a fool. "I thought you were someone else."

He grins a one hundred percent movie-star smile. "I get that a lot." He thinks I don't know who he is, but of course I do.

This is the guy I was going to marry when I was fourteen years old.

This is the guy I tucked away in the back of my brain, along with my childhood and teenage hopes and dreams. Along with the grief for my mother. Along with my feelings.

But now I've allowed myself to breathe, look back, and feel. And *this guy* isn't the man who will make me happy. Not the fantasy of him. Not the reality of him.

And it's not a man like Jed either.

All I can think about is Ben.

"Can I buy you a drink?" he asks.

If my mom were still alive and Daniel De Luca slid onto a barstool next to me and offered to buy me a drink, I would have said yes before he'd gotten the words out of his mouth.

But not today.

Not now.

"Good to see you, Daniel. I'm a big fan." I drain my glass and slide off my stool. "But I've got somewhere to be."

Even if our love story is only going to last a few more days, I want to make sure I don't miss a frame.

CHAPTER THIRTY

Apparently, there's been some kind of power outage at Coffee Confide in Me, and there is no coffee. It's the reason I'm in line at the place down the street, trying to not judge the way the barista seems to be moving at a snail's pace. It's only been a few weeks, but I'm going to miss Coffee Confide in Me as much as I'm going to miss seeing red buses everywhere. I can't believe it's my last weekend in London. I fly back to New York tomorrow.

I sigh at the sloth-like movement of the line and jump when someone behind me taps me on the shoulder. I'm full New Yorker furious when I spin around . . . and come face-to-face with Ben.

"Hey, Wednesday."

His dimple undoes me. I go from furious to grinning like a puppy on ecstasy. Humming *The Addams Family* theme tune, I click my fingers twice. The corner of Ben's mouth turns up and he shakes his head.

"Did you finish your packing?"

I'd left Ben's place last night to come back to the hotel and pack. And maybe because the more time I spend with him, the more I worry about how difficult I'll find it to leave.

Even though I saw him less than twelve hours ago, it's so good to see him, I ache inside. "Apparently it's not just me stalking people this morning."

"Last night, I found myself watching the end of the Daniel De Luca movie we started together," he says. "The one where he agrees to marry his boss for a green card. I thought finding you here was more . . . in keeping with our theme."

"Our theme?"

"Yeah, I figure our theme is Daniel De Luca romantic comedy tropes. There are so many tropes between us, I can't keep count. You're new in town—like De Luca in *This Old Town*. I'm a grumpy billionaire, like the one he plays in *Love Me Like a Boss*. Apparently that's a thing."

"Yeah. That's definitely a thing." I grin. *This guy.* "That's two."

"Mistaken identity—like in *What a Feeling*. You thought I was Daniel De Luca. You stepped on my toe in the queue at the coffee shop—that's number four."

"Standing in line at a coffee shop definitely isn't a trope."

He narrows his eyes with a look that says, *Don't argue with me. I know I'm right.* "I'm sure there was one. Then of course, fake engagement."

"My favorite."

"The primary trope in our movie."

"We're in a movie now?"

"Isn't everyone the star of their own movie?"

"I don't know." I'm not sure I have been up until now.

"But!" He holds up a finger. "We've missed an important one. I think we need to put it right."

"Okay. What did we miss?"

"Holiday romance."

"But it's not Christmas."

He rolls his eyes. "Americans. 'Vacation romance,' then, if you insist."

He's put a lot of effort into his argument, which I have to admit is compelling. "So how do you suggest we put it right?"

The corner of his mouth twitches. "I'm glad you asked. Turns out I have a light day at work. You're new in town, only here for another day. Thought you might want a tour guide."

Warmth swirls in my belly. The duchess's reminder about it being the small things that count plays in a loop in my head. "Nothing I want more than a grumpy billionaire tour guide."

The line inches forward and we shuffle along.

"What's on your list that you haven't seen yet? St. Paul's, Westminster Abbey, The Tower of London?"

I wince. "I haven't seen any of them."

"What have you seen?" He groans. "Don't tell me—Green Park where Daniel first met Julia Alice in *Love Me Like a Boss*, and the lobby of the hotel where he's staying while he films his latest movie. It sounds like you haven't seen the most beautiful, most important things London has to offer. Well, I'm here to show you."

"It's very sweet of you."

"I'm not sweet."

"I beg to differ."

"Aha, I see what you're doing," he says. "You're making sure we've covered enemies to lovers, like in *A Duchess for a Duke*. But you see, I'll never be your enemy." He looks me straight in the eye, and his gaze warms me from the inside out.

We finally reach the start of the line and place our coffee orders. I play it safe with a grande latte with a caramel shot, and he insists on ordering a medium filter coffee. Whatever.

"So what now?" I ask. "Cue montage of us enjoying ourselves at various London landmarks?"

"I guess. Where do you want to start?"

"With a plot twist," I reply.

"What do you have in mind?"

"I want to take things to the next level."

The dimple is back. I don't even mind that I can tell exactly what's on Ben's mind—and it isn't PG. "I'm all about the next level."

"Bring your boring coffee and come with me."

Ben's growling as we climb out of the car and stand in front of The Fairfield Hotel. Black wrought-iron railings fence the almost too-green hedges around the outside of the building, so immaculate it looks like they were trimmed with nail scissors. Three flags fly over the entrance. One is the British flag, another American, and another in the middle reads *The Fairfield Hotel* in scrolling script. A doorman waits for incoming guests at the top of eight marble steps clad with red carpet. He's dressed smartly in a gray coat, and he's spotted us but can't decide whether we're coming in.

Apparently, neither have we.

"When was this place even built?" I ask. I glance up at the redbrick building and gargoyles stare back.

"Eighteen sixty-three," he says without missing a beat. Why would he know that? What is it with this place? Why is it so important to him? "It's a nice example of Gothic Revival."

I know stuff. I went to college. I can hold my own in a room full of suits when they're discussing whether interest rates are going to tank the market. But even I have to admit, I don't have a clue what he's talking about. "Gothic Revival, huh?"

"Of course the Palace of Westminster or Tower Bridge are more famous examples, but Sir William Henry Barlow didn't do a bad job here."

Oh, we're talking architecture. He's clearly done his research, but I have a feeling a love of architecture isn't the reason Ben wants to own this hotel.

"Show me around," I say. "I want to see the place that meant you gave a near-perfect stranger thirty thousand dollars."

"No," he snaps. "Is that why you brought me here? You want to go inside?"

"We're sightseeing. This is a sight. I want to see it."

"It's a hotel, Tuesday."

"But it's important to you. And it's been the reason for a lot of my experiences here in the UK. You've told me I'm bad at asking for what

I want, so I'm telling you as clear as day: I want you to show me the hotel." We've spent so much of our time together over the past weeks making decisions and taking steps connected to this hotel. I want to know what's so special about the place.

He folds his arms and stands rooted to the spot.

"Come on. Let's get a coffee." I dump my coffee in the trash and walk toward the entrance.

"We've just had a coffee." The softness in his eyes has completely gone, and his expression is bordering on furious.

"Champagne, then," I say. When he still doesn't budge, I add, "Tell me why this place matters to you."

"I buy and run profitable businesses. That's what I do." His walls are up, his windows are shuttered.

But I'm not giving in.

"I know it's more than that."

Silence wraps itself around the two of us, binding us in a bubble in the middle of a bustling street in Knightsbridge.

He hasn't left. He's still standing here next to me. I'm taking that as a win.

"So what if it is?" he asks eventually. "What does it matter to you?"

It's a good challenge, and I don't have an immediate answer. "I want to understand. Then I want to brainstorm with you and come up with a different plan for you to get it."

Ben laughs, but it's an empty sound that makes my ribs rattle. He checks his watch. "And that will take us until lunchtime. Shall we then try and broker world peace in time for dinner?"

"I'm serious," I say, a little frustrated with his resistance. What's he hiding? "I'm new in town, remember? I get to choose which sights we see. I'm telling you what I want, Ben. Don't you want to give it to me?"

"And what about you?" he asks. "Why don't we figure out the direction your life is taking? Maybe that's what should occupy us this afternoon."

I tilt my head and hold out my hand. "If you follow through with The Fairfield, you can help me compile my vision board."

"Your what?"

"My plan for my future. I've been thinking about what you said. I think I've just been going along the path of least resistance for a long time. Prioritizing other people's needs. Acting out of fear instead of passion. I want that to change. I'm trying to figure out what exactly I want."

"Oh, your personal life plan." He takes my hand, and the sparks of electricity jump between us. "Deal."

At the top of the stairs, through the entrance, is a lobby that's larger than looks possible from the outside. There's a huge chandelier hanging from the ceiling and a round table beneath it, covered in vases of every shape and size, holding white lilies and orchids.

I glance over at Ben to find him stopped, facing a battered old oak desk that looks a little out of place in the lobby of such a grand hotel.

A member of staff appears out of nowhere. "I see you're admiring our fine concierge desk, sir," the short, blond-haired woman says. "We're very proud of that desk. It was the desk Sir Winston Churchill sat behind at Downing Street when he was prime minister."

Ben nods slowly. To the casual observer, it might look like he's interested in what she's saying, but I know him better. He already knows who the desk belonged to. Is that why he wants this hotel? He doesn't strike me as a man who collects trinkets, but maybe he's a Churchill fanatic.

"We're here to get a coffee," he explains. The woman leads us toward the back of the room, to the sun lounge.

I glance around, trying to find more clues about Ben's fascination with this place. Meanwhile, he buries himself in the menu.

"Is it the desk?" I ask. "Is that why you want the hotel?"

"Partly," he answers, which, of course, is entirely infuriating. He's offering me a breadcrumb when I want the whole loaf and a slab of butter.

The waiter appears with our coffees. "I'd like to order the strawberry shortcake," Ben says as the waiter sets down my cup in front of me. "Would you like anything?" he asks.

I shake my head, then remember Ben saying something about strawberry shortcake when we were first getting to know each other. I change my mind. "Actually, make that two." Ben isn't a guy who indulges in dessert. Even when we went to stay with the duke and duchess, he never ate more than a mouthful. If he's ordering the strawberry shortcake, I can't pass up the opportunity. Even if it is only just past nine a.m.

"Certainly, sir, miss. I'll just get that."

"Strawberry shortcake?" I ask.

He shrugs but doesn't give any more away.

"You like this room?" I ask. "Any more items of furniture that catch your eye?"

"It's a fine room, but not my favorite."

I try the silence thing, hoping he'll answer the question that hangs in the air: *So what is your favorite, then?* But he doesn't. He sips his coffee, staring out at the empty chairs.

"What do you think they're talking about?" I nod over to two men in suits at the other end of the lounge.

"Maybe they're asking each other what *we're* talking about."

I laugh. "So you already knew about that desk, didn't you?"

Ben nods.

"You've been here before?"

He nods again as he sets his coffee down on its saucer.

"Did you use to work here?" I ask. Is that what this is? Some kind of weird score settling?

"My dad worked here," he says finally. "For thirty-five years."

It's like I've cracked the world in two and molten lava is flooding out. I'm not quite sure what to do.

"That's a long time," I say, like I'm trying to avoid stepping on anything hot. "He must have enjoyed it."

"He loved it. He loved people." He shoots me a look that says, *I know what you're going to say before you say it, so save your breath.*

I shrug. I'm not going to make some lame joke about how the apple falls so far from the tree it thinks it's an elephant. It's not a time for telling jokes. "Way too easy."

"That was his desk. It *is* his desk, as far as I'm concerned."

"That's why you want the hotel? For the desk?"

"Not just the desk. While he worked here and even after, when he retired, he'd regale us with stories from the hotel. The rich and famous who crossed the threshold. The waiters who made more money than the managers. The chefs screaming at each other. His mother, my grandmother, was Irish, and you could tell by the way he could—and sometimes still can—tell a story. He could capture the attention of Wembley Stadium. He still has a magnetism about him. A charm. He can pull people in and keep them entertained for hours. This hotel is so much a part of him. And a part of him and me that . . ." His voice cracks. It's like watching steel turn to cotton.

I slide my hand over his, and he lets me provide that small bit of comfort.

"There's a lot of memories here," he continues. "The way he proudly brought me to visit the place on his days off. The way I'd sit under that desk—that he was so proud to work behind—during school holidays when my mother was ill. I'd sit cross-legged by his feet and listen to him arranging trips, charming restaurants for reservations, researching destinations and guest preferences. He took his work tremendously seriously. He was my inspiration." His voice doesn't crack this time, but only just.

"Did anyone know you were under the desk?"

He smiles. "The staff all knew. Apart from the manager. But never the guests. I'd sit so quietly while he spoke with people. I always had a book with me, and Dad had a pocket torch as well as a Swiss Army knife he'd charge me with while I was there. But I didn't read much. I was too fascinated with everything going on. Every now and then, when Dad knew it was going to be particularly busy, housekeeping would smuggle me into one of the guest rooms and put the TV on. Someone always brought me a plate of strawberry shortcake."

This man is so special.

"I bet you know every room in this place."

"Like the back of my hand."

"So that's why you want it? To relive the memories?"

Ben sighs and shakes his head. "My dad was—is—a clever man, but his father before him was a farmer. They came to England for a better life. For their children to have a better life. And Dad had a life his father before him could never have dreamed of. My father's wages weren't generous, but in summer months, wealthy Arabs flock to London to avoid the heat of the Middle East. It still happens now. The tips would flood in like rain. We lived a comfortable life. But he could have done so much more if he'd had the opportunity. I'd overhear him talk to my mum about what he'd do with the hotel if he was in charge. The small changes he would make. The large shifts all the staff agreed on. He was on the ground. He knew what he was talking about."

It's like when a painter starts on a canvas—there's no hint of what the picture will look like in the end. But Ben has just put down his palate knife, and everything has become clear. I understand him so much better now. "You want a chance to do all the things your dad talked about."

He nods. "He's older now. Too old to come back. He has joint pain, probably from being on his feet so much over the years. And his memory sometimes fails him. He's having some tests. They think it might be the early stages of dementia. I want to show him, before it's too late, that his hard work laid the foundations for what I've been able to achieve. I don't know a better way to do that than buying this hotel and making all the changes he wanted to make."

My throat tightens and I can barely get my words out. "I think you're wonderful."

Ben is not some tropey, grumpy billionaire. He's real and sweet and loyal and so, so wonderful. I can't bear to think what would have happened if I hadn't mistaken him for Daniel De Luca. If I had never gotten to know him.

"Have you ever thought about telling the duke the truth about why you want the hotels?" Surely anyone would be moved by Ben's story.

Ben shakes his head. "He's focused on maintaining his legacy. The financials have to be sound. He needs to have confidence that if he sells, the person is going to be able to continue what he started."

"Is it possible to have both? You can prove to him that you meet his competence criteria, that you understand the financial aspects of the hotel, *and* that you have a truly personal connection to the business he built. You don't even need to buy all of them. Why not see if he'll just sell you *this* location?"

He takes his time, and I appreciate him listening to me. He doesn't dismiss me because he's the billionaire and I'm just some random American who works at a bank. He respects me enough to consider what I'm saying.

"Last time we spoke, he pretty much closed the door. He said he wasn't ready to divest. And I'm not surprised. Our engagement may have even worked against me. Maybe he sees me as someone who can't hold on to what's valuable." My heart inches higher in my chest at his words, at the thought I might be valuable to him. "Serves me right for lying." He shuts his eyes. "I should never have been so dishonest. That's not how my father raised me."

"No, but isn't it worth telling him about your family connection to The Fairfield?"

"He might see it as attempted manipulation."

"It's the truth, Ben."

"Tell me more about your vision boards." He's not subtle when he wants to change the subject, but I can't blame him. He didn't even know I was going to bring him here today. "What does that involve?"

"It's fun. Just grab a bunch of magazines, some card stock and glue, and we're off." I don't tell him I've already wasted an afternoon with a bunch of magazines and didn't come up with anything. I ended up lying on my bed, scrolling through photographs of my time in London.

"You create your vision for the future?"

"Exactly. I used to do them all the time before my mom died. Since then, I lost sight of what I want my future to look like. I've focused too much on everyone else."

"Ben? Tuesday?" I snap my head around to find the duchess coming toward us. "I didn't expect to see you here. Together." She's beaming. I can tell she's hoping this means we've reconciled. For real.

"Darling," she calls. I follow her gaze and spot the duke having a conversation with someone at the entrance to the lounge.

He breaks it off when he sees us.

We stand and greet them like old friends, and they join us in seats around the low table in front of the sofa we're sitting on.

"We didn't expect to see you either," I say.

The duchess orders tea for her and the duke. After we confirm we don't need anything, she asks, "What are you doing here of all places?"

I glance at Ben. He's not going to tell them, and I can't help but think they would be entirely charmed, knowing Ben's connection to this place.

"Do you mind if I tell them?" I ask.

Ben mumbles but I make out, "If you must."

"Ben's father worked here for thirty-five years. Ben has such wonderful memories of the place, I insisted he bring me to see where his ambition was born."

"Your father worked here?" the duchess asks. "How long ago?"

"He retired just under ten years ago," Ben replies.

"His name?" the duke asks, looking puzzled.

"Harry. Harry Kelley."

The duchess raises her hands. "You're Harry Kelley's son? We love Harry! How is he?"

Ben pushes his hands down his thighs. "Very well. Thank you for asking."

"He was a very good man," the duke says.

Ben clears his throat. "Still is, sir. The best of men."

"Ben was just sharing that his dad would smuggle him into the hotel to sit under the Churchill desk for the day while he worked."

The duchess roars with laughter. "Did you ever know that, George?"

"Certainly not, and neither did my managers. I'm sure we would have been in breach of at least a dozen laws. But GMs never have a clue what's going on with their staff. I've always said it."

"He didn't do any harm. It was years ago," the duchess says.

"It's probably still happening. People think owning hotels is a walk in the park. Let me tell you, it's a headache."

"So that's why you want to own these hotels?" the duchess asks Ben, ignoring her husband's grumbling.

Ben slides his hands down his legs again. "Partly. I'm sentimental. Tuesday's right—this place is where my business brain was born. And it would mean a lot to my father."

I don't miss the look exchanged between the duke and duchess, but nothing more is said.

"And the two of you being here together," the duchess says. "Can I hope for a reconciliation?"

Neither of us says anything, but I feel Ben's gaze on me.

The duchess leans back. "You two are meant to be. You're going to figure it out. I just know it."

She believes that just like in all Daniel De Luca's romantic comedies, there's going to be a happy ending for us. Our story might be tropey, but I don't see how everything ends wrapped in a bow.

Even if a happily-ever-after with Ben is definitely on my vision board.

CHAPTER
THIRTY-ONE

London doesn't feel like home; it just feels like it *could* be home. I've loved it so much. This city—the whole trip—was exactly what I needed. I can't believe I'm thirty minutes away from taking a cab to the airport to go back to New York. I spent my final night with Ben last night, and we left it how we always leave it—like we'll see each other in a couple of hours. Except this time, it was the last time.

Just enough time to get one final coffee from Coffee Confide in Me. There's only one person in line, and they've moved to a table by the time I reach Ginny with the bright-red hair.

"Hey," Ginny says. "Venti cap with an extra shot, half almond milk, half oat milk, a shot of caramel, extra foam, and cinnamon sprinkles?"

"Yes, please. My last one before I leave to go back to New York."

"Oh, bummer. I'm going to miss torturing the baristas with your order."

The British aren't cold and stuck-up. They're just not interested in strangers. They're private more than rude, and I've grown rather fond of their idiosyncrasies.

Someone taps me on the shoulder, and I know before I spin around who it is. Who else could it be?

"Hey," I say, coming face-to-face with Ben. His hair has grown since he last had it cut, just before we went to Fairfield for the weekend. The extra length suits him. It hits me that I won't get to see how it curls over at the front when it gets long like this anymore.

"Ending as you began: Ginny sneering at your New York coffee order." Ginny? He knows her name? He bends to kiss me on the cheek, and it sends shivers across my body. "You look beautiful."

"Gets me every time," Ginny says. "Got your filter coffee coming right up, handsome."

Ben drops a twenty-pound note on the counter, and we move to the pickup station.

"Just like old times, right?" I ask.

"I thought meeting you here was a proper ending—one you'd get in a Daniel De Luca movie. Finishing at the beginning, but forever changed."

"Except we don't know if you're going to buy the hotels. And I haven't really figured out what I want out of my life other than an apartment that looks like your house."

He grins. "It will all become clear when they roll credits over still images of me standing in front of Fairfield and you killing it at whatever you end up doing."

"You really have been doing your research," I say. The way Ben has embraced Daniel De Luca's back catalog is impressive. "You have me to thank for broadening your horizons."

I expect to see the dimple, but instead Ben looks at me intensely, as if I've just told him the location of the Holy Grail and he needs to commit the coordinates to memory. "You have no idea," he whispers, then snakes his arms around my waist. "Actually, I have news on at least part of our . . . What would you call it . . . epilogue?"

"Go on," I say, gripped by how his story might play out.

"The duke's assistant called me last night. He wants to see me to talk about Castles and Palaces."

"Wait, what? Are you serious?!"

"I'm not getting my hopes up. But it's progress. Progress I have you to thank for."

"I'm feeling a little smug right now. I'm earning that money you insisted I take."

"You did that already," he says.

I'll miss him, his dimple, and the way it always feels like the Fourth of July when he touches me. I'll miss the way he listens to me without making up his mind before I've finished what I have to say. I like the way he clearly took time off work to spend a day with me earlier in the week, even though we probably won't see each other again. And I like the fact he finally let me in.

"I have a good feeling about you and the duke. I think he sees the man you are under your gruff exterior."

He closes his eyes in a long blink, like he's enduring the pain of a memory or something, but he doesn't say anything.

"You'll have to keep me posted on whether you get to hide under that desk again," I say, trying to lift the mood.

"Who would I be hiding from? Some American woman who thinks I'm a movie star?"

Jealousy blooms in my chest and I frown. "Yes! I definitely want to be the only one of those in your life."

Our coffees are delivered to the counter. Ben releases me, we collect our cups, and head out.

"Thanks, Ginny," I call over my shoulder. "See you around."

Outside on the street, Ben's car waits. "I've had your luggage put in the back. My driver will take you to the airport."

It's the little things, the voice in my head whispers.

"That's very sweet of you, Ben. Are you sure? How will you get back to the office?"

"I'll take the bus."

I burst out laughing. He smiles, and I don't know if it's at his own joke or because he likes my laugh.

"Let me know you're home safe."

I nod. "Absolutely. I'm going to take some time to figure out next steps."

He smiles, steps forward, and kisses me on the forehead.

"If you're ever in New York," I say.

"Is that where you'll be?" he asks. "We never got to do your vision board."

I shrug.

He reaches out, swipes his thumb over my cheekbone. "Time ran out . . ."

For what? The vision board? Me in London? Us? "It's a work in progress."

Our gazes lock, and it feels like he wants to say something. But what can he possibly say? That he's going to come to New York to compile my vision board with me? That he wants me to stay?

"Still planning to go back to your job with the bank?" he asks.

"It's not where my heart is, but I need time to figure stuff out. Bills to pay and all that."

"Does that mean you might not end up in New York?"

I narrow my eyes, trying to figure out what, exactly, he's asking me. "I haven't . . . Everything's in New York . . ." My voice trails toward the end of the sentence. I don't have an apartment in New York. Or a job that I actually want. And my friendship circle is . . . I thought it was tight, but the only person I've heard from more than once since I got on a plane is Melanie, and we're ride or die no matter where I am in the world. It wouldn't matter if I lived in Iceland—Mel and I would still be close.

"Maybe there's a guy in New York who needs a pretend fiancée?" I take a half step back from him. "I'm pretty good at that. Would you write me a reference?"

Ben catches my hand and presses it to his lips. "I'm not sure I like that idea. Fake fiancée is our trope."

"Don't forget holiday romance."

He pulls me close and presses his lips to mine. His tongue is searching and urgent, and I'm this close to pulling the buttons from his shirt and feeling his hot, tight skin against mine. I can feel his heat as he holds me against him, the rise and fall of his chest, the *boom, boom, boom* of his heartbeat echoing mine. It feels so warm and right, like this is exactly where I should be.

Without warning, he steps back and opens the passenger door.

I want to slam it shut and jump into his arms. But life isn't a fairy tale. And this isn't where my story ends.

I get into the car and wind down the window.

"What are we doing?" he asks as our eyes meet.

"Saying goodbye?" I suggest.

He looks away. I know I've said the wrong thing, but I don't know how to put it right. What could I say that would make this moment okay?

London has been a balm to my broken heart. The perfect escape, the most exciting, vibrant, uplifting place to lick my wounds. Now I have to go back to real life. I have to figure out where my career goes from here, where I'm going to live and who I am when I'm not engaged to Jed. Ben has made me realize my life, and maybe my past, are just the previews; I'm about to start living the main feature.

He shakes his head but doesn't say anything. I want to reach for him, but I know I can't. If I do, I might never leave.

I swallow, trying to stop my throat constricting. It's impossible I'm this upset. I can't let myself cry over the end of a vacation romance when I barely shed tears over my fiancé dumping me after ten years. I want to suggest maybe I call Ben or he comes to visit and we can do this again, only in New York—not continuing things, just repeating them. But it's just prolonging the agony. We're not going to end up together, so we should skip to the end right now instead of drawing things out.

Then I can focus on my future.

"It's been a blast," I say, trying to keep my voice steady.

"Bye, Thursday."

"Now promise me you won't swap that billionaire status for stand-up comedy."

We grin like we're going to see each other next week, rather than walk away from each other for good. But that's Ben: He makes me smile, no matter what.

Ben nods. "I still think you're lovely."

"I still think you're wonderful."

He turns and walks away. It's like clouds have filled the sky, blocking out the warmth of the sun. I feel the chill right down to my bones.

CHAPTER
THIRTY-TWO

I'm the second person at the gate. I wasn't deliberately rushing through the terminal; I was just too busy thinking to go slow. About London. About the bank. About Ben. I didn't get pulled in by the perfume and keepsakes in duty-free. I already have memories more valuable than anything I can buy, and my Ralph Lauren wardrobe is a souvenir in itself.

I take my boarding pass from my bag. LHR: JFK. Six letters, three thousand miles apart. I came to London scared to lose my job, and now I'm leaving, scared to keep it. Well, not scared, exactly, but I know it's not the career I want going forward. I didn't really choose my job at the bank. I didn't really choose Jed. Or our apartment, or really anything in my life before coming to London.

I stuff my boarding pass into my pocket and pull up the picture of my partially completed vision board.

There are plenty of blank spaces on the picture—gaps to fill among the images of a beautiful apartment, people having fun, and orange-pink sunsets. There are also images of airplanes. This trip to London has fed my soul. I had no idea how undernourished I'd been until coming here, or how soul-affirming I'd find international travel. I want to see other places on the planet. Experience new things.

A picture of Daniel De Luca made it there, too, albeit smaller than it was on my last vision board. After all, if it hadn't been for him, London wouldn't have been quite the same.

And if I squint, it looks like Ben.

My heart falls through my chest.

And then I know.

I know the person I want standing next to me when I bring this vision for the future to life.

Ben. I want Ben.

I glance down the wide corridor, flanked on one side with windows overlooking parked planes, the other side with seats. People are swarming toward the gate. We're all headed to the same destination.

Except I don't want to go where everyone else is going.

In *Sunshine on a Rainy Day*, Daniel De Luca turns up at the airport and proposes to Jennifer Elm.

But that's not my story with Ben. We've been engaged, even if it was fake. And I know he's not coming to the airport. He could have asked me to stay many times before this moment, and he didn't. There were plenty of opportunities for him to confess his feelings for me, and he didn't act on any of them. Then again, neither did I. *Lovely* and *wonderful* were as close as we got.

I let the realization sink in like pebbles resting on a riverbed. If he wanted me, he'd have told me, right?

Except I never told him either. He knew I'd spent my life being carried along by other people's decisions. Other people's desires.

Maybe he was waiting for me to choose him for myself.

Adrenaline shoots through my body and I jump to my feet. I'm not ready to go home. I don't even know where home is anymore. But I'm starting to understand it's nowhere Ben isn't.

My relationship with Ben deserves a feature-film ending. He's not just going to wave me off in his sedan. We need grand gestures or one of us running after the other in a rainstorm.

It's me who should be barefoot. I'm the hero in this tale.

Pulling my carry-on, I chase down the corridors into the throng coming toward me. The old me would have been carried along by the flow of people, but I'm not the old me anymore. I want to go in the opposite direction.

I have no idea whether or not it's possible to exit the airport once you pass security. It can't be physically impossible. All the people who work in the shops and the restaurants in the terminal don't live here. They must get out at some point. Maybe I'll have to sneak through a staff exit. I charge left and find an elevator. Without thinking, I punch the call button, the doors open and I get in.

Eventually, I find my way to passport control.

It's like I just landed.

I expect to be stopped at some point—to be asked where I came from—but no one bothers me. Everyone's more interested in something else. I line up, and when it's my turn to face the immigration officer, he doesn't even notice I've only exited the country an hour ago.

"Is your trip business or pleasure?" he asks.

"It's personal," I reply.

"When are you leaving?"

I'm not about to tell him that it depends on how Ben reacts when he sees me.

"Two days," I blurt out. By then I'll know what I'm doing.

He stamps my passport and hands it back to me.

"Thank you," I say a little too effusively. I speed off before he can detain me for acting suspiciously.

Now what?

Time for a movie-star ending.

CHAPTER THIRTY-THREE

I have no plan, no place to stay, and I've just officially missed my flight back to New York.

I'm standing in front of Coffee Confide in Me, wondering whether I should have gone right to his house or his office.

I'm not thinking straight. I don't know what I'm supposed to do next.

A crack of thunder makes my bones rattle, and I look up, only to be splattered in the face by the beginnings of a rainstorm. I suppose the universe has the set right. A rainstorm makes total sense. I'm just missing a love interest.

I need another cab to take me to his office. I should call him to ask where he is. He could be in a meeting. Maybe I should be practical and rebook a room at the hotel.

I pull out my phone. I start to type.

Where are you?

I delete it.

Do you want a coffee?

I delete it.

Can we meet?

I delete it.

Damn it. Grand gestures weren't meant to be made via text.

The rain is coming harder now, and I glance up and around to see if Coffee Confide in Me or the hotel is my best chance of shelter.

As it turns out, the answer is neither. Because Ben is coming toward me. He doesn't see me at first. He's looking down at his phone, completely ignoring the rain.

Then suddenly he stops and looks up, right at me, as if he knew I was here all along.

He continues toward me until we're just a foot apart, neither of us speaking. He doesn't look confused, like he bundled me into his car a few hours ago and sent me back to New York, only to have me reappear on the sidewalk. It's like he expected me to be here all along.

"Hey," he says finally.

"I choose you," I reply.

He closes his eyes in a long blink, and I exhale. We're right where we're meant to be.

"For so long, I've been the heroine's best friend. Best supporting actress. Or the lead of the subplot. You saw it before I did. I've been going along with everyone else's story. It's time to be the lead in my own."

He still doesn't speak, but I understand at my core why. It's for the most selfless reason: He doesn't want to influence me. I need to pick. I need to know what I want and ask for it. He wants me to have the life I choose.

"I pick you. I want you. I know this was just supposed to be a vacation romance, but I've never felt for anyone what I feel for you. And for the first time, I'm not scared of losing someone. I'm scared of not living my life with them.

"I'm in love with you, Ben. Be with me. Be mine."

I step toward him and feel him exhale, his body nearing mine with every second.

"You don't know how long I've waited, how much I've held back, how hard I've had to work to try not to love you," he says, circling his arms around my waist.

My heart lifts in my chest. I slide my fingers up to his jaw, drawing his lips down to mine.

"Nothing worked. I fell in love with you anyway," he says.

His words carve into my soul. I feel a sense of belonging I've never felt with anyone. But I've seen it before, between my parents. They were soulmates—each other's happily-ever-after.

And now, with a little guidance from my mom and a couple of nudges from Daniel De Luca, I've found mine.

"We're in a rainstorm," I say. "I'm not barefoot, but I'll happily toss my shoes if it will show you how much I want you."

"I'm not going anywhere for you to come after me," Ben says. "And honestly, I can't think of anything less romantic than being barefoot in this city. Keep the shoes on, Monday Morning."

He releases me and pulls out a ring box from his suit pocket.

"Is that . . . ?"

"I never returned it," he says. "I hoped you'd be back to claim it."

My apple-pie smile shines up at him.

"You've felt like mine since the first time you slipped on this ring. It was like an internal earthquake rattled through me, and I've never recovered from the seismic shift you created. And I don't want to. I want to eat popcorn and watch movies in bed with you. I want to waltz around rose gardens. I want to hold hands in the back of taxis, build a swimming pool, have a family. I want to do life with you.

"Marry me. For real this time."

It's the traditional ending for a very untraditional love story.

"I want you to be my leading man forever. Not because you asked me, but because I want to marry you more than I've ever wanted to do anything. Ever."

"Finally, you figured it out."

"That you're marriage material?" I ask.

"What you want."

I nod. "And that's you."

The thunder cracks above us again, and Ben slides the ring on my finger, cups my face in his hands, and kisses me like the hero he is.

And for the final camera shot in our movie, I kiss him back.

Roll credits.

EPILOGUE—ALMOST ONE YEAR LATER

There are a thousand people in the hotel suite, and I have no clue what at least half of them are doing. How did this wedding get so complicated? I just needed a dress and a ring. Maybe some flowers. Things have gotten a little out of hand. None of it is my doing. Ben and I met with the wedding planner, and every time she suggested something, Ben said yes to it. And she suggested a lot of things.

Even though I'd have been happy to go a different, much simpler route, I kind of like that Ben's so completely into it. Strike that. I *love* that he's so completely into it. If I didn't, I wouldn't have gone along with our ever-expanding plans, and Ben wouldn't have wanted me to. Who'd have thought my haughty Brit would turn to mush so easily?

I smile at myself in the mirror, and Meera, the makeup artist, pauses in a silent admonishment. I drop my smile.

"Nearly done," she says.

"Then it's my turn," Melanie says. "And I'm going to take until three days after the wedding is over because of this." Yet again, she points to a zit on her forehead. "Do you have prosthetics? Like, could you put a layer of rubber over it to cover it up? Or maybe we should lean into it and make a feature of it?"

Meera laughs as my phone goes off.

It's Ben.

Meera and Melanie continue to talk about her zit, and I send up a silent prayer that she doesn't end up convincing Meera to cover it up with a picture of Captain America or something. I'm not concerned with a fancy wedding, but I'd really like a good picture of me, Melanie, and Ben.

"Are we allowed to speak?" I ask as I pick up the call.

"We're allowed to do whatever we want. It's our wedding." Ben is steadfast in his independence and equally committed to me having *my* independence. That doesn't mean he won't stand in front of a bus for me; I know he would. And I for him. I love him wildly. I love him fiercely.

I'll love him forever.

Life feels so different from what it was before Ben. It feels like the sun shines a little brighter because I have my biggest champion right next to me. The past hasn't been buried, but has been left in the past.

The door to the suite swings open, and my dad appears, followed by three people carrying flowers.

Dad's already got his boutonniere. But there's my bouquet, plus Melanie's and Elizabeth's. Nick's wife has become one of my closest friends. She's really good at translating American to British and vice versa—a much-needed skill I'm happy to take advantage of. Thanks to her, I don't use the term "fanny pack" anymore.

"How is everything going down there?" I ask Ben.

"All that's missing is you."

My heart inches higher in my chest. "I miss you."

"Same."

"After today you get to have me forever, so there's that."

I can hear his smile at the end of the line. I get these calls every day. He doesn't call to say anything in particular, just to hear my voice. Just to connect. These little moments have become the best parts of my day. The way he can't go more than a few hours before checking in is one of my favorite things about him. That and his nice ass.

"The duke gave me some written directions to our honeymoon destination."

"Google Maps doesn't work?" I ask.

"Apparently not. The route is through private land."

Scotland might not be the first choice of honeymoon for a lot of married couples, but when the duke and duchess offered their place there for our use, Ben and I were thrilled. I can't think of anything better than being in the middle of nowhere with Ben, wrapped up in a tartan blanket in front of a roaring fire, which is what I'm told we'll have to do to keep warm in August in Scotland.

"And the duchess sends her love," he adds.

If it hadn't been for the duke and duchess, Ben and I wouldn't be about to get married. We've got a lot to thank them for. The duchess thinks our love story should be turned into a movie. I'm not sure the silver screen could capture how magical it is, being with Ben. And who would play him? Anyone, including Daniel de Luca, would seem like a poor second next to my soon-to-be husband.

"I can't wait to see everyone as I walk down the aisle," I reply. "I'm excited."

"Before you do, I'm going to get some photographs with Dad. And Mum."

"Maybe do one at the Churchill desk."

"Yeah," he says. "I think that would be . . ."

"The full-circle moment you've been working your entire life for?"

He chuckles and I can picture his dimple coming to life. "Something like that."

Ben's father is on a new drug trial for his early-onset dementia. Ben found the best doctors in the world, and for now, his father's symptoms have stabilized. It means that Ben got to experience telling his dad he'd bought The Fairfield Hotel. He got to bring his parents back, not as employees, but as VIPs. Ben never said anything, but I knew it felt good to him, like he'd waited a lifetime to do it. Suggesting we hold the wedding at The Fairfield was like giving voice to a foregone conclusion.

I imagine the staff were slightly less enthusiastic about hosting the wedding of their new boss. The hotel is beautiful and the perfect location for the start of our lives together.

Along with Ginny, I invited some of my friends from New York. Obviously, Melanie's here. Ginger and Callie as well. But the others couldn't make it, and I don't think we'll stay in touch. There's no animosity, just the gentle dissolution of relationships that stopped being meaningful. My mom used to say people are in our lives for a reason, a season or a lifetime. I didn't know it at the time, but a lot of my New York friends have turned out to be seasonal. Jed was definitely in my life for a reason, and although it wasn't nice being cheated on, splitting up was definitely the right thing for us both. And not just because I met the love of my life just after.

Ben, on the other hand, will be in my life for the entirety of it. My best friend, my lover, my husband.

"You're done," Meera says. "Are you happy?" She nods toward the mirror.

"Couldn't be happier," I reply and slip off the chair. It's true, but it's got nothing to do with what I look like.

My eyes snag on Dad, who's sitting in the corner, reading a newspaper amid the chaos. I can't explain why, but I want a few moments with him before I'm married. "I gotta go," I tell Ben. We swap *I love yous*, then I hang up and head over to Dad. He stands.

"You look beautiful," he says, and his eyes go glassy.

"Thanks, Dad."

"It makes me so happy that you're . . . happy. Not just happy, but with someone like Ben," he says. "He's a good man. I always worried with . . . the other one." Dad won't say Jed's name since he heard about Fifi. "I worried it was too much of a compromise. I blame myself for that."

"Blame yourself? Why would my boyfriend be your fault?"

He pulls in a breath and puts his hands in his pockets. "After your mother died, I was . . . a wreck."

I close my eyes at the memories of him in those early days after Mom died.

"And you did everything not to make yourself a burden," he continues. "To keep me happy. I knew it at the time, but I had no energy to stop you. I wasn't the parent you deserved during those times."

I slip my hand through his arm. "Don't say that. You did the best you could."

"It wasn't good enough. You deserved more and I'm sorry."

"I love you so much." What else can I say? I don't blame him for those days. Not at all. But the reason I stayed with Jed so long was probably because I was good at not being a burden. I was good at keeping someone happy at the expense of what I needed.

"Ben's a good man," he says again.

"The best," I agree.

"I have something for you." He reaches into his breast pocket. "It's nothing fancy, but I thought you might like it today." He pulls out a small leather jewelry box that I recognize from my mother's dressing table.

I glance up at him, searching his face for an explanation, but he's focused on the box.

Inside are a pair of diamond earrings. I never saw my mom wear anything like this. We never had enough money for something so extravagant.

"They don't quite match," Dad says. "You can see that this one has a slightly different setting, just to keep it more secure."

He glances up at me as if to check that I'm following.

"They're beautiful," I say. They look exactly the same at first glance, but the one on the left has an extra claw.

"The right one is new," he says. "The left one is . . . the stone from your mother's engagement ring." His voice falters on the last word. I tip my head back and blink to stop the tears from falling.

"Dad . . ." I say, almost lost for words. "I love them."

"I wanted you to have something that was hers and something that came from me as well. This seemed like a good idea."

"It's the perfect idea." It's so sentimental and beautiful and completely perfect. I get to have something of both my parents with me as I walk down the aisle.

"I guess it fits the criteria for something old and something new. But don't feel you have to wear them today."

"Of course I'm going to wear them today." My eyes start to well up again at the thought of my mom. She would have loved Ben and our love story and having a daughter whose husband looks just like Daniel De Luca. Except better, in my very humble opinion. I've missed her more than ever, planning this wedding, choosing my dress, and picking the invitations. She would have taken so much joy from the entire process. The only thing that makes it okay is that I know she would have been so happy for me. I know she would have loved Ben and how he loves me.

"She loved you so much," Dad says.

I try to swallow down the lump in my throat. "I know. And I'm so lucky that I got her for as long as I did."

Dad nods and pulls a tissue from his pocket. He hands it to me, then takes another for himself. He's come prepared. "Absolutely. We were both lucky."

"Are you sure you won't move to the UK?" I dab the corners of my eyes.

Dad pats my hand. "I'll be a frequent visitor. I have no desire to leave a house that's seen so much joy. And I look forward to my grandchildren spending summers with me, adding to the memories."

I nod, thinking back to my summers in Madison County. "They were the happiest times."

Dad pulls in a breath. "There are plenty of happy times to come."

I know he's right.

Before I can respond, Lila, the wedding planner, bursts into the room. "Where are we up to? Are we fifteen minutes away from being ready? The groom is getting restless, and I'm not sure how long he's going to last without coming up here and ruining everything."

I laugh. "He can come up if he wants, but I think we're ready, aren't we?" I glance around. Melanie's still in the makeup chair, but at least she's smiling.

"Zit-gate is under control," Melanie calls. "We're good to go."

Everyone in the wedding party files out. Lila hands me my bouquet as we exit the suite and head downstairs.

I see Ben's broad back through the crack in the door to the ballroom and smile when his shoulders lower at the opening strains of the processional music. My soon-to-be husband isn't a patient man. That's why I know I'm so important to him—he waited for me far longer than he wanted to. Nick looks toward the doors, straining to see what's going on. Ben is probably threatening to march up the aisle himself and drag me to the altar to speed things up.

The doors open, Ben turns, and our gazes lock. I know I should take in the faces of those seated either side of me, who have all gathered here to see Ben and me get married, including the duke and duchess. But all I see is Ben.

The man I mistook for someone else when we met.

The man I pretended to be engaged to.

The man I thought was a vacation romance.

"You look beautiful," he says, voice hushed, as I stand before him.

I smile, never taking my eyes from him. "Did I ever tell you that you look like a famous movie star?" I ask him.

I hadn't believed in happily-ever-afters for a long time, until I met Ben. Now we're in ours every day. We're living the scenes the credits usually roll over. And it's the best part of our entire story.

MORE GREAT READS BY LOUISE BAY

The Boss + The Maid = Chemistry

A grumpy, reclusive New York billionaire meets his match in the maid who makes his bed (in more ways than one).

When an older guy with a dirty grin and an expensive suit flirts with me from the next barstool, I don't realize I'm about to have a one-night stand with the man I desperately want to work for.

After a night that leaves my world (and body) shaken, I start my summer job housekeeping in a five-star hotel even though I'm determined to kickstart my career in tech. As I dust and polish the Park Suite, in walks Mr. Dirty Grin—now with an icy glare.

Why is the man from last night who was so charming (and good with his tongue) so furious this morning? As I piece together the puzzle, I discover the guest in the Park Suite is none other than Ben Fort, the reclusive tech mogul I want to work for.

Ben has kept his identity hidden for years and he wants to know how I figured him out overnight.

As he questions me, I don't waste time telling him he's a (super-hot) grump who needs to lighten up—and give me a job.

I don't want to sleep my way to the top, and he doesn't trust me. But neither of us can resist the sizzling sparks that fly every time I fluff his pillows.

Fake Fiancé

What's a heartbroken American to do when she's in London trying to get over her ex? Find herself a fake fiancé. Obviously.

I'm walking past Big Ben, trying to get over the world's worst breakup, when I slam into a hot hunk of British man.

And pour scorching hot coffee all over him.

My caffeine casualty not only forgives me for ruining his shirt, but when I ramble on about needing to distract the press from my recent heartbreak, he agrees to be my pretend Prince Charming faster than you can say "espresso."

Our agreement is clear: nothing is real.

Except the more time we spend pretending to be a couple, the harder it is to keep my side of the bargain. And his smoldering stare tells me he might be having the same problem.

And then we have a game night. Maybe it's naked Twister that pushes us over the edge.

I'm starting to think my fake fiancé might be husband material.

For real.

For more, visit www.louisebay.com.

ACKNOWLEDGMENTS

Wonderful readers, thank you so much for reading!

This book started off inspired by Leonardo DiCaprio's reputation for dating women under twenty-five, as described in a song in a YouTube I saw by @natalieburdick (which I still look up regularly when I need cheering up; I recommend it). It didn't end up anything like the book I expected to write, and any inspiration from dear old Leo has been entirely erased. But it's proof that you can get an idea anywhere, and even if it's completely useless, you just need to start somewhere. Note to self. Underline. Highlight.

To Hazel Bradbury, thank god you slipped me all those Judith Krantz, Jackie Collins, and Sidney Sheldon books that I devoured in the sixth form "study" room! Yes, I would have had better A-level results, but I got a more important education.

Thank you to Rebecca Heyman for helping me shape this idea and holding my hand every step of the way. It's come the distance, but why wasn't it easier? Because sometimes when it's hard, the end product is better? I live in hope. Always.

Kimberly Whalen, thank you for being so patient and encouraging and completely kick-ass. It's all better with you in my corner. We need some champagne, stat.

Thanks also to Lauren Plude for believing in this book and Krista Stroever and the entire Montlake team. Thank you, Kelly and Judy.

Lenora, thank you for being my overriding reason for doing anything in this world.

ABOUT THE AUTHOR

Louise Bay is the *Wall Street Journal* and *USA Today* bestselling author of more than thirty contemporary romance novels—the kind she likes to read. Louise was inspired by such bonkbuster authors of the eighties as Judith Krantz and Jackie Collins, but wants to be Emily Henry when she grows up. She loves the rain, *RHOBH*, London, days when she doesn't have to wear makeup, hanging out with her kid, elephants, and champagne (not necessarily in that order). For more information, visit www.louisebay.com.